Brendan Conboy

For Honour, Truth & Justice

Published by
Yellow Dog Publishing

First published July 2022

Cover design
Brendan Conboy

Printed and bound in Great Britain
ISBN 978-1-9169000-8-0

Special Thanks:

To Jason Parker, for his patience in searching for errors in my writing and for helping to make this book what it is today.

To Heather my wife, for her patience and belief in me and for understanding my need to escape into fantasy worlds of words.

To the members of the Association of Christian Writers, whose encouragement has enabled me to grow as a writer in so many ways.

To NaNoWriMo (National Novel Writing Month) – about a third of this book was produced by this.

And of course to God,
for telling me that He hasn't finished with me yet.
For enabling me with the power to overcome the curse and to be able to call myself an Author (see short story in rear of book)

My prayer for you the reader.
May you read more than just the story, formed by the words that are on these pages. Although this is science fiction, woven throughout the story is truth.
May you know the truth and
may the truth set you free.

Dedication

This book is dedicated to you the reader.
It fills me with joy to hear from someone that enjoyed reading one of my books. After all, why write if no one ever reads it. My books are just a part of the legacy of my life. We all leave a legacy, so make sure that yours is something to benefit others.

LEGACY of the MIMICS...

beyond the void...

The story so far...

The Mimics arrived in 2012
and their presence was felt for over seven decades.
They were finally defeated in 2085
which saw the end of their oppression.
Using our bodies to host their
consciousness was worse than slavery.
It gave birth to profound confusion,
desperation and hopeless chaos.
The older the victim was,
the more severe the symptoms.
Imagine waking up in your 60's
after 36 years of sleep?
The strong will survive, but what is survival?
Desperate people do desperate things.
Any waiting predators can now act.
Now the Mimics have gone...
...they will take advantage.

This is the LEGACY of the MIMICS.

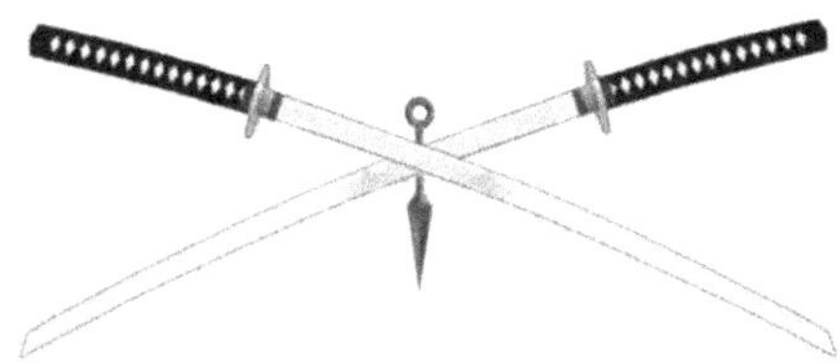

For Honour, Truth & Justice

PROLOGUE

No matter what happens in life, be good to people.
Being good to people is a wonderful legacy to leave behind.
Taylor Swift

Imagine, if you can, losing your memory. Questions fill the void that is the emptiness of your mind. Who are you? Where are you? What do you do? How did you get here? Floods of confusion pour in to fill the vacuum. The evidence before you enable the assumptions, the make-believe and illusion. The illusion leads to even more confusion.

You have a limited understanding, you can communicate, even speak. You can identify objects, but not people. You look at those around you with a clueless gaze and wonder who they are? Mother? Lover? Friend? Enemy?

Panic and fear arrive to devour what is left of your sanity. You're completely on edge, heartrate elevated, skin, sweaty and clammy. Eyes dart left to right, up and down. It's decision time. All that you can rely on is instinct. What does your human nature tell you?

Fight or flight? It's time to choose but this could be life or death.

Imagine, if you can, the person stood next to you, as they experience the same void and emptiness; the same amnesia and vacuum; the same feeling of hopelessness. Some of the others around you are so overwhelmed they're unable to run away or get ready to defend themselves. All they can do is stand and stare. Some have already collapsed.

Everyone in the same building as you is experiencing one or more of these incredibly intense feelings. Now imagine the whole country. Imagine the entire globe engulfed in gloom, doom and despair. Can you even begin to comprehend what it would be like if everyone experienced this void, all at the same time? A pandemic of simultaneous amnesia!

Fear overwhelms; oozes, infects, contaminates. It grows, develops, emerges, like an ominous, iniquitous, beast. The beast waits patiently in readiness to pounce. The beast's name is fear and it makes a choice, to feed. The weak are captured first, the easy prey which then generates more panic and even more fear. As it grows, intensifies, reproduces, then matures, bringing wickedness, evil and darkness.

Animal instincts kick in. Feeling trapped. Ensnared. Getting caught. Need to escape. Need to hide, to recover. Have to recuperate and pull through the confusion. Such chaos and panic! Need to survive, to move beyond… beyond the void…

Chapter One

I don't fight for the money. I fight for my legacy.
I fight for history. I fight for my people.
Khabib Nurmagomedov

Billions of things happen every second; at the moment that humanity was freed, Gideon had died, Ashia remembered and a gate began to open.

An eerie thick mist moved slowly over the desolate barren landscape. Its brownish-yellow hue deposited a stench of burnt sulphur. Mortemus lingered with Fonias, they breathed in the foul taste of the vapour and bizarrely savoured every moment. They sensed a new beginning, new opportunities, prospects to tip the balance, restore power; their power. They had waited patiently, stalked, and roamed the land of their banishment, the realm of Erebus. Their wait was at an end, the sentence nearly over. These creatures and more like them would soon be free again.

The sky was ablaze with fireworks booms and echoes, accompanied by multiple-coloured flashes of light. The explosions and sparkles transformed the dark silhouetted outlines of the horizon. It had been a year since the first VM Day, the 'Victory over the Mimics' had of course saved mankind and set them free, but it had cost her brother his life. "Absence makes the heart grow fonder." These were the parting remarks that Jeru had made to her, when he left, over six weeks earlier. At the time she regarded the comment as a flippant, almost humorous thought. Now amid the party and celebrations, her impulsive nature and lack of patience incubated the thought within the petri dish of her mind. Amidst the confines of the crowded harbourside, her mind struggled to process her thoughts.

A man, full of excitement with a beaming smile, grabbed her arm and encouraged her to dance, "Happy VM day," he grinned, as she shrugged him off with a look to kill. Her mind drifted on, as she thought more about Jeru's comment. *'Journeys always create an absence, but grow fonder? I'm not sure about that. I never enjoy the journey! Jeru says that I lack patience. I simply want to reach the destination in the fasted possible time. Is that me being anxious? That isn't anxiety, I see it as efficiency. I need quick answers and my question is, what did Jeru really mean by that parting comment?'* She wondered if he was frustrated with her irritable ways. She had been that way since Gideon had died and she knew that she could be difficult. The words *impulsive* and *impatient* popped into her mind and she reacted by speaking out loud to herself. With a shrug, she said, "Yeah, that's me." She always needed an instant solution to a problem. "There's nothing wrong with that", she vocalised her thoughts again as if Jeru stood beside her side.

The firework display was nearly over. A message on a pontoon, anchored in the bay reminded the gathered crowd, what they had to celebrate; it read '*HAPPY V-M DAY*'. Her thoughts had been momentarily distracted by the atmosphere, so she closed her eyes and continued to speak in a hushed mutter, "I thought I had improved over the year." Now, her nerves felt on edge and she feared that she had run out of patience. Tears began to leak from behind her eyelids and above the cacophony, she screamed, "Oh, Gideon, why did you have to die?"

As the fireworks fizzled out, she heard the hubbub of the crowd. After the barrage of explosions, it now seemed almost serene. She gazed at the empty darkness overhead which gnawed away at the emptiness within her. She missed her brother so much, and constantly yearned for him, but ultimately the emptiness within remained. The desperate words of her brother's final plea to her back in the work camp, resonated within that same petri dish of her mind, *'Ashia, you must fight, you have to fight.'*

Those words now haunted, festered and grew out of control, in the unstoppable way a bacteria breeds within that dish. Within the same flashback, she vividly recalled that she had promised her brother that she would use her knife. That knife had long since gone, but ever since the day that she had been released from Apateon's grip, she had calmed her fears and always carried a reliable blade. She had affectionately named the lethal weapon, '*Honour.*' The idea for the name was in her mind one morning as she woke. She liked the idea of a knife with a name, it comforted her. She reached down to her slender thigh, where the weapon was inconspicuously concealed within its sheath, inside her black jeans. She drew reassurance from the touch of the hilt and felt safe; though she was far from secure.

Smoke from spent fireworks still lingered and hung like a shroud in the Angolan night sky. Her gaze was drawn toward it, as a gentle breeze punched a hole within the veil-like mist. The sudden sight of the exposed Moon and stars beyond shook her already nervous senses. A further tear trickled and slightly warmed her cheek, as she inwardly mourned for her brother. The Moon was his grave. She could never visit, but every night she could see it, no matter where she was. Sometimes she made a conscious decision to look up and at times she would speak out loud to her deceased brother, the hero that had saved mankind at the cost of his own life. Tonight, was an unconscious decision, she just happened to somehow direct her gaze, through the hole in the veil. This time something felt different. As she peered toward the celestial ball of light, she felt a new connection with Gideon's spirit. Something stirred, deep within her core, which stimulated a new sense and resurrected something dormant. An image in her mind cleared, like an old-fashioned television set as it was retuned, to reveal a picture. The image in her mind continued to change, pixel by pixel. It appeared to be a dancing silhouette of a person – a man. Not just any man, but the one that tried to dance with her earlier. He grinned, the same grin. Then the Tsunami of shock and fear hit her hard in the gut before it rushed to her head!

A familiar voice from behind startled her thought, "Beware, sis, he's an assassin!" She had no doubt who it was. They had lived, fought and survived together most of her life. The last time she had heard him, he told her that he would find Trenchant and that Trenchant would set them all free. She turned, in expectation to see Gideon, but alas, she was alone. The words grew louder, "HE IS AN ASSASSIN!" She sensed a deep love in her brother's voice and it caused the anxiety and fear to subside. Again, she heard his voice, this time with the familiar words that she had heard as they had parted company in the work camp, over a year earlier, "Be strong my sister, use your knife!" She should have questioned; how could this be possible? Instead, she accepted it, as if it were natural. Gideon seemed to be alive and somehow able to communicate with her. The warmth of reassurance swept over her and as it did so it filled her with new confidence. This new sureness instantly drove out any fear and nervousness that remained. She felt a new strength.

She turned around and gasped as she came face to face with the deadly dancer, who now stood still. She felt safe at a distance of about five metres, as he made no threats or gestures. He just stood, waited, and glared, with deep, dark, empty eyes. His face was set like stone, expressionless and cold. She wondered briefly if he could be possessed by a Mimic. Her memory of before her time as a Mimic host was intact and something troubled her. He continued to stare back, vacant, lifeless, and vacuous. She returned the stare, in a kind of stand-off, which seemed to last several minutes. Gideon had given another warning, "Be careful Ashia, look at him closely."

"I am looking, Gideon. What do you think I'm doing?"

"Look closer. Don't just look *at* him, look beyond, look *into* him, but be careful."

She felt slightly confused. What did he mean, to look beyond and *into* him? As she thought about this, she could feel another presence emerge within her. At first, it felt like a warm, fuzzy, tingling sensation, but it continued to change, it grew, propagated and energised. The energy vitalised her, spread, awakened, distributed throughout her body, into every extremity. The power equipped, readied and stabilised her. Adrenalin poured into the mix, as her muscles twitched in readiness, but in readiness for what? Her brain neurons charged with electricity received and sent signals; like a computer making rapid calculations. The new presence had a sense of familiarity, like a reunion with an old friend. The friend did not need to speak, just the presence was enough. She had been told about the Pneuma power and especially the stories about Gideon and the other Sixers. Jeru had told her the stories over and over. Now, she recognised that this was most likely the Pneuma. It filled her and prepared her. Then something incredible happened.

The darkness of the African night suddenly became lighter and the air felt warmer as it comfortably caressed her body. It is a scientific fact that our eyes become more alert in the dark. As her pupils dilated, it enabled increased light to enter her retina with enhanced sight. What she now saw was far beyond anyone's natural ability as she crossed into the realms of the supernatural. She could now see beyond that which was physically before her. "Is this what Gideon had referred to?" She was thinking out loud again as she stared into the dark pools of the eyes that belonged to the man opposite. Now she could discern more. His eyes had a red, fiery glow that cut through the darkness and provided a threatening ominous, ghoulish appearance. Fear tried to fill her mind but was swiftly crushed by the love of the Pneuma's presence. Gideon had told her to, *'look into him,'* so that is what she now did. She could see that he was in pain, he felt lost and then she had a sense that he was not in control of all that he did. Her discernment continued to improve, her vision became clearer, then, she repulsed at the sight of the open, painful wounds just below his eyes. The wounds had festered; deep gashes, as if he had been clawed by a bear.

She felt sorrow for the man, then, Gideon's words echoed within her head, *'BE CAREFUL!'* With the thought, she sensed another presence. It had an aroma of rotting flesh and just briefly she sensed the danger, like a beast lurked to devour her. Her mind switched and doubt began to question, "Is he really dangerous? He doesn't seem to be a threat? He's just stood there? Just waiting, but what is he waiting for? What is he?" Then she inadvertently stopped thinking and asked the question aloud. "Who are you?"

"Ashia, don't you mean, WHAT am I?" came the slow, mono-tone reply.

She drew in a sharp intake of breath, uncertain as to how to respond and tried to disguise her shock. More questions filled her mind, "How does he know my name? What does he want with me? What is he waiting for?"

Panic attempted to undermine her fortitude and courage. It unnerved her and weakened her resolve. The Pneuma continued to fill her, pushed back, and exerted its presence. The manifestation comforted but didn't control. She felt safe and secure, despite the unsettled remark. The threat seemed to subside, so she quipped across the five-metre expanse, "What are you waiting for?"

His face twisted and he snarled a wide grin, at which she had confirmation once again that he wasn't a Mimic. She seemed to wait for eternity for an answer, then, when he eventually replied and for the first time since the encounter, she began to feel threatened. She was in the presence of danger, "Wait – Just wait – Wait and see."

His voice had a reptilian hiss and menace in the tone. It pierced her comfort zone, and evoked her unease, though he still hadn't moved. She appeared puzzled and confused and he sensed her uncertainty and weakness. After a long delay, he continued with, "Not long now – Waiting soon be over – Not long now."

"Not long now? What did that mean?" She assessed, calculated, mentally prepared, changed her physical

stance and pitched forward into attack position. Her sweaty right hand lightly stroked the hilt of *'Honour'*. She too waited, then, she wondered if they both waited for the same reason. The crowd had now dispersed considerably and she started to feel more alone, more vulnerable. Confusion swamped her mind until in the distance she noticed a familiar figure, which moved with a confident swagger and assurance; it was Jeru. Her heartbeat increased instantly in the knowledge that he was there, but he hadn't yet noticed her and was, therefore, unaware of the strange stand-off and the possible presence of danger.

Mr Dancer followed her gaze, his eyes instantly locked onto the approaching target. It was now time, the wait will soon be over, time for a dual-kill, to kill two birds with one stone or in this case one Beretta Px4 Storm, a semi-automatic pistol with a silencer attached. Her eyes sent a message to her brain. Her brain responded with a message to her sweaty hand, '*Stop stroking – Time for action – KILL!*' The hilt slid into her hand, blade in-line with her now straight fingers, thumb clasped tightly to secure the weapon in place. She didn't use an up-in-the-air, over-the-shoulder type of method that you might see a knife thrower use in a circus or a wild-west show. Instead, as she grasped the handle, she rapidly reached her arm backwards but kept it downward. The jerk back was instantly followed by a swift swing forward and at the appropriate time, whilst aimed towards her opponent, her thumb released the deadly blade.   Honour, flew, direct, precise and unwavering. The gun was still being raised towards Jeru, looking to engage the target, when the cold steel of the blade sunk deep into the exposed throat and nicked the carotid artery with surgical precision. As 100 millilitres of blood pass through the artery, at each beat of the heart and 65 beats per minute, there is considerable pressure within the small pulsating tube. The fatal nick and the sudden exit of blood produced a gruesome sight before her.   A crimson, fountain sprayed half of the distance between them.

The stricken man slumped to his knees. The look on his face conveyed fear. He knew that his life was about to end. In the next 30 seconds, he would be dead. Ashia watched as the twisted, contorted grin changed to a semblance of 'normal.' His whole form changed, as did his voice. In a soft, apologetic tone he gently spoke, "Sorry, please forgive me." From his knelt position, he slowly fell back upon his bent legs. The body came to a halt, his face upward toward the sky. Ashia instinctively rushed forward, partly to retrieve the knife, but also a reactive shock to the change that she now saw in the man. Whatever the creature had been before, it was gone. All signs of menace had disappeared. The lifeless eyes that glared back were bright blue and normal. She had saved Jeru's life but had killed a man. She could no longer sense the presence of the beast that once lurked within the man, though she felt as if it was still nearby, watching, waiting. She sensed that this wasn't the end. Whatever she had witnessed would return.

Jeru arrived heavily out of breath, as she made a hurried attempt to extract *Honour* from the bloody neck. Then, after a couple of wipes on the dead man's clothing, she concealed it back in the sheath within her jeans. It had been less than a minute since she launched her pre-emptive assault and the onlookers had only just started to gather. The comforting arm of Jeru around her shoulders sparked a fresh awareness. "Time to leave," he commanded and her intuition knew that he was right, as they blended easily into the dispersing crowd.

Fonias had already taken his vaporous form and was in the process of retreat from the scene. Now he appeared as an innocent-looking mist that lingered over the harbour. He knew that he had failed and that Mortemus would be angry, but he was out of practice, as they all were. More than 70 years of prison had made him slow and weak, but he would be back…back to kill more, regain his strength and assert his superiority.

Chapter Two

Legacy is not what I did for myself.
It's what I'm doing for the next generation.
Vitor Belfort

Sagami Province, Cipangu, the year 1290

He was no stranger to battle and all of his warrior senses told him that this one was going badly. He sensed that this could be his final fight, his last day, the end of his life; then he saw her. For a brief moment, it seemed as if the battle paused and all around him had calmed. Pain from the wound in his arm jolted his awareness back to the imminent threat. His reputation had previously struck fear into any opponent foolish enough to approach him on the field of battle. This horde, however, seemed fearless and unstoppable; as if they were possessed.

His usual tactical manoeuvres of ducks, dives, rolls, thrusts, and parries, seemed ineffective and the numbers around him continued to increase. For each enemy that he killed, two more replaced them. He was under immense pressure and his energy drained. His helmet had long since been discarded, so dirt and blood filled his ears and eyes sweat poured from his body and filled the rest of his armour. All of his senses were dulled. His strength had been replaced with exhaustion. He knew that he was now in his final seconds, then, he saw her again, but failed to allow the sight to distract him.

Instinctively he reacted as another assailant approached from his left; drop, roll, tuck and thrust. His blade pushed through the flesh and the twist of his wrist caused maximum damage to the internal organs of his assailant. The lethal Katana withdrew from the stricken target, momentum continued to rip through the man's belly and the stench of his intestine spewed forth. Death was all around.

The gutted attacker was a short-lived victory and he failed to see the potentially fatal blade, behind and above his head. Though, he sensed a new smell. Amongst the reek of death, carnage and destruction, his nasal cavities filled with strange, scented perfume. The unseen enemy blade dropped, on target, poised to shatter his skull, but then, a fraction before his appointment with death, he felt an invisible force push him. It was gentle, with a warmth and pleasing aroma. What was that fragrance? What was that smell? After the push came the fall; inertia in his clogged-up ears told him that he was about to hit the ground but the enemy blade had only removed a slither from the top of his ear.

From where he'd fallen, he glanced toward where his instincts told him the blade originated, but his assailant was already dead beside him. Someone had saved him.

"Masamune, stay close to me!" The voice commanded, yet was also gentle. He turned his head toward the voice and through his cloudy vision, found what he thought was an apparition. He attempted to brush the dirt from his battle-sore eyes and identified the woman. Close up he noticed her ferocity and forcefulness. Her movement was swift, exact and precise; as her hand reached out to clamp hold of his.

"I'm Meiyo", she said, "Now shut up and fight. Stay close!" As she touched him, he felt a surge of energy fill and restore him. His vision cleared, muscles revitalised and his brain switched back to fight mode. He didn't remember the clamber to his feet, he simply found himself next to her, back-to-back; hack, chop, slice, slay. He did as she had commanded, he stayed close. Every time the gap between them widened, he seemed to weaken. She appeared to radiate energy, a strange force and it strengthened him even more. His mind tried to ask questions. No time for questions, they can wait, need to survive, stay alive; win, live. Yes, live!

The battle rapidly turned and all across the battlefield, his comrades had also found a fresh zeal to survive, to win. Instead of death, he was rewarded with life, a newly invigorated life. The questions flooded his mind. Who was this woman? Where did she come from? Where did she learn to fight like that? Suddenly overwhelmed by his sense of relief, he dropped to his knees and wept. Unaccustomed to such an act of outward weakness, he momentarily felt embarrassed and averted his gaze. She stooped to his level and touched him for the second time. Her fragrance intoxicated his brain. She placed a gentle hand lightly on his shoulder, although in his mind, it seemed as if she caressed him; he felt loved, over-whelmed and for the first time in his life; complete. Who was this woman?

"I know that you have questions, Masamune, but you have been chosen."

"Chosen, what do you mean? Where did you come from? Who are you and where did you learn to fight like that? Questions, you're damn right I have questions." He shook his head in bewilderment.

"All will become clear in time, but I am here to protect you and help you to fulfil your destiny. You are a great Samurai warrior, with many victories, but you are destined for even greater things."

"Destined? Greater? What do you mean? Where did you come from? I've never met anyone like you before?"

"My name is Meiyo…"

He cut her short, "Yes, I heard you say that in battle."

"I am a friend…"

"Well, I gathered that", cutting her short again.

Why was he being so abrupt? He knew that he was doing it, but was unable to stop. He always knew but never could change. This was his way. He was well known for his rudeness. She could see his true nature. The tears had stopped. Time to be real! He stood to his feet and she mirrored his motion, then, he stared directly into her eyes. Deep blue eyes; like small oceans, beautiful eyes; eyes that seemed to speak. They said, '*I love you more than you realise.*' It was as if he heard her voice, yet her lips remained still. Her whole demeanour remained calm. The calmness seemed to intimidate and threaten; it was alien. His warrior instinct struggled to comprehend what was happening. Why did he feel so threatened? No sword was drawn, no blade to his throat, just a presence, a power. The power didn't attack; instead, it seemed to calm him. He sat back down on the blood-stained ground.

"Sorry, I'm tired." Once again, he was aware of his words, but couldn't stop talking and now, he didn't want to stop. "Thank you."

"What are you thanking me for?" She seemed to play with him, teased and smiled. Her face appeared to shine and for the first time, behind her blood-spattered appearance, he saw immense beauty. He had never seen anyone with so beautiful and his jaw dropped, speechless.

"What are you thanking me for?" She repeated her question and pressed him harder for an answer. He realised that she had asked the same question again and how foolish he must have seemed. He attempted to pull himself from the ground and once again, she reached out a hand to help.

"For saving my life", he said with a smile back at her. His brothers in arms slowly made their way from the field of battle. As they passed by one occasionally patted him on the back or shook his hand. Most simply nodded a tired head, but no one ever smiled or acknowledged her. War was brutally painful and the losses always suppressed any likely smile. His smile now puzzled them. He appeared to be stood, smiling and talking to himself and they assumed that he was dazed from the madness of battle.

She briefly turned away from him. Gratitude was not what she was after and she didn't know how she should respond. She had a mission to complete and saving his life was only the start of it so replied, "Think nothing of it."

"I still have questions."

"I know, but let's find somewhere more comfortable to talk."

Finding his horse, they mounted it and left. As they rode, deep in thought, they contemplated the despair and destruction. His mind now gave birth to fresh new questions. When will this madness end? Why do we always try to solve a problem with war? She had different questions. How do I tell him? How will he react? Will my mission succeed? It must, it has to the future of mankind depends on it; on us.

They journeyed through Paddy fields, where industrious rice farmers stopped to wave at what appeared to be a lone soldier, as he made his way from the horrors of battle. Their trek led them into a dense forest of spruce and bamboo. Masamune knew the route and so did the horse; it was, after all, his retreat after most battles. The trees grew tight together, with no path defined, yet the horse found the way through. Suddenly he pulled hard with his left hand and the horse obeyed. A hidden path directed them to a clearing with a bamboo hut. The sound of running water indicated a stream nearby. He dismounted, helped her down and gestured, '*this way*' and she followed. At the deepest point of the stream, without hesitation, he stripped and jumped in. She did the same, revealing her full beauty. He was glad that they were not talking, as once again he was lost for words by the sight of her body and his mind asked a new question, "What are you?"

Chapter Three

It has been said that time heals all wounds.
I don't agree. The wounds remain.
Time - the mind, protecting its sanity - covers
them with some scar tissue and the pain lessens,
but it is never gone.
Rose Kennedy

Jeru and Ashia came away from the harbour focused, determined and swiftly moved forward. Life preservation was their priority; no distractions, don't look back. His arm reassured, comforted, protected. She was in a slight state of shock and bewilderment, her mind raced, computed, factored, and questioned. What just happened? Was that real? Her legs stumbled ever-so-slightly as they proceeded up the slight slope towards the security of the base that they both knew as home. Through the checkpoint, the guards recognised them and casually waved them through. Her stumble became a stagger, as they proceeded along the cracked concrete paving. Adrenalin had drained, so too had the supernatural energy that she had experienced. Eventually, they crashed through the doorway into the small house that they shared. Neither had spoken a word for the entire distance from the harbourside to their home. Now they just sat in silence in a fog of contemplation as their minds tried to make sense of the information. They each held back emotions.

Jeru knew that Ashia would one day discover the Pneuma. He had anticipated it and expected it long ago, but he wasn't prepared for it to happen in such a dramatic way. He felt angry with himself, partly because he had said nothing in advance. He had bottled up his concerns for some time, in an attempt to protect her from what he knew was to happen, but nothing could have prepared her for this. A feeling crept over him. It spread out of control and he considered himself to be a failure. He never really felt good enough. He had loved Gideon like a brother, deeply admired him, and wanted to be like him, but he couldn't. He never would. He creased his brow into a firm frown, and then, as he bit down hard on his bottom lip, he became even more incensed with the taste of blood on his tongue.

He believed it was his duty to protect Ashia. Her brother and his best friend, Gideon, had protected him and he deemed it his responsibility to do the same. She heard him grind his teeth in frustration and watched as he wrung his hands together in a desperate bid to steady his thoughts. Adrenalin still coursed through his hot, sweaty body fuelled by anxiety. He was ready to fight. His muscles tensed and he tightened his right

hand into a fist before planting it into the palm of his
other hand. His attention quickly focused on his head
and he started to pound the fist into the side of his
temple. He was losing control. He had failed! This is
what his brain told him and his response was to lash
out at himself. He believed it was his duty to protect
Ashia and he had neglected her. He couldn't bring
himself to look at her face. His emotions told him that
he was a disappointment and he continued to slap
himself and punch his chest, like a frustrated ape. His
feet stamped like an angry child and restlessly, he
stood, walking and sitting, like an expectant father.
His mind thought of Gideon, he had failed him too, let
him down. He had never felt as good as Gideon,
always second best, never good enough, permanently
in his shadow. These negative thoughts only added to
his frustration and worthlessness. He believed it was
his responsibility to protect her and he kept repeating
to himself that she could have been killed. He tried to
think, to prepare his words, but his irritated brain
struggled to comprehend. He knew what he had to say,
but struggled to start to express himself calmly. This
made him feel even more inadequate, more of a failure,
and more uncomfortable, as he fought hard to suppress
the anger that rose inside. Then a tear trickled down
his cheek and reminded him that he was only human.

In the time that it took them to scurry home, Fonias,

in his vaporous spirit form had already rendezvoused with Skia at the equator. Due to the secluded location of the meeting place, they both chose to meet in their true corporeal form. Fonias was tall and slender, though he appeared to stand with a crippled stoop. His once muscular body had withered over the decades in exile. He needed to kill, he wanted to kill; it was his nature to do so. Abaddon himself had given him his name and explained to him the meaning, Slayer. He knew his primary objective was to slay, kill and slaughter. He also knew that with each drop of human blood, he would grow stronger. Puss oozed from numerous boils which covered his greenish-grey, shrivelled hide.

The scarlet red of his eyes had faded to a dull glow, where they were once acutely focused and sharp, now they were almost lifeless. His ears, like all Erebusians, were slightly pointed and honed for hunting. Talons and Teeth were his weapons, with signs of dried blood visible from his latest victim. If he had his way, he would continue to kill, indiscriminately. However, he was under orders from Mortemus to tread carefully, stay undetected and eliminate strategic targets.

He had managed to secure an invitation into the southern hemisphere five months earlier. He tricked a gullible southern soldier, who was on a routine mission into the north. Fonias had used his very limited ability to deceive and appeared in the form of a beautiful woman. He could only hold this form momentarily, so had acted quickly. The soldier wandered from the group and when 'she' appeared, she threw herself at him and kissed him. He was happy to oblige and kissed her back. The embrace sealed his fate. Fonias leapt onto his victim's back, stuck his lethal talons into his face and took control of him. Outwardly, the soldier looked the same, inwardly it was a different situation entirely. Soon after returning to the south, the soldier was found dead; an apparent suicide. Fonias no longer needed a passport and the meal had made him stronger, although it would take many more before he would be fully restored.

He stood facing north, facing Skia, who was unable to cross the invisible and deadly (to him) line of the equator. In comparison to Fonias, he seemed insignificant; everything about him was much smaller and non-threatening, but he could stir up great fear in most of the weak and insecure humans. His small stature enabled him to hide and creep about undetected. He was given the name Skia, because of the matt black colour of his skin, because it meant 'Shadow.' He could conceal himself within any form of shade, which is why so often the humans had feared him. They feared what they could not see and what they fear lurked within the shadows. He had smiled every time that he had heard a reference to things that hide in the shadows. Little did they know.

He was a messenger to Mortemus, who wanted an update on any progress made by Fonias. "It's good to see you again my old friend and Mortemus is pleased with your success of entering the south. What news do you have?"

"I have located my primary targets, but they were too strong for me, I am sorry to report."

"That's not good! Mortemus won't be happy to hear this news and I know that he will react badly when I tell him. The last time that I reported with bad news he had me flogged. I think I might take the long route home and feed to gain strength."

"Sounds like a wise move."

Jeru had stopped pacing and was now perched on a chair. Ashia successfully encouraged him to calm down, by telling him that she had already been through enough stress for one evening. She now sat opposite him in silence. A simple, utilitarian table created a barrier and a place to rest his elbows. His head was in his hands, as it hung low.

He raised his head slightly, but still held onto it, in a subconscious attempt to feel secure, "I made a promise and I feel that I almost let him down, I'm sorry."

"Nearly let who down? What are you talking about?"
She was confused. They could have both been killed
and he seemed to be full of self-pity.

"Gideon, I promised him… Years ago… When we
were much younger… He made me promise…"

"Promise what?" Her tired voice screamed as her
patience ran thin.

"To protect you… If anything, ever happened to him…
I have to protect you and tonight I nearly failed; on the
anniversary of his death, you could have died. I
couldn't live with that."

"I never knew." For a moment the look on her face
was one of shock and concern for him, but that quickly
changed with a fresh realisation. "But why are you full
of so much self-pity?" She had said it and there was no
turning back, "you say, you couldn't live with that?
What's that supposed to mean? Stop feeling guilty,
you and Gideon both rescued me. I think that about
pays off that promise and besides, I did a pretty good
job tonight. I looked after myself pretty good, don't
you think?" Her eyes glared at him and she made a
cheeky smile, as she waited for an answer.

"That's just it", said Jeru, "I don't think you did do it
by yourself."

There was a hush in the room whilst he allowed her time to reflect over what had happened at the harbour. Her head dropped as another realisation occurred. More moments passed before she eventually admitted, "I… I killed a man."

"Yes, you did, but I think that you had help." His tone was gentle and reminded her that he did care, but she wondered if it was just because of an old promise. Then she remembered her energy, the inner strength, the knife timing and accuracy and the voice; Gideon's voice.

"Gideon *was* there." She stopped and thought about how stupid that must sound, her brother was dead. Jeru said nothing, just pitched his head slightly, as if she had said something of great interest, then he waited. She looked at him as if he already knew something, another thought, '*did he know something?*'

"Well err, what I… What I really mean is that he spoke to me." She stopped again, did that sound stupid. No, he was nodding and smiled as if he understood, so she continued, faster and more excited.

"It was amazing really, really amazing like he was there, but he wasn't, if you know what I mean, of course, you don't know what I mean, I mean… What do I mean? Oh, well… it felt like I heard him." She began to blush with embarrassment and looked away to conceal it.

"I believe you", he said and immediately she felt a sense of relief and thought, *'maybe I'm not going mad?'*

"You do?"

"Yes, of course, I know exactly what you mean. I've had my own experience of it and Gideon did as you know." He paused momentarily as he tried to clear a lump that swelled in his throat. To mention his name wasn't too bad, but to reflect on the memories took his emotions to a place that he struggled to cope with. "I've waited for this, anticipated it. I've learnt that, as far as the Pneuma is concerned, to expect the unexpected. If you say, that Gideon spoke to you, I believe you, but I am anxious to know what he said?"

"He warned me… about the man, ah err…or whatever it was? He looked like a man or at least he did when he was dead, before that, Gideon told me to look beyond, look into him."

"Look into him?" He queried.

"Yes, I didn't understand at first, but as this power grew inside – and it grew fast – very fast! As it grew, the appearance of the man changed. He appeared to be in great pain and I think that he had something in him that controlled him. I can't be sure but I sensed that it was a power similar to the Pneuma, but not as strong and not good." She paused and thought again then shivered. "No, not good… Not good at all… definitely evil. The man's face was twisted and contorted, with painful-looking gashes."

She continued to fill him in with every detail and as she did so, she knew that she wasn't alone, she never would be, the Pneuma's presence was still in her. It didn't feel as strong as it did at the harbour and she thought that perhaps it will be there more when she needs it.

She still had many questions, "I wonder who he was? Why did he want to hurt us? What was controlling him? Was it another creature or a force? Is this another threat, another enemy? Will it come back? **Will it come back?"**

"And that, I think, is the most important question. Will it come back? I don't have any answers to your questions Ashia, but I think I know someone that might. It's late, let's eat, sleep and go pay him a visit in the morning."

As her head hit the pillow and before her eyes closed, she looked once more to the moon. "Good night, Gideon, I wish I could tell you what has just happened to me, but I think that somehow, you may already know.”

Chapter Four

Love is our true destiny.
We do not find the meaning of life by ourselves alone
- we find it with another.
Thomas Merton

In the pool of water, Masamune was mesmerised by her athletic, muscular body. He could appreciate the effort that it took to maintain such a high standard of physique and by comparison, he was out of her league. She was perfection. This was something that he had always aimed for in all that he did. Unfortunately, he knew that flawless excellence was always going to be out of his reach; because the human race is not perfect. Besides her physical stature, there was something else, her skin appeared translucent with a slight glow. During his transfixed stare, he mused to himself with a thought, *'I wonder if she shines in the dark?'*

The glow seemed to increase then decrease as if she controlled it. Another muse, *'What is she?'* This question nagged at his mind, but he didn't wish to ask it again. He was a patient man and a holy man. Like many holy men, he had learned to fight, to protect, not to persecute. He had studied the way of the Samurai, like his father before him and he knew that honour was everything. He now honoured her and allowed her time to give him the answers that he searched for. He would not press her and he respected her, not just as a warrior, but as his saviour on the battlefield.

There was something else that he couldn't explain. He sensed a familiarity and another question occurred to him, 'did he know her or know of her?' He could usually remain in the cold stream for a long time, but now the water seemed colder than usual and uncomfortable or was it just him? He didn't want to leave before her so he waited. She seemed to sense his sudden discomfort and said, "Let's get out." He wondered again, 'how did she know?'

They dressed, walked the short distance to the wooden steps and made their way up and into the small hut built on stilts. Inside it was light and airy, with plenty of ventilation. The space was graced with a small bed and a stove. He lit the stove with such ease, a demonstration that said, *'I know what I am doing.'* All the while she just stood in the middle of the room, this was his domain, he was master and she respected that. A large stone storage jar stood in the corner and he drew water with a ladle. The aroma of the tea as it brewed said, *'now we are civilised, cleansed from battle, time to relax.'*

He offered her a fine porcelain bowl of hot black liquid and their fingertips touched as she received it. Her smile said, *'thank you'*, though no sound came from her mouth. They had been in silence since entering the building. Now, as he reached toward her, the sting in his arm reminded him of the wound. The icy water had slowed the blood, now warmth from the fire restored the feeling. A fresh red line flowed downward toward his elbow, then, she spoke.

"Please, allow me to help you."

Under normal circumstances, he would not have allowed it. He would have been alone and managed to stitch and dress the wound himself, as was his normal post-battle routine. Under normal circumstances, he would have already done it and be asleep on the bed, but this wasn't normal. Under normal circumstances, in a battle such as it was, he would have been dead; he should have been dead. So, he did the not-so-normal thing and accepted her offer of help.

The stitches were neat, like those of an accomplished seamstress and he knew that he was not the first casualty that she had sewn up. The bandage was in place and she had even smoothed a healing balm to his now straight tipped ear; as she did so, she tried hard not to laugh.

"It's not funny", he said, then immediately burst into

laughter, smiled at her and said, "Well, maybe it is."

"It could have been a lot worse", she quipped.

"It should have been a lot worse! I should have been dead, where did you come from?" He didn't press her for the answer, he had asked before and she had explained that he would have his answers.

"There is much that I need to tell you." She brewed more tea and they both sat on the floor; she was ready.

"I've already mentioned that you have been chosen, now I will explain what that means, but you also have a choice to either accept or reject what I tell you… but know this, the future of mankind rests on what you decide. This will not be easy. If you accept what I ask, you will experience great blessings and live a long and happy life. You will also be called to make sacrifices, unimaginable and impossible sacrifices that no human should endure. However, I will help you and provide you with strength beyond human ability."

He interrupted, "What do you mean? What are you? Tell me?"

"I am Elafrian, from a place called Elafria."

"The people of light, I have heard of you, but I thought you were a myth, really, are you for real? Sorry, I don't know why I'm even asking you that, I already know the answer. I sensed something different about you, something so mysterious and deeply spiritual. I've read about Elafria in holy writings, but they are so vague, we know so little. I also believe some people elaborate on stories, they warp the truth, which is why they become myths and unbelievable. Where is Elafria?"

She evaded the question for now. "Masamune, you have been chosen because of your purity and strength, but also because you believe. I know, that despite all the elaborations, exaggerations and far-fetched stories that you have heard, you still believe. You believe that there is a place called Elafria, therefore you believe in me. I hope also that your belief, your faith, will help you to choose wisely."

"What is it that you ask me to choose?"

"All in good time, but first more about Elafria. It's a beautiful place, without pain, war, disease, suffering and death." She paused and waited for his reaction, but there was none so continued. "It's not of this world, not a physical place. It's a realm that is really hard to imagine or explain. You have to see it, feel it; experience it."

He spoke without thought, "It sounds incredible... Well, actually it sounds like heaven." A moment of brief silence allowed the words to sink in, "So what does that make you? Yes, I know you're Elafrian, but WHAT is that?"

"I'm not human." She said it and he didn't seem shocked.

"I kind of guessed as much. On the battlefield, I've never seen anyone move like you and your body, well it's amazing, plus, well I somehow feel a connection with you. It's strange… It's err…well, like when I pray, I feel like you know my thoughts, but it doesn't feel invasive, it's kind of… well reassuring. I felt it as soon as you touched me and energy; that energy, it saved my life."

"Don't keep saying that." She struggled to take credit for what she had done and he thought that she was just being modest. "Sorry, I struggle to relate to receiving any thanks. In Elafria, everyone feels so thankful all of the time. We have all that we need, it's provided by the One."

His expression said, *'tell me more.'*

"Yes, Elio, the One is the First and the Last, the Author. He is known by many names. He is the One who made us. He sent me to you, on a mission, because He is the One that chose you. Is this too much? Do you want me to stop?"

He didn't and he asked again, "What do you mean chosen? Chosen, what for?" He shrugged and waved his hands in an enquiring gesture.

"You have been chosen to live a long and fruitful life. To create a child; a beautiful, strong, healthy and perfect child. This child will provide you with three equally strong, beautiful and healthy grandchildren, who will bring you great joy into your old age and you will be happy, so happy."

His puzzled expression told her to stop there a moment as he processed the news that he had been given. He believed it, why wouldn't he? He had believed in Elafria for most of his life and had heard stories of the blessings associated with it, but still, he was puzzled. "I don't doubt what you say, I believe you, but to have a child, I would require a mate. I'm a holy man and as such, should desire no such thing. How…Who…How will it happen? Can you tell me more?"

"Yes, of course, I too have been chosen. For me it's easy, I simply follow the command of the One, but you… Well… You have to first accept me. There are other tasks that you will also need to accept, but this is the first of three. So, do you accept?"

"Hold on, you want to mate with me, to make love and make a baby?"

"Yes, Masamune, but there is more, I also wish to live with you, as your wife, for the rest of your physical life."

"My PHYSICAL life, what does that mean?" He wanted the bigger picture, the full picture.

"If you accept, then when your human body dies, you will live in Elafria, you will be given a new body, become an Elafrian. The children will be a blessing, but you need to understand something; to live in Elafria is the greatest blessing of all, as it will be for eternity."

For the very first time he started to believe it was too good to be true; a beautiful wife, a beautiful child and to live for eternity. "It all seems too good to be true, what's the catch? I understand the first task and even though I'm a holy man, I'm sure I can cope with such a tough challenge." He smiled a cheeky grin with his mouth and a loving smile with his eyes. She giggled, rapidly catching onto human ways and humour. "You mentioned three challenges, are the other two so, err… Well, let's say pleasurable?"

"The second requires learning a new skill and you will become the greatest of its kind throughout the world. You already know the sword, another reason why you have been chosen. You know how to wield it, to maximum effect; but now I will teach you to make them. You will become the greatest swordsmith in history, Masamune the legend and no one will ever surpass your skill."

He couldn't quite comprehend it, yet he did; he did believe and was so excited. He had longed to learn the craft of the *'Yoshi Hara yoshindo'* – the master swordsmith. From a young age, he had watched the masters in the Sōshū school and they were of course very familiar with him. They had made his Katana and a pair of Wakizashi. He hoped that they would accept him into the school but would they be willing to teach him? He didn't know how that would happen, but he had growing faith in her.

"I am very happy to do that", he said. His smile grew even stronger and he wondered if it was his birthday. He pressed another question, "Does that mean no more battles, no more killing? What about the third challenge?" He imagined that he had rubbed a lamp and a wish-granting Genie had just popped out with the offer of three wishes. They weren't wishes though, they were challenges, tasks. He waited with bated breath. The not knowing tested his patience but at the age of 26 years old, he had become a patient man. Then, something inside of him touched him, seemed to lift him, give him strength in preparation. He had a sense that this task was not going to be an easy or pleasant one.

"My name, Meiyo, means honour. You have been chosen because you are an honourable man. When you have mastered your craft and when you have been blessed with three grandchildren, it will be time for the third task. It will require all of your strength, courage and honour. We, the Elafrian people hope that, with all of your blessings and promises for more, you will honour the agreement we make today." She paused, mainly to delay telling him, but he just waited, listened in silence.

She continued, "We will call our son, Ketsueki, which means blood. He will be a Nephilim, half-human, half-Elafrian and his blood will be powerful." His confused look told her he wondered where this was going, so she hesitated at first, then, just blurted it out. "His life… Err, his life will be required, more specifically his blood. His blood will be needed!"

"How? Why? Is he to die with honour in battle? The third task, what is it?" He anxiously waited, wanted to know, needed to know.

"You will make five very special blades, two katana and two Wakizashi, plus a Shuriken knife. I will teach you a special technique of folding and forging the metal. The blade will firstly be quenched in water. After multiple folds, it will be quenched in venom from 50 Mamushi snakes, the deadliest snake in the whole of Cipangu. Finally, it will be plunged into blood to cool… Our… Our son's blood." Her voice quietened as she said the next words and she was hit by a flood of emotion with the reality of killing her own son.

"He – must – die." They both had tears in their eyes. The boy had not even been conceived and they were discussing his death. He had been offered amazing blessings only to now hear this.

It seemed bittersweet.

She felt the need to explain the reason further and to offer more encouragement. These five blades will be known as the '*Honour Blades*' and together they shall be a powerful weapon in the fight against evil, both now and in the future.

He remained silent, deep in thought.

She continued, "Ketsueki will also join with an Elafrian, like me. His children will also be Nephilim; they and their children will be the '*Shison*', descendants of Masamune. They will be a warrior race and their destiny will be to fight all evil in Cipangu and beyond. I realise that this must be difficult for you, but there is one more thing. When Ketsueki dies, like you he will go to live in Elafria, you have to sacrifice him, but you will see him again and spend eternity with him."

Masamune considered all that Meiyo had told him and after some time spoke with surety and conviction. "Yes, I accept the three tasks, I have made my choice." They lay down together on the narrow bed and made love.

Chapter Five

The events in our lives happen in a sequence in time,
but in their significance to ourselves, they find their own
order; the continuous thread of revelation.
Eudora Welty

Ashia awoke and felt as if she hadn't slept. She heard Jeru as he hurried to make breakfast. He always woke early and joked light-heartedly that his 'demons' always came in the night. Although they weren't physical demons, his nightmares always felt real. He had been this way since that fatal mission on the Moon. Mankind may have been delivered, but he was there and witnessed his friend give up his life, first-hand. At times, he would wake, having dreamt that he was still there. Survivor's guilt consumed him every night and he tried to combat it by protecting Ashia. She briefly stuck her head in the kitchen, and smiled at him already dressed in his black boots and khaki fatigues. He looked ready for action, but the patient composure on his face told her to take her time. When he was not on a mission, this was the usual way of things.

This morning she was also in a hurry and annoyed with herself that she had once again delayed their departure. She jumped into the shower for just two minutes to wash off the tropical, night-time sweat. Another minute and she was dressed in her favourite, ripped, tight-fitting, grungy, black jeans that said don't mess with me. In contrast and in her hurry, she grabbed a loose-fitting, semi-see-through, floral blouse, which would have been more suitable for a trip to the beach. Finally, she loosely laced her calf-high, black and shabby combat boots, with knife safely concealed.

No words were necessary, all communication by body language and gestures. She grabbed a slice of cold, dry toast and crammed it into her mouth, further restricting any verbal communication. Simultaneously she poured lukewarm, strong, black coffee into an insulated mug, then, dashed for the door.

Jeru broke the silence, "Oh, OK, let's go." It wasn't a command and sounded more like a commentary. They both stepped out into the cool, autumnal, African breeze. The fog still seemed to hang thick in places and the gentle wind caused it to swirl. It seemed natural and innocent, but this was the day that Ashia's destiny would change. She would soon learn that not everything is always as it may first appear.

Masamune spent a restless night, as he drifted in and out of sleep. He prayed that the day would be taken from him, that he would not have to proceed with the task, yet Ketsueki had accepted his calling long ago. He had been created for a purpose, but how could a father sacrifice his own son? Masamune wiped the sweat from his hot clammy hands and made some tea. His heart hammered, palpitated on the inside of his chest cavity and caused his mind to ask even more questions. Is there another way? Why him? Why his child, his sweet child?

He agonised in physical pain, as his mental anguish became unbearable. He was known as a strong man, rarely visibly emotional. Now he felt weak, nausea rising from the pit of his stomach and in silence, the tears began to flow. The warmth and comforting aroma of the fresh brew calmed him for a moment until Ketsueki appeared and stood, silhouetted in the moonlight. The strong, handsome, gentle, young man spoke quietly, "I'm ready."

"Father, this is my destiny and I am honoured… It is time. We have talked about this many times and you know that I was made for this purpose. Are you ready Father?" He sounded confident, resolute and Masamune felt a new feeling; an overwhelming sense of pride. A fresh vigour began to fill him as it exuded from his son; his sturdy, muscular young son. "Come father, we have time for a walk on the beach before we must start work."

They walked and talked, with Masamune repeating over and over that he loved his son. As the sun rose, they returned to his workshop. Meiyo and Mitéra, Ketsueki's wife and mother of his three beautiful children had already lit the fire of the small forge. Five unfinished blades lay innocently in wait on the master's workbench. Each had been forged and folded multiple times, creating a watery pattern on the finish of the blade. Each had been previously quenched in venom from 50 Mamushi snakes. They were now ready for the final stage and each of them would play their own part in the process. No instructions or commands were necessary, Meiyo had already shown Masamune, the master swordsmith how to forge these special blades. The final stage now required them to be heated to cherry red heat, allowed to cool until purple and finally quenched.

Ketsueki worked the bellows. For anyone else, it would be difficult work, but with his strong, well-toned biceps, he could have been wafting a lady's fan. As he pumped hard, the coals heated and sparks began to fly. Mitéra took his hand gently, and looked deep into his eyes, with such affection that he could not hold back the tears anymore. She squeezed tighter and through the tears and smoke, his broad smile appeared with perfect white teeth shining back at her. Her lips moved, to form the words, *'I love you'*, but no words were heard. He returned the same silent words, with an even tighter grip on her hand.

Meiyo and Masamune held onto each other for comfort, but no amount of affectionate embrace would ever take away their pain. She released him from her hold and watched as he gathered up the five blades into his arms. He thrust each one firmly into the glowing white coals and even more sparks flew. As each was placed into the correct position, Meiyo now spoke out each of their names. The Katana pair went in first, "Truth and Justice", she declared. These were shortly followed by the shorter Wakizashi swords. As he thrust them in, she spoke out in authority, "Sure and Steadfast." Finally, the Shuriken knife went into the fire, "I name this blade after my own name Meiyo, Honour. Though it is small, it will make a mighty difference. These are the *'Honour Blades.'*"

Ketsueki knew that it was almost his time. He had been prepared for this moment his entire life and believed it was his destiny. He left the bellow and moved away from the intense heat; Mitéra stepped in to take over. He knelt on the uneven, stone slabs of the workshop floor, removed his arms from his Kimono and rolled down his top to expose his well-developed physique. Poised in traditional Samurai self-sacrifice position, arms outward, angled toward the ground, palms faced upward, he was ready and signalled to his anxious father with a firm nod of the head.

Masamune retrieved the pair of Katana and turned his head away from the glow of the red metal. Though he had done this process many times, he could never manage the extreme heat of 900 $°F$ on his face. He waited... They all waited... Until the red glow had faded... Until it was purple. Ketsueki broke the silence, as he tipped his head backwards, he stared up into the rafters and cried out, "I love you father."

His father responded with an emotional tone but managed to stay focused on the task. "I love you, my son, please forgive me." Then, plunged both hot blades into his chest, piercing his son's heart, before finally protruding through his back. Death had been instant, a warrior's death. Masamune froze, gripped the swords and supported the now limp, lifeless body of the young man that he had created; his son that he loved. He signalled to Mitéra, who now ceased bellowing, in order to support her dead husband's body.

Meiyo was already crying out in agonising pain. She shrieked words that Masamune did not understand, "Elio, Elio, Kṛpayā malā'ī sunnuhōs. Kṛpayā yō baccālā'ī tapā'imkō rājya mā svīkāra garnuhōs, meaning: Elio, Elio, please hear me. Please accept this child into your kingdom.

The smell of seared flesh began to fill the workshop as the same procedure was now performed with the three blades that remained. Masamune had seen many horrific battles and lost many brothers in arms, now he considered the scene in front of him to be the most grotesque he had ever experienced. As Mitéra gently and lovingly lowered his body to the ground, the sound of metal swords clanged in his ears. His senses returned and he reacted rapidly, pulled the five blades from his son's corpse and launched them across the room, with even more clatter. The sound awakened him even more and he stared at the blood on his hands. He felt the thick, warm liquid ooze between his fingers. Immediately he dropped to his knees, grabbed Ketsueki in his arms, pain filled his chest, the pain of a broken heart and he cried a long deep cry at the top of his voice, "W.....h.....y....?" It was a father's natural reaction, which triggered a supernatural response.

Suddenly the room filled with incredibly bright light and both Meiyo and Mitéra instantly dropped to their knees. A most gentle voice spoke from within the light, though the intense light concealed the being within, "Masamune, I know you are in great pain, even though you have known that this day would come, nothing can ever prepare you for it. I know that you have questions and that you feel you will never recover from this moment. Trust me; I have been where you are… I too had to sacrifice my own son, for the greater good. All will be as you have been promised and you will eventually be reunited. Until then know this; there is power in the blood of Ketsueki; that power is now within these five blades and within his descendants, your Sishon."

The voice stopped as the light moved slowly towards him and engulfed him. Within the white cocoon, he saw a figure walk toward him. His broken heart instantly overflowed with uncontrolled love, as he realised that it was Ketsueki. He was alive, healthy and smiled at his father. They hugged; no words necessary, both overwhelmed by an incredible sense of love and Masamune understood. He understood everything.

Every time that Jeru made his way up the steps into the building he thought of Gideon. He first made this walk with his friend by his side, a little over a year ago. The memory triggered his guilt again as he looked briefly at Ashia next to him. She sensed his pain and smiled back in an attempt to ease his mind. Once inside, he transformed into a professional, confident Jeru. He was ready to debrief on his mission to the north and that had to be the priority or so he thought. Ashia would need to wait until she was called, after all, it was just a story about a crazy man, who she now regretted killing. General Benjamin Jacobson, his superior officer met him at the open office doorway. He had anticipated his arrival and they greeted like old friends, then, Jeru briefly glanced back at Ashia before disappearing behind the closed door.

The gripes in her stomach told her that she needed food, so she turned toward the busy breakfast buffet. She had become accustomed to the hostile looks from some and understood why they must feel this way toward her. She had, after all, been Lucy Apateon and had fired nuclear missiles into the south and massed a huge invasion force, (although she had no first-hand knowledge of any of those deeds). A hand reached from behind and grabbed her hand gently. She instantly turned with her loose hand clenched into a fist, ready to defend herself. This was who she was, who she knew she was, who she thought she was; a fighter, survivor, on guard, defensive. The friendly, familiar face smiled and her anxiety levels immediately reduced.

"Hello Ashia, it's really good to see you, I've been planning to come to chat with you."

"Oh, hello professor, it is good to see a friendly face… err, to see you, it's been a while."

Professor Emmanuel Elias peered over the top of his half-moon spectacles, as he strained his neck up to assume eye contact. Though short in stature, he had a superior brain and a big heart, making him an incredibly, intelligent academic that cared about people. When the Mimics were defeated and her brother killed, Elias, as he preferred to be known, had been there. He was the first person that she had spoken to when she became fully aware again and he had supported her ever since.

"My child", he always referred to her in this manner and she found it reassuring. "I'm so pleased to have found you. Some new information has recently been found and it may explain how Gideon was so connected with the Pneuma. Though the island of Japan is in the northern hemisphere, it too has been protected like us by an invisible barrier. Throughout the seven decades of mankind's enslavement to the Mimics, we have remained in contact with the Japanese authorities and they are our allies."

Her impatience made her irritable again and she started to play with her badly platted hair, force a fake smile and raise her brow. He sensed her impatience and decided to forego the background information and jump to the exciting part.

"Just recently, in the last year, the remains of a Samurai warrior were found. When archaeologists further examined the site, they discovered a very rare and precious sword. The sword is of exceptional quality and believed to be one of the lost treasures of Masamune, the great swordsmith. Now, here's the interesting thing, hidden within the handle, they found some ancient Japanese writings. I'll tell you more about that shortly, but first, the most exciting news that I can't wait to tell you. You are…"

His flow was interrupted by Jeru's return from his debrief, "Hello Jeru, sit, I have exciting news, you both need to hear this.

Chapter Six

If absolute power corrupts absolutely,
does absolute powerlessness make you pure?
Harry Shearer

He brought Jeru up to speed and continued, "The remains of the Samurai warrior have been tested for DNA, to try to establish who the poor unfortunate fellow might have been." Elias stopped, smiled, readied himself for the revelation and reached out across the small table. Then, he took her hand in his own soft hands and spoke in a hushed tone, "My dear, we already have your DNA, Gideon's as well and I can tell you that you are related to this Samurai. Gideon was also related. We also know that it is Mitochondrial DNA, which tells us that your mother is also related. The writings suggest that the dead warrior was a direct descendant, the *Sishon* of Masamune himself. You are a Masamune Sishon, a direct descendant of the greatest swordsmith that ever lived. The sword itself is remarkable and said to have great power, but especially when wielded by a Masamune Sishon."

She stared back at him in semi-shock and disbelief, her mind filled with questions and she had a sense that there was still more to come. Her anxiety rose through her chest and burst out of her mouth at a volume that attracted attention, "Come on Elias, I know you. I know that there is more, what are you not telling me?"

"Shush, shush have patience Ashia. There is a legend that talks about five powerful blades called the 'Honour Blades.' The writing contained inside the handle now confirms that this sword, a Katana, is one of them. The blade is engraved with a name, *'Truth'.*"

He told her the writing revealed the names of the other three swords and the legend of how they were made, about the sacrifice made by Ketsueki. Finally, as he felt it less significant, he told her about the small knife, "…and that one was given the name, *'Honour'*, named after Masamune's wife." He went on to describe it to her, but he stopped in absolute shock, as she reached down to her boot and produced the small, but lethal weapon.

A Shuriken

"I think this is what you might be describing", she said. Her hand held an ornately decorated hilt, with twisted red and golden thread, tightly wound in a helical pattern and protected in layers of lacquer. He acknowledged a small, black steel ring on top of the hilt, which would have been used to thread it onto a cord. The deadly end glimmered in the rising sunshine, now breaking through the window. From the handle, for a distance of 4cm, the blade widened to about 2cm, and the next 10cm length tapered down to a sharp point, which made the overall appearance of the blade an uneven diamond. Elias's attention was immediately drawn to the blade engraved with Japanese letters, 名誉 and he gasped, as he placed his hand over his mouth.

Eventually and after great scrutiny, he said, "You have '*Honour*', the shuriken, but how?"

"Yes, she said, "'*Honour*', that is what I've always called it. It was with me when I awoke a year ago. I don't understand the engraving, but when I saw it, I just thought of honour. I had it when you captured me as Apateon and although I was thoroughly searched it wasn't found, maybe because, at times it becomes invisible. At first, I thought that I was imagining it."

"Incredible, this was named after '*Meiyo*', the wife of Masamune, Meiyo means '*Honour*.' The legend states that Meiyo was not of this world, she was some kind of being from another realm, a supernatural realm. So, the invisibility? Well, let's just say, I believe you."

He told them the legend of Ketsueki and how he sacrificed his life, but that his sons would carry his bloodline. "The bloodline that you belong to, you are part of, both you and Gideon are what are called 'Nephilim', you are part human, part supernatural being. This is why Gideon was so connected to the Pneuma and why I think you will be also." He paused, "And of course your mother if she is still alive. I think you both have the same potential."

32 years earlier

Her heart pounded, thumping to break free from her already naked chest. She had waited her whole short life for this moment. She knew the procedure well, as she had been through the ceremony many times before. She knew the disappointment of rejection, the feeling of not being good enough. Anxiety swelled within and with it the hurt and pain. A small tear trickled from the corner of her red and swollen eyes. It instantly froze on her goose-bumped, pale flesh.

The snow fell as always. It had been that way for as long as she could recall. Joash could see the queue in front of her had progressed and she sensed her anticipation rise. She had been in the camp since she was 10 years old and worked as a slave, although she knew (or rather she sensed), that she was destined for something greater. She briefly averted her eyes from the altar up ahead and glanced down at the number tattooed on her left forearm. It had been there since her birth and it designated her future, but first, she had to be transformed.

She tried to contain her yearning within, but this was now her 49th attempt at the enlightenment ceremony and each time, she had experienced the deepest sense of rejection. Since her 20th birthday, every month she built up her hopes, only to have them dashed. Her excitement was like that of a pregnant woman in labour, she even felt the physical pain. For a brief moment, the pain subsided as she approached the guard, who waited at the altar. She smiled a naturally broad grin, so much as to say, "This is it, it will happen, it has to happen!"

The expression on the guard's face never changed, she knew that it wouldn't, but that was what she yearned for. She longed to change and for her enlightenment. She felt a sudden chill on her exposed breasts and once again glanced down, slightly embarrassed at her nakedness. The guard mumbled a few unrecognisable words and the ceremony was over. Now, all that remained was to sleep in a nice warm bed. She liked that part the most; it was luxurious in comparison to her usual cold bunk.

As she slept, she would dream. Memories from her

deprived life would pass before her, but they would fade, and so too would her consciousness. She had thought that she would awaken and feel like a transformed being, but she was wrong. As she slept, her mind switched off and a new Joash awoke, then looked into the mirror. The process had worked. Her expressionless face peered back at her and a new yearning entered her mind, or was it? She instantly knew her first duty; she needed to breed, though the real Joash was completely unaware. She would never know that enlightenment had been a deception and that she had lost her freedom to the 'Mimics.'

31 years later, Joash had no knowledge of the abuse that her body had been subjected to. Oblivious to the fact that she had given birth to 7 children and unaware of where they were. Gideon and Ashia were her children, her blood, yet she had no memory of them. After she fulfilled her use as a breeder, she was transferred back to the same camp that she had grown up in, where she served as Governor and persecuted so many of the camp's young slaves, even her own children, without knowing.

On VM day, she was standing in her office when it happened. She gazed out of the window into the cold night-time air, at the continually falling snow. Joash couldn't understand why her legs buckled, then, as she fell, she developed a sense of fear for the first time in thirty-one years. She couldn't understand where the feeling was coming from or what she was suddenly afraid of. As she hit the floor, she felt a new sensation all over her body, it was shock and her vision rapidly blurred, as if the retina had lost connection to the brain.

The shock to her senses heightened her state of alert. From a cowering position on the office carpet, she looked up and around the room, but failed to recognise where she was. As far as she could recall, she had never been here before. Her mind struggled to compute and understand. She was unaware that this was her workplace. Her desk slowly came into focus in front of her. It was the workstation that only minutes before she had worked at, as a Mimic slave. She looked at her hands and touched her face and desperately clawed into the depths of her mind to search for a fragment of who she was, who she is. She felt nothing but a dark, hollow, void. Confusion increased, grew and robbed her of the inkling of sanity that seemed to roll around the shell of her skull, like a grain of *'sand in a clam'*.

The stench from the filthy floor repulsed her, as her nostrils flared and sucked in decades of decay and grime. Reflexes kicked in and she jumped back into an upright stance, as her hands continued to investigate her body, a body that she struggled to remember; with no familiarity whatsoever. She wondered if she was dreaming, then tried hard to remember the last time that she was awake. At first, she had no recollection, but gradually, as she became more lucid, she remembered. Her last memory was her enlightenment ceremony. Immediately she felt a sense of disappointment, yet another failed attempt.

Her fears escalated to a new level as she could make out the cries from others outside. They too sounded in fear outside of her window. She turned to investigate the source of the sound and continued to feel her face in deep exploration. Then as she moved closer to the glass, she noticed another face staring back at her. The face was also being touched by hands. It was then that the grain of sand within the shell evolved into a pearl, as realisation dawned. The face that peered back at her was her, her own reflection. She could hardly recognise who she was and what she had become. She had aged and gawped speechless at her 55-year-old self. She wiped a tear away with the back of her bony hand and wondered if it was a tear of joy or fear. The feeling in the pit of her stomach confirmed that it was fear and she remembered it from her youth.

The restrained memories now unleashed, rushed in like a flood of emotions…. recognition, reminiscences and recollections… it overpowered, downloaded and overloaded her now conscious mind. She realised where she was and worked out that she had been there for what must have been decades. Her mind was void, unaware of her time at the breeding farm, where she had been systematically raped for six years before she ironically returned to Javelin Park camp. She had transformed from victim to persecutor, punished those that she had once been friends with and nobody had come to her rescue until now. She was free, but her mind bore the scars of captivity and abuse.

The doorway had remained sealed for decades. The inhabitants trapped behind it lay in slumber and waited for their moment, as they conserved strength until it was time. That time had at last arrived and Mortemus, the *Bringer of Death* slowly slipped through the crack, over the threshold into the domain of his enemy. He would not rush. He would patiently bide his time, in search of the key. His predatory senses told him that Joash was that key, that she would play a significant role. "She will be an easy target," he thought to himself, as he hovered over the vulnerable, unprotected northern hemisphere. In addition to his own manoeuvres, he had already dispatched his Lieutenant, Fonias, the slayer, to the south. He would use all of his skills of deception to gain an invitation into the south, before taking lives, in his role as assassin.

With haste, Joash grabbed her protective, long down, winter coat; hurried into the freezing night-time temperature and was greeted by a scene of bedlam. Many were as she had been and struggled to pull themselves from the madness that now engulfed them. For some, the shock had simply been too much and they had instantly dropped dead at their posts. Making a quick study of each of the corpses, she rapidly ascertained that they all appeared older than her. The strain of deliverance from the hold of the Mimic presence had all been too much, after so long and they were now at peace, but Joash still knew nothing and remained in the dark.

The chill of the air made her feel vulnerable and afraid. She couldn't understand why, she just knew that she had to retreat to the warmth and security of her office. She ran through the door, turned the key and locked it before she turned to see a handsome young man stood before her. "Don't be afraid, Joash, I know that you are confused, but I am here to help you. I can tell you things; things that will help you to understand. I know that things may seem chaotic. So many of you are struggling at present, but I can help you. I can help you all, but you are my priority, I would like to help you first. I can bring clarity to your confusion and provide the answers that you seek. If that is what you want, all that you have to do is seal the deal, with a shake of my hand."

He seemed friendly and helpful, as he offered her encouragement. She needed to know what on earth was happening, she wanted clarity. He told her things that she didn't know, that she had been used for breeding, produced seven children and that she was in charge of this facility. He promised to help her find her children and offered her even more knowledge and power.

Tempted by the offer of more power, she wanted to know more, to know the truth, so reached out and tentatively grabbed his hand. It was enough, the handshake was an invite and Mortemus took advantage without delay. In a flash, he disappeared from her sight, leapt onto her back and savoured the enjoyment as he sank his long, razor-sharp talons into her skull. He was now in control.

Chapter Seven

The biggest adventure you can take
is to live the life of your dreams.
Oprah Winfrey

Jeru nudged her like a little schoolboy, as he tried to contain his excitement, then the words burst out, "Tell him! Ashia, tell him what happened."

She turned to him with a scowl on her face and a slight shake of her head. She still didn't know if she imagined the whole experience and didn't want to sound stupid. The professor waited patiently. Patience was one of his great virtues and Ashia knew him well enough to know that he would sit and wait until she decided to speak. "Oh ok, ok… I think that I may have already experienced some of the Pneuma presence in me. It's not as strong now, but I think it is still in me."

She started to tell the story about the incident at the harbour, but as soon as she used the word *'assassin'*, he stopped her and suggested that they take this to General Jacobson. The big soldier listened to every word without any form of expression. The professor helped with the link to the *'Honour Blades'*. When she had finished her story, he absorbed, waited and processed the information before his comment, "When the Mimics arrived, no one was aware. Their presence grew slowly, as they gradually took control. We underestimated them and it was our weakness, it resulted in the downfall of the human race. We should learn from history, from every conflict and every bone in my body right now tells me to be on guard. I don't know what from, but this old soldier has a sense of when danger is close. I can't explain the nature of this assassin, but he was a clear and present threat. You say that he seemed to be under the control of something or someone, not a Mimic, something different. So, I'll make some assumptions here." Although he was the most superior person in the room, he nodded to the professor for his approval.

The professor gestured for him to continue, "We know that the Pneuma is a supernatural presence, a power and we know that it protects us and for some enables them with abilities beyond what we would call *'normal'*. So, we can all believe that the Pneuma is good. What then, if there is another supernatural presence that isn't good? What if this assassin was possessed by something evil, it would explain things. I would also suggest that the Pneuma warns us to be on guard as well?" He blustered to an end, slightly embarrassed and unsure of his sudden assumption, but the professor agreed and made him feel instantly better.

The military man summed things up simply, "We have a potential new threat. It could well be supernatural. Ashia seems to be developing a connection with the Pneuma, like her brother and also has this, err… Masamune connection. Somehow, these swords seem important; we need to find them all." He looked directly at Ashia and continued, "You need to go to Japan, get that sword, then try to track down the other three. This is your mission!"

"My mission? What are you talking about? I'm not a soldier, I'm a civilian? I don't take commands from you? Whatever happened to freedom of choice? I had enough of not having any choice as a Mimic slave!" Ashia never did like being told what to do and she made her feelings known.

"Oh, I am sorry"' he replied with a hint of cynicism, "You are correct; I have made another assumption. I thought that you would want to be like your brother, to embrace this gift that you are being given and to use it to fight against evil. I am sorry if that isn't the case. I had you down as a fighter, some kind of survivor, but I was obviously wrong." The General employed trickery and psychology to convince her, but she would not relent to these tactics and remained quiet, shut down, arms folded.

"My dear," the professor lightly touched her arm.

"What is your destiny? Aren't you just a little inquisitive to know more about your ancestry? What do you think the Pneuma would want you to do?"

"I don't know, it's all a bit much at present. I don't know if I can be bothered about destiny and about dead relatives, swords and… and well, what the Pneuma wants me to do. It's all too much to take on board. I'm sorry, I can't just agree to do this '*mission*' of yours"

She turned, ran from the room and headed home in a confused state. Jeru waited for permission to leave. The professor placed his reassuring hand on the young man's shoulder, "Give her some time to think before you go chasing after her."

Unlike being controlled by a Mimic, Joash had an awareness of all that she was now doing, but could not stop herself. A crowd gathered outside. The guards, all previously Mimic slaves, were in a state of confusion and unaware of what had happened. The younger inhabitants of the camp were now free to roam and had freed anyone that had been locked up. It was only a matter of time before someone naturally asserted their power to become the new leader of the disorderly assembly. Mortemus knew he could not allow that to happen; he must take control of the situation and gain superiority.

A young man in his early twenties stepped out of the crowd and climbed onto the altar. "Friends, most of you know me. I have looked out for all of you young ones, protected you from those that have persecuted you. I can't begin to imagine what has happened here, but clearly, the guards are no longer any kind of threat to us it would seem…"

Mortemus cut him off, "No threat? It would seem? Clearly, you do not have a clue what has just happened here. Your oppressors, who you refer to as the Mimics, they are defeated, they are no more and it's all thanks to me; I have freed you, I am your liberator."

The young man laughed back at Joash, "We all know who you are and we all know that you are our persecutor, not a liberator. So many have suffered under your hand, so many have died and you expect us to believe what you now tell us." He mocked her and his voice trailed off with more laughter.

"Yes, you are quite right, I did kill, but no one else needs to die if you just shut up and follow me." It was a demand, not a request. Mortemus had issued an ultimatum.

Life is full of choices and the mocking man was about to make his last. "Haha, not one of us will follow y…" His sentence was cut short as her hand sprung out and grabbed him unexpectedly by the throat and he gasped for air as her fingers sank in deep drawing blood.

"It didn't have to be like this", she hissed with a reptilian tone, then, with a quick twist and a pull, she ripped his trachea from his neck. The group in their early twenties surged forward in a natural retaliation, their leader was dead so a void had been created. The first five to reach Joash suffered the same fate as their leader and with each fresh kill, Mortemus, '*The Bringer of Death*', grew stronger. "I am your leader now!" Joash screamed, Mortemus made her scream, he was in control and now he controlled the crowd. This was the start of his army. The defeat of the Mimics created the longed-for void and he had rushed in to take advantage. He was now in control and the strongest of this rebellious group would be selected and more Erebusians would arrive to control them. Joash had been their first strategic target, now they would target the seat-of-power.

<hr>

Another battle now took place, the battle in Ashia's mind. Her anger told her to explode with rage. She knew anger well, it had protected her, strengthened her and kept her alive. Anger was a good thing, but she also knew enough to know that it can also be bad. Her anger now battled with her love, her love of life, her love of her brother and her love of Jeru. He was like another brother, so of course, she loved him, but was there more? On her arrival home, she made a mug of coffee and then the battle had started. Anger flared up again as she threw the mug in her hand across the room.

Love tried to reason with her, '*Gideon was your brother, your brother is family, family is everything, your bloodline is important…*'

Smash! Her foot kicked out, boot launched coffee table. Crash! "Why should I do this? I won't do this! This isn't my destiny! What does Elias know? What does HE know?" She screamed out loud to an imaginary person.

In her mind, love tries to interject, '*What does he know? He knows a lot and you know he does; you know that he's right. Follow your destiny.*'

Bang! The table lamp hit the wall opposite her. Anger had won the battle as she yelled, "I don't care, the bottom line is, I just don't care and I don't want to care. Gideon cared; he cared too much and see where it got him! It got him dead and I don't want that! I'm not him, not Gideon, not my brother. So, you can all just leave me alone."

Jeru stood outside the door and listened, unsure if he should enter, the sound of her rage struck fear in him and he didn't scare easily. He wanted to do the right thing, to restore peace, not to upset her more. He wondered if this terror was because he cared for her so much. His mind wandered and wondered some more, did he care for her more than he realised? Did he love her? With that thought, came another thought, *'love conquers fear'* and suddenly his anxiety subsided.

As he entered the room he saw her, spent, exhausted; as if she had been through a physical battle. He could see no bruises, no wounds, although the battles within the mind do leave scars and she had many, far too many, she didn't want anymore. She wanted protection and peace. For the last year, he had fulfilled that role and she was comfortable with it. *'Why couldn't things stay as they are?'* she thought.

He did what she wanted as if he had read her mind and placed his strong comforting arm around her, "It's alright, I'm here." He had stated the obvious, she could see that he was there, but she still didn't feel alright. Is he lying to me? Is he really my protector? What does he really want? Doubt crept in; anger and fury would take the supreme victory as darkness descended into her mind. During her race back home, she thought nothing of the patch of sea mist that she hurried through and inhaled. It was Fonias that was now playing with her mind, as he took advantage; he would eventually consume her mind, drive out her sanity and cause her to take her own life. Her anger had made his task easy. Although he did not have a full hold of her yet, it would be enough.

Jeru decided that actions would speak louder than words, so wrapped his arm around her tighter. She felt the warmth of his sweat from his chase after her. His heartbeat played with her own, already thumping heart, they seemed to be harmonious. His odour, manly, musky, aroused her, in a seductive manner. She felt comfort, reassurance and more. He stepped toward her bedroom; guided and supported, she felt obliged, attracted, and compliant. He released her, pointed at the bed and she complied again, lay down, breathed out, and relaxed. He gently removed her boots and lay down alongside her, held her tightly, lovingly and safely. Although neither of them was tired, they both fell asleep.

It didn't take long for Joash to search the installation and discover the Mont Blanc connection. More information was available on the location of the closest airbase and a plan was made. With access to an assortment of trucks, transport to the airbase was easy. Upon arrival the scene was further chaos, the void had not yet been filled. Mortemus soon established his leadership at the expense of a few airmen, which caused him to further strengthen.

On the runway sat two giant Lockheed Martin, Super Galaxies, the C-5M, fuelled, loaded and ready to roll, one contained five Apache helicopters and the other six Mine-Resistant Ambush Protected (MRAP) vehicles. An arsenal of assault weapons was also available and combined with their other weapons, confusion, disarray and fear, it would be enough for the task.

Less than an hour after they seized command of the base, the small army was in the air and en route to Geneva airport.

Chapter Eight

The best remedy for those who are afraid,
lonely or unhappy is to go outside,
somewhere where they can be quiet,
alone with the heavens, nature and God.
Because only then does one feel that all is as it should be.
Anne Frank

Before her enlightenment, she had always slept with one eye open. Since being released from the Apateon creature to her fully aware self she had always struggled to sleep. A year of tossing and turning, sleepless nights had left her irritable and she knew it. Jeru also suffered from insomnia, but he would try to play it down with comments about his demons. His attempt to screen the issue with humour would work with most people, but not with her.

Now, Ashia stirred from what felt like the best sleep ever. She rose like Sleeping Beauty, from a deep slumber. Although she had never heard the Sleeping Beauty story, she wondered about her life, her 'destiny' and whether it would all end happily ever after? As she slid out from underneath his embrace, she glanced back down at Jeru. He was sound asleep, his arm still in an outstretched, curved position, as if he still hugged her.

Drowsiness was still upon her, as she crept along the passageway to the open-plan kitchen, lounge/diner. Sleep was still in her eyes, so instinct told her to rub them and the blur that she saw when she opened them, told her that someone was standing before her. She didn't feel threatened; the person was friendly, almost familiar.

"Hello Ashia", the voice was gentle, firm, reassuring and recognisable. The recognition brought her to her senses, her mind raced, *'What, it can't be?'*

"It CAN be", he said, as if he had heard her thought. "It's me, Sis, it's Gideon."

The doorpost steadied her, as if it were a third person, while she gathered her breath and her thoughts. "Gideon, how is this even possible? You're dead! Aren't you? You died on the Moon, a year ago. How can this be happening?"

"Look", he said, "Touch me, hold my hand." He reached out and took hers, which took even more of her breath away and caused her knees to wobble. His response was to grab her in his brotherly arms and steady her. "I love you, my sister."

As soon as she heard those words, she knew that it was him. "I've been sent to you to help you. There is much that I need to tell you, to show you what you need to know. The mission that you have been asked to do is vital, but first, I must tell you that you are in danger."

"Oh no… not you as well… I just want peace." She paused, shook her head and turned away briefly, then switched onto the offensive, "What sort of danger? I can take care of myself and how the hell did you get here? You can't be real? Gideon is DEAD. Now just get lost, you're just in my imagination."

Although it was only a slight hold, Fonias held on, he told her to reject him and it seemed to work.

Gideon was not perturbed, "The Pneuma… I need to tell you about the Pneuma… The Pneuma is far more than we could ever realise…" Every time that he mentioned the Pneuma, she felt a deep desire to know more and Fonias could feel his grip weaken.

At first, her response was gentle, positive and submissive, "Yes, I would like that, to know more, understand more, maybe to have what you have… err, had, I'm not sure what to say." Fonias scratched at her mind, "I don't know what I want, what to think, how did you get here?" Fonias had sowed a single seed of doubt and it had taken hold and Gideon could smell it.

He knew that doubt, when left unchecked would turn to lies and lies would breed hate, fear and destruction. He knew that so much hurt could come from doubt and that he had to act fast.

"I don't want to hurt you, but I need to show you, just trust me for one second." Then he touched the palms of his hands to her temples and they were transported to a place with bright light, everything white, nothing else to see, just white. Suddenly she felt calm and at peace as if a weight had been lifted. For the first time ever she felt safe, free and loved. Her pent-up anxiety, aggression and disbelief had gone. A new feeling filled her, a new realisation, she must fulfil her destiny.

"What just happened? What is this place? I understand some, but not everything, but I want to know… what is my destiny? I understand yours was to die on the Moon, I understand that we all die at some point, we can't avoid it, but it's what we do with our lives that will make a difference. I don't feel scared anymore? What… I mean, *where* is this place?"

Fonias had lost his grip. He had as soon as she was transported. He had been in her mind and now her mind was in a place that he was forbidden to enter.

"Welcome back Sis and welcome to Elafria. Let me show you your destiny. Human beings talk about destiny in such a small, linear way. You think that my destiny was to die on the Moon, but that was just a small part of the process of my destiny. Elias, Jacobson and even Jeru will encourage you that your destiny is to find the *'Honour Blades'* and they are both partly right. You do have to find them, as your true destiny depends on it. Elafria is your true destiny, to know the Pneuma power as I do, to feel one with him, but come and see."

As he finished speaking, the blank canvas of white changed. The first thing that she noticed was the sky. It was every colour in a rainbow, constantly changing, colours merged and mixed like oil on water. No clouds were present until she thought about that detail, then they just appeared as beautiful shapes and not just white, they too were every colour under the sun and the sun. It was indescribable and she felt the warmth of its rays. They seemed to caress her skin, to welcome her.

Her eyes bulged in astonishment at the stretched-out vista of fields, trees, flowers, strange animals and mountains. A river cascaded from a high cliff top, meandered through the meadows and flowed into a gigantic lake or, was it the sea?

"This is your destiny… this is Elafria. Come, we don't have long and there is much that you need to know and people that you will… well I think that you'll like to meet them."

From within a wooded glade, two figures emerged, an older man with a young man, both oriental in their look. The similarity of features indicated that they may be father and son. Even from a distance, they seemed vaguely familiar as if she should know them. "You already know of the *'Honour Blades'*, well now it's time to meet their makers. This is Master Masamune and his son Ketsueki; they are the start of our bloodline and they would so much like to meet you."

They talked for what seemed like hours and told her that all sacrifice is painful, so should only be carried out when necessary. The pain will always leave scars, but we should be proud of scars. Ketsueki showed her his nine scars, "Without these, this sacrifice, there would be no *'Honour Blades'*." At some point Ashia reached into her boot and produced the Shuriken, *'Honour.'* For a brief moment she tried to recall when she had put her boots on, but her thought was broken by the reaction from the pair.

"She is a beautiful specimen. She hasn't changed since we first met. So powerful, purposeful, truly reliable." Ashia wasn't sure if they were talking about the knife or a person until the old man gestured to her to turn around and said, "Meet Honour, my beautiful wife; she looks the same now as she did all those centuries ago and she is just as powerful."

"Hello, Ashia, I am so pleased to finally meet you." As she spoke, Ashia was mesmerised by the glow of her skin and she finally came to accept that she was in a completely different world. The three men had previously explained about Elafria, but to see a true Elafrian was what it took to finally convince her that this was all real.

"Ashia, you have been told many things. In your world, you have a mission that you do need to accept, but what you have not been told yet…. is that you will not be alone. I don't mean, Jeru and others that may be with you, I mean myself. I will be there for you. You may not see me, but I will be there and will protect you, fighting the unseen forces…. but when the time is right, we will need to combine our forces. Gideon will also support you, as best he can. The time when you return here will be unknown to you, but remember, this is your destiny."

She turned to look at the three men behind her, but only her brother remained. Her head swivelled back to Honour, but she too had disappeared. She felt that she still had so much to learn.

"Gideon, I'm not sure if I'm ready for this? I'm not you. I have so much to learn."

He smiled at her and said, "You will always be learning, you will never know everything. You only '*think*' that you don't know enough. Maybe you even '*think*' that you are not good enough for this task, but Elio himself has chosen you. He is the One that created all that you see and he wants you to just step out in faith, believe that you can do what is needed and be at peace with that. Now I need to tell you more and give you something. Hurry, we do not have much time left."

Lying on her bed, Ashia stirred slightly and Jeru wrapped his arm around her even tighter. His reassurance caused her to drift back to sleep, even though it was the middle of the day.

Gideon held her hand, as he took the lead, anxious to fulfil his task. After a short walk, through trees with orange bark and purple leaves, they were greeted by a wide pasture, adorned with thousands of species of unknown wildflowers. A multi-coloured river flowed gracefully through the meadow, fed from another tall waterfall cascading from, she assumed a majestic clifftop. The top, and therefore the source, was too high to identify. Dotted evenly along both sides of the river bank were huge, sentry-like trees.

"This is the '*River of Life*', said Gideon. "When you

drink from this, you will never thirst again. It is the source of all life; it gives life and renews life. Just one drop will restore the righteous and reveal the evil. It never runs dry."

He pulled out a chain from under his garment that had hung around his neck with a small triangular-shaped crystal glass flask attached. He lowered the flask into the strange glowing water and filled it before he handed it to her.

"Take this Sis, keep it safe, you will need it on your mission. You must also find two more similar flasks, one will contain Ketsueki's blood and the third will be empty. This last one will need to be filled with the breath of an Elafrian. Remember you need to find the remaining '*Honour Blades*'. Take great care though, there are enemies all around, especially in the north, but even in the south. They are the '*Erebusian*'. Like the Elafrian, they are ethereal beings but DO NOT underestimate them they are a dark and evil power. This flask will help to protect you however, without the three flasks and the swords, you will be no match. They will grow stronger and they will overpower, so you have to act swiftly. Remember we will meet again, but you MUST succeed in your quest... I love you..." His words faded, as did his image, then he was gone.

Ashia opened her eyes and just lay there in the stillness, thinking about the unusual dream that she had experienced. As she reflected, she felt different, as if new courage and boldness had filled her. She tugged on the arm that still caressed her, and shouted, "Wake up Jeru, wake up, I had an amazing dream."

She recalled every vivid detail as she spewed out the story, "I met Gideon and it felt so real…" She moved quickly onto her encounter with Masamune, Ketsueki and Meiyo, but she was going too fast.

"Whoa, slow down, let my brain wake up." Then he noticed it and questioned, "Where did that necklace come from?"

Without any thought, she blurted out the answer, "Gideon." She paused and thought, '*What does that sound like*', then continued. "Gideon, gave it to me… in my… dream…but how can that be?"

Chapter Nine

Hoping for the best,
prepared for the worst,
and unsurprised by anything in between.
Maya Angelou

She slowed down, told him the whole story and when she finally finished, he simply said, "It wasn't a dream."

She already knew that but felt reassured that she wasn't going mad. Then she remembered something, "Jeru, I owe you an apology. I was angry and rude towards you and I didn't mean to be."

"That's OK", he said, "Think nothing of it." He realised that she had been under considerable stress; it was less than 24 hours since she had killed a man.

"No, you don't understand it wasn't me; something seemed to be in me, it took control. I don't know how, but I couldn't stop myself from saying those things and I even felt bad about myself... like I might even hurt myself. It was powerful... somehow, I think that I let it in, but it's gone. Going to Elafria must have somehow removed it."

He hugged her even tighter than he had done before and held her safe, "Don't ever let that happen again, the Pneuma will protect you… I will protect you." As he tried to contain his emotion, a tear welled up. When he wiped it away, he had his confirmation, his heart seemed to burst, as he realised that he did love her, not as a brother, this was a new kind of love.

A year earlier Ashia's mother, Joash had experienced her own awaking. The two monstrous aircraft landed safely on the Geneva runway and the heavily armed assault force rapidly overpowered the bewildered forces on the ground. Those that were not killed had succumbed and joined the growing deadly force.

There had been no victory celebration for taking the airport, for it had been a stepping stone to achieve their current objective. Mortemus, directed his puppet, Joash and she had easily and fearfully convinced the Apache helicopter pilots and crew to accept her authority. As they did, each of them had unknowingly submitted to Mortemus. Now his Erebusian army trickled through the still invisible gate, latched on and took control of their new victims.

The Apaches were the first attack wave on the Mont Blanc stronghold and within just three days of the victory over the Mimics, a new enemy took control of the seat of power. In the year that followed, the gate widened but still remained unseen and even more evil passed through the gate. This enabled them to take control of the majority of the remaining population of the northern hemisphere. The Erebusian tactic was brutal, submit or die. Mass killings occurred all over the frozen, barren wasteland. The accepted explanation was people simply losing their minds, having been suddenly released from the grip of the Mimics.

Each time a human life died, the evil force grew stronger, the gate opened some more and although the Erebusians were greatly outnumbered by humans, they drove fear into mankind. In just twelve months, the northern population had been depleted from eight to four billion. An elite force of Erebusians known as 'Choani', had the skill to hop from one host to another. Though there were moments of slight relief as they left, the host would never fully regain control of themselves long enough, before the *Choani* returned. In comparison, the Mimics had been quite humane as they wiped out all memories. Mankind now existed in a living hell and in the worst affected areas, the living now fed off of the dead.

After a year of torment, mass murder and cannibalism, Mortemus, within Joash had grown strong and was even feared by other Erebusians. Only one was more fearful, Abaddon. He would remain in Erebus until his minions had control over the whole of the earth, and the gateway was fully, visibly open. Mortemus gloated that he knew it was only a matter of time before they eliminated any hope for mankind. In Africa, his Lieutenant, Fonias would not fail, he had never before failed. Mortemus eagerly awaited news.

Skia, tried his best to enter the room stealthily, just as Mortemus snapped the neck of another victim and fed off of their life. "Skia, report to me, tell me good news, STOP LURKING in the shadows! What news of Fonias?"

"My Lord, O great Mortemus, Fonias has done well, he has successfully gained a foothold in the south and he has located his primary targets, the '*Sishon*' and her mate."

Mortemus forced a smile onto the face of Joash. He briefly sensed that victory would soon be theirs, but he also knew that Skia held back news. "Tell me everything, are they dead? Did he succeed?"

"My Master, I fear to tell you. Fonias is weak, he desperately needs to feed, his weakness caused him to fail. The Sishon still lives and she grows strong."

He grabbed the petrified messenger by the throat, "Then report back and tell him to feed, but pick off the weakest and the elderly, stay undetected. He must follow her, confine her and then kill her. Now leave me!" As he bellowed his last command, Joash released her hold and he was forced back by the power of his energy, which blasted him out of the mountain stronghold and he tumbled down the snow and ice-covered rock.

Ashia did as Gideon had urged her, accepted her mission and began preparation for the next two months. She learned fast, as the Pneuma power in her filled her with even greater combat abilities than Gideon. The flask remained around her neck at all times, which filled her life with even more power. Being on the base, with Jeru, the flask and the Pneuma presence made her feel safe and secure, but little did she know that she was being watched.

Fonias was there whether awake or asleep, his vaporous form drifted into the local villages, picked off the weak and he grew stronger. Records would indicate that there had been an increase in the death rate, but each loss could be medically explained. Therefore, he remained undetected. His orders were to follow, confine and kill, but confinement had not yet been possible. She grew stronger, faster than him, so he fed faster, and unexplained accidents started to occur throughout Angola. Every night, more unexplained deaths happened and soon Fonias knew that he was ready, but how would he confine her.

During his 'following', he had discovered that her mission would lead her to Japan and he reported this intelligence to Skia, who promptly told Mortemus. Consequently, Joash had started a bombardment of the small, sheltered country, but the shield of protection had so far held.

Ashia was ready. She had become a leader. Jeru was her number two and her strike force of '*Sixers*' assembled. Their journey to Japan would be under the ice, in the confines of HMS Trenchant and Fonias couldn't believe his luck. She would be '*confined*'. All that he had to do was slip aboard the submarine, wait until they reach Japanese waters (within the protective shield), kill her and Jeru…then wreak havoc across Japan. He would be a hero of Erebus and maybe even greater than Mortemus. He drooled a mix of saliva and blood from his last feast, as he sensed victory within his grasp.

HMS Trenchant waited in the misty harbour of Madagascar and history seemed to repeat itself, as a single Chinook helicopter flew low over the land to rendezvous. The ten-strong strike force felt ready for anything, although none of them was aware of the extra passenger, Fonias, in his ethereal form, moved gradually from one to the next. His invisible form savoured each moment, he sensed their weaknesses and their puny skills. He felt stronger, knew that he was. Their Pneuma power would be no match for him. He had feasted, devoured flesh, consumed life and now he would take theirs.

Chapter Ten

Once you believe things are permanent,
you're trapped in a world without doors.
Genesis P-Orridge

The cumbersome aircraft landed with remarkable grace on the harbourside, just a stone's throw from the mighty, dark and ominous outline of HMS Trenchant. The machinegun turrets were manned, as expected during any wartime or conflict and although there was a clear and present danger, the enemy slipped past unnoticed. Fonias, (the rival force of one) grinned and drooled, as he drifted in the early morning sea mist. His plan now unfolded as he had hoped and he entered the same hatch in the deck that Gideon had climbed out of over a year earlier. He brushed past the occasional submariner. Each man experienced a sudden onset of nausea, yet still, he remained undetected. He soon arrived at the location that he considered to be the safest place in the vessel, the nuclear reactor. No human being could survive for long in there, but he was not human.

Ashia knew her role and the responsibility that it

carried, but as she stepped onto the deck and stared at the open hatch, she sensed a chill and froze. "You all go on ahead", she gave the command, trying to sound authoritative, but she thought that it sounded weak. Her feet seemed glued to the deck, as she stared intensely at the hatch.

"Is everything Ok?" Jeru approached her from behind with the last of their equipment, but she couldn't turn to face him. Something gnawed at her, warned her, an internal alarm rang in her head – DANGER.

"Sure… err… yes, fine." He grabbed her by the arm, ripped her off of the spot and dragged her away to a quieter part of the deck.

"Ashia, I know you well enough to know that you are not alright. Something bothers you, what is it?" She knew that she couldn't lie, not to him, so relied upon her own knowledge and experience to determine her problem. The Pneuma tried to warn her, but she was still learning, still naïve.

"I guess I just thought about Gideon. He was here and travelled on his mission in this same vessel. I had a sudden chill, a fear, I thought that something bad was going to happen." As she finished talking, she glanced up at the moon as it dropped in the Madagascan morning sky.

Jeru made an attempt to reassure her, "Your feelings are only natural. During my first mission, after Gideon died, I just felt terrible; as if I was missing an arm or something. I still struggle without him, but he would want us to get on with life. Come on Ashia, you've got this and the Pneuma has got you."

She sensed the Pneuma power fill her, since she had failed to discern the warning, it now did the only thing that it could do, prepare her for the danger that she had chosen to face.

"Yes, come on let's do this, time to get below." She gave the command; she was back in control.

<hr>

Captain Harry Hanson soon had the submarine underway on a direct route to Australia. There they would take on fresh supplies, before navigating north, through the Indonesian islands towards danger. He addressed the team, "Welcome aboard… You are all brave… Trenchant is a safe place and it is your home…"

It was his standard welcome speech, but after he had finished, he spoke quietly to Ashia and Jeru. "I was sorry to hear about Gideon, he was a great man and he made a great sacrifice for mankind. My prayers are with you and I pray that you will stay safe on your mission."

"Thank you, Captain. That is very much appreciated…" It was the usual niceties that they had become accustomed to since Gideon's heroic death; all politeness and mannerly but never truly understanding their loss.

The team made the most of their downtime, during their four-day cruise to Australia they spent time getting to know each other and began to bond as a unit. Jeru gave them the name, the *'Honour Squad'* for obvious reasons and slowly, as they sensed no danger, they all lowered their guard. They anticipated that they would first engage the enemy when they left the safety of Japan and head on into the unknown.

After stopping in Australia, Fonias became anxious with a need to feed and have some fun and he selected a target.

At 6 feet tall it's not surprising to hear that Alan Collins was more commonly known as *'Big Al'*. The truth is though, he was given his nickname on account of having a big heart. He really was a man that cared about others. The 36-year-old soldier had been born into the military and his father and grandfather instilled within him how important it is to look out for and support your comrades. He was the oldest member of the Honour Squad and although he was of a lower rank, they all looked up to him with great respect. The younger ones especially saw him as a father figure and often joked with him, calling him, '*Dad.*'

The diver's wristwatch told Al that it was morning; his stomach confirmed it, as it let out a long, slow rumble. One more thing informed him that it was a new day; he needed to make his regular stop at the '*Heads*'. He had grown to enjoy his quiet moment sat on the lavatory seat. It was his peaceful quiet time. In that tight space, he was alone, or so he thought.

It only took a single second to take his life. Fonias was the strongest he had ever been and one blow from his tightly clenched fist was all that it took. His kill had been clever, cunning and surgical. The cause of death will be initially considered a heart attack. Only a full post-mortem would reveal the true nature of his death; his heart exploded from a huge blunt force trauma, yet no outward bruising was visible.

At the moment before he struck, Fonias had materialised in the cubicle in his true corporeal form. Al had been shocked by his grotesque, definitely-not-human appearance and in that instant, he knew that the mission and the team were all in danger. He wanted to shout out, but fear and shock seized the big man.

Fonias savoured the moment, absorbed the life force of the stricken soldier and grew even stronger. He wanted to rampage indiscriminately through the occupants of the craft, but he knew that he had to restrain himself. He had selected Big Al as he knew how much his death would impact team morale. It was all a game to him and he enjoyed playing with his food..

In the confines of a nuclear submarine, it didn't take long before his body was discovered. The medic declared it as natural causes and the Honour Squad dropped into a depressive state of disbelief and mourning. With no facilities to store a corpse, Hanson made the decision to bury the man at sea. So later that day, whilst navigating north, the team and some of the crew assembled on deck. Fonias drifted alongside as a mist, behind the gathered line of mourners.

Not one person shed a tear, but they all felt the numbness, confusion and questions associated with any death. Various people said a few words about Al, including Ashia as their leader. Then Hanson concluded with brief comments saying, "Let's bow our heads and say a few words of prayer."

The Erebusian was well aware of the human weakness of prayer. He considered the averting of their eyes toward the ground and especially closing them, to be a sign of stupidity. *'These humans are so predictable',* he chuckled and sneered quietly so as not to draw any unwanted attention, then he moved.

As a lion selects a gazelle from the outside of the herd, he struck. He could now move fast and in a heartbeat, his rough, scaly hands were placed over his next victim's mouth, razor-sharp talons dug deep into his temples. His huge body mass instantly dragged the man over the side and to his death. This stealth attack was so well calculated and so well executed that no one even noticed they were yet another man down.

Pete James was just an average sixer who dreamed of one day being able to live in peace. To have children with the woman that he loved, whom he had recently married and to live out his life raising ostrich on a small ranch. His dreams ended that day and his young wife became a widow without a body to bury. They would never find him, as Fonias rapidly fed, devoured his flesh beneath the ocean and grew even stronger.

Fonias, the slayer, once again safely ensconced within the reactor, mused over the fact that no one had missed the man. He considered the value of human life and decided that their lives must be even more worthless if no one misses them when they are gone.

In silence and disbelief, the crew and the Honour Squad returned to the bowels of the submarine. Big Al was as fit as any of them and they all considered their own mortality, their fate and what happens after death.

Al's body had been discovered soon after he was killed and most of the squad had missed breakfast, so they all headed to the small mess room for food. As they scoffed at the chef's special of the day, which no one dared to ask what it was, Jeru arrived with a tray of nine small shot glasses. Each contained some kind of alcoholic drink. "It's customary", he says, "To drink to a fallen comrade and although Big Al didn't fall in battle, he was on a mission and he was part of this team. So please raise your glasses to Big Al and the rest of the Honour Squad."

A single glass remained on the tray untouched, which raised the question, "Who is missing?" Ashia looked around the room, she had memorised their names, faces and just about everything else about them all.

"*Cowboy*, where is he? Has anyone seen him? Did he even come back in from the deck? Everyone, start to look and find him."

As they were now submerged, they knew that the only place they could look was inside, so they split into four pairs to cover the sub as quickly as possible. "Something doesn't feel right here, so make sure that you all stay in radio contact and report anything strange. Report back here when you finish your sweep.”

As cousins growing up together in High School, Xander and Chuck Okoro had always worked well as a team. It was as if they were telepathically linked and as Sixers, they quite possibly were. One thing was certain; they could sense each other's movements and thoughts just before they happened. This phenomenon is often common among twins, but these cousins had an even closer bond. Their synergy made them a great asset to the squad, as between them they had the potential of four average Sixers. They had been assigned the section of the lower deck housing the reactor. They knew that they had more ground to cover than the others, so moved fast.

“Slow down Xander; someone is sure to find him. He can't go far on this old tub.” Xander Okoro knew that his cousin was right, but he was famished. He hadn't eaten much when they had realised that Pete James aka *Cowboy,* was missing.

“Yeah, I know you, Xander, you're hungry again, nothing new there. I don't need a special Pneuma connection to know that.”

Xander was first to the top of the metal, ladder-type stairs. Shiny, parallel, metal handrails, polished with use, ran the length from ceiling to floor. Steep, open metal treads, were evenly spaced to be able to ascend and descend. He was in hurry and so jumped both feet on the handrail, to make a rapid, fireman style, descent. His hands also gripped the rail to slow his fall. His boots stomped on the steel floor as he landed.

Chuck stepped slowly onto the first step, even slower onto the next, then, he sensed something that he couldn't explain. His intuition told him that there was danger nearby and Xander picked up on it too. "Xander, something's wrong, this doesn't feel right."

His cousin responded, "Yeah, I feel it, best call it in."

"Roger that." Chuck touched his finger to his throat mic and started to speak, "Unit 4, all call signs. At the reactor, someth…argh!" He stopped mid-sentence as something reached through the steps from the shadows, then forcefully pulled both of his legs, until his knees crashed onto the patterned tread. For a fraction of a second, he perched there horizontal, face down. The someone, *(or something),* still held onto his ankles. There was no time to think or speak before he heard the snap. The pain seemed to come in the next second, as his anguished scream was heard over the radio, both of his legs had been snapped and ripped off at the knees. Gravity then took over as the rest of his now limp body pitched downward toward the metal floor.

Xander froze and stared at the sight of his cousin as he

plummeted. Chuck frantically squeezed out one word, "MOVE." Then his skull smashed open on the steel floor.

Xander heard the word before it was spoken and already reached for his combat knife, as a long, gnarly dark arm reached out from the shadow and grabbed him by the throat. Fonias, undeterred, moved closer and stomped on the fallen soldier's skull, which made it pop like a party balloon. The slayer now lifted his arm and raised Xander into the air. Xander figured that the beast was being careless and he took advantage as he thrust his knife into his assailant's chest.

Fonias just smiled an evil grin and hissed, "Who do you think you are? You and your Pneuma are nothing compared to me and as for your feeble weapon, you will need to do better than that pathetic excuse of a knife. Your flimsy weapons can never harm me."

Fonias used his free hand to grasp the wrist holding onto the knife and snapped it like a twig. Xander screamed, then unable to hold the knife, he let go and instinctively held his broken arm up to his chest for comfort. Fonias deliberately and dramatically pulled the blade from his chest, as if drawing it from its sheath. In the same movement, he lifted the man higher to stretch his neck, then sliced it open.

Blood spattered the narrow passageway, as his head

drooped and his eyes closed and he took a final glance down at his cousin's broken body, then, he was also dead.   As a celebration, the slayer clawed and dismembered both bodies, just for fun and to instil fear in whoever found them. He then decided that he was tired of hiding. His handiwork would soon be found. It was time for a new strategy, so he concealed his form and drifted up through the submarine.

Chapter Eleven

It's OK to have your eggs in one basket
as long as you control what happens to that basket.
Elon Musk

Rebekah Bekker was almost rejected from the team, but not because of a lack of combat skills, fitness, ability or experience. She was a seasoned soldier, who had never been reprimanded, always followed orders and at the age of 27 years old, had already been promoted to the rank of Lieutenant. She was an impeccable soldier, but she was a woman.

During selection, Ashia had been impressed by her ability to achieve the task, she had been the obvious choice based on points, and she was an excellent Sniper. Despite her credentials, Ashia still had concerns. Rebekah Bekker, Beck Bekker or *'Beebee'* for short, was beautiful. Ashia had struggled, questioned herself, *'Is it her beauty that concerns me or something else? I'm a woman… I should stand up for her… Can I trust her? Can I trust the men with her?'*

Her Jewish and Scottish heritage had given her rich red

hair, which she kept short. Deep, alluring, mahogany eyes shone out from her smooth tanned skin. Her smile was cheeky and potentially seductive. With a tall, slender body, like that of a decathlete, she stood out in a crowd. Did Ashia want someone that stood out? They all needed to blend in and this woman would struggle.

In addition to these concerns, her personality was bubbly, outgoing and flirtatious. The rest of the squad were men and so she could be considered a disruptive influence, but in the same way, she could also be a distraction for any potential enemy. For Ashia, Beebee was a head or heart decision and her head was saying '*no*'. In the end, Ashia decided that the Pneuma had given her skills and she had proven herself so therefore, the Pneuma convicted her heart to accept her.

Chuck's last radio transmission said that they were at the reactor, now Ashia and Jeru were almost there. They hurried, panted and Ashia tried to raise them on the radio, "Unit 4, Chuck, Xander, are you there? Chuck, come back? Xander, come back?" As she reached the top of the stairs, she hollered some more into the hole toward the floor below and noticed the blood below. She made hand signals to Jeru to hold his position and stepped onto the stairs.

After Big Al's send-off, Captain Hanson had briefly spent some time in the control room and now enjoyed a cup of tea in the small officer's stateroom. The name was something of a misnomer, as there was barely enough room for the three officers that slept in this space. Beebee didn't knock, just walked straight in and found him sat at a small fold-down desk. She had startled him from reading a report that the medic had provided on Big Al. "Hello, it's customary to knock before entering? What are you doing here?"

She didn't answer but smiled her alluring smile. All of Ashia's concerns were about to be justified. He wanted to tell her to get out, but her presence was hypnotic. He had noticed her on the first day that she came on board and had felt an instant attraction. His senses screamed out to him, told him that this is not appropriate, but she just raised her index finger to her plump, moist lips and said, "Shhh... No one will know."

The combination of smile and words intoxicated; over-powered, then, she reached out to him. As she pulled him to his feet, she embraced and kissed him. He was happy to kiss her back passionately.

The still-warm blood dripped from the stainless-steel handrail and acted as a lubricant. Ashia's hands slipped down faster than intended, it caused her to trip on the steps and land in an undignified heap at the bottom. There she lay on the floor, between the two corpses and covered head to toe in blood and brain fragments. Her natural reaction was to check the bodies for signs of life, but in an instant, she realised that their wounds were fatal. She recognised the claw marks as similar to those she had seen before on the *Dancing Man'* assassin on VM Day, only considerably worse. In a calm, quiet manner, she spoke back up the stairs to Jeru, "I think we may have a problem."

"Are they dead?" Jeru was slightly in shock and asked the obvious.

"Yes, both dead and now I wonder about Big Al and how he died. I don't think it was a heart attack and as for Cowboy, I don't think that he is even on board."

"That means our squad of ten is down to six and we haven't even seen any action yet."

"Or have we? Are we in the battle right now and we don't even realise it?

"Someone's coming, be quiet."

The footsteps scurried towards him, multiple sets and

he waited in anticipation. Two of the crew were out in front, both armed with pistols. The captain closely followed and behind him came Lieutenant Bekker with her team partner Tommy Lopez. Lopez was without doubt the ugliest member of the squad, but he was also the meanest. He used to think that these were the reasons why he had never been able to attract anyone of the opposite sex. Then he realised that he was attracted to other men. It was for these reasons that Ashia had teamed him up with Beebee. Tommy's partner waited for him back home and they had plans to set up a home together after the mission.

By the time they had all arrived at Jeru's position, Ashia had already climbed back up the stairs. "Turn around and put your hands behind your back, you're both under arrest for the murder of your own teammates. Cuff them." The captain had given the order and his crewmen promptly obeyed. Lopez and Bekker looked on from behind, speechless.

Jeru and Ashia, both protested, "Take a look at the bodies, this wasn't us. You're making a mistake. We're not even armed. We're all in serious danger."

Their pleas were ignored as they were frog-marched to separate interrogation rooms. Hanson and the guard took Ashia into a small room that had evidence of old dried blood… the remains of the many Mimics that had been terminated within the tight space.

The guard forced her to sit at a steel table before he stood slightly to the side and in front of her. Hanson stood opposite her with the table in between and started to ask random questions, just to satisfy the guard, but it wasn't his voice that she heard.

"Ashia, look beyond him. Look into him." Filled with a sudden peace and comfort at the sound of Gideon's voice in her mind, she challenged the captain, but not so as to sound too confident.

"Are you really so afraid of me that you need to keep these cuffs on? You know that I'm not a threat. You know that I didn't kill them. So, let's be civil." She teased him, tempted and tormented him until he succumbed.

Harry Hanson sneered back in silence and indicated to the guard to remove the restraint. As he did, she followed her brother's instruction and looked beyond. This time it was easier than the first time she tried this on the harbourside. Now she could fully make out the entire, hideous form of Fonias, the slayer and her stomach repulsed. She hid her reaction well and the Erebusian was unaware that she could she. As far as the guard was concerned, nothing had changed, apart from her hands being freed.

She now moved fast, with a supernatural speed, flipped

open the bottle that hung around her neck and flicked it towards the captain. The water revealed Fonias, so the guard could see what she saw. He pointed his weapon at what he now determined as an intruder. Hanson responded with an instant, single punch to the guard's face, sending him flying into the steel wall, where he collapsed unconscious.

"You think that you are soooo clever, but you are no match for me. I am soooo much stronger than when we first met… yes, we have met before, when you killed that weak creature. Go ahead, why don't you kill this one… I'm going nowhere."

"That's what you think, I'm also stronger." She moved fast, leapt from her crouched position into a flying dive and reached down to the concealed Shuriken. Fonias forced a wide grin onto Hanson's face. The captain cringed at what he was doing, but he was not in control of his actions. Fonias braced himself to smash her frail body and gloated with pride. His pride blinded him to the knife in her hand, not being thrown this time, not aimed at the human host. She targeted the bulging red eye, a clear target on the dark scaly, Erebusian skin.

Unlike the blade that Xander had managed to plant in his chest, this one was smaller, but far more lethal, especially to an Erebusian. This was *'Honour'* and though it was the smallest of the *'Honour Blades'* it was made with the blood of a Nephilim. It penetrated the eyeball and her hand continued forward into nothing, as Fonias had gone, banished to roam Erebus.

Her momentum continued to move her forward into Captain Hanson and they both joined the guard, who stirred on the floor.

Hanson spoke first, "Sorry, that wasn't me."

"I know."

"Thank you, but it was your Lieutenant Bekker, she must be working with that thing."

"That's interesting, why do you say that?"

"Because she came to me and seduced me. As she kissed me, I lost control."

"That wasn't Bekker, I believe these things can transform, imitate us to deceive us, so we need to be extra vigilant."

"Well, how are we supposed to defeat an enemy like that?"

"Not by our own might and not with conventional weapons, but by the power of the Pneuma. We are facing an enemy far more deadly and deceptive than the Mimics. We should trust no one, but also do not allow fear to consume us. If we do that, then they have already won."

Mortemus didn't need Skia to tell him the news; he sensed a loss, as if a small light had been ignited within the darkness. He knew that Fonias, his beloved slayer, had gone. He also knew that a small flame of light could spread if it was not extinguished. In his frustration and anger, he wanted to shout at someone, but he was alone, so he shouted at Joash, though it appeared that she shouted at herself as she stared at her reflection.

"Your daughter thinks that she is so clever, but she will fail. We know her plans; you humans are so predictable. I don't know how she managed to kill my friend, but it won't happen again."

Joash heard his words; they had come out of her mouth and they had mentioned her daughter. She had a daughter. The mother in her tried to cry, but she could not, she could not control her actions. Then, in hate and anger, Mortemus made her give the command to increase the bombardment on Japan.

Chapter Twelve

Japan, 1ˢᵗ August 1945

Haruto Tanaka observed for most of the day, as men unloaded the endless stream of captured enemy weapons. The curator of the Imperial War Museum, now wondered how he would start to catalogue every new weapon. A propaganda exercise of the Japanese Imperial Supreme War Command had ordered that their spoils be displayed as a mark of their considerable victories.

Soldiers and museum staff rushed to complete the monumental task, as continuous truck-loads arrived without any time for rest. The task began to take its toll on the aged historian who now felt weary, unable to focus clearly. Never in his 37 years at the museum had he ever experienced such chaos. Deep down, he disapproved of the exuberant show of glory. Nevertheless, his Japanese culture would not allow him to question or judge his superiors and he understood their desire to show the people that it looked like they would win this war.

Akio was amongst the team of soldiers and had been to-ing and fro-ing throughout the day. His mother had told him that his name means bright and as such he had always tried to dream up bright ideas. He had started various business enterprises, but unfortunately, each of them had failed. The war had given him an opportunity to reflect on his life. He tried to determine where he had gone wrong and he concluded that each venture had failed due to a lack of funding. Quite simply he had no money. Now, however, he thought he saw an opportunity and was determined to take advantage.

Amongst the bedlam, he spotted what he believed could be his investment for the future. The Samurai Katana had first grabbed his attention, with a single word inscribed on the blade *'Justice'*. It took pride of place on an open display above the two smaller swords and a small knife. The description on the display used the name Masamune and he knew enough to know these blades were very special and perhaps valuable.

Amid the mayhem, it was an easy task to slip the unprotected swords into an empty packing crate, then, load them onto his truck. He knew that as a deserter, he would be executed and so Akio ran and hid. Haruto

Tanaka, although he was tired, soon discovered that the swords were missing along with Akio, but that was the last anyone ever saw of him.

If Akio had known the significance and power of these blades, he may not have removed them, but to be fair, not many people alive in 1945 would have been aware. Though separated from the fifth blade, these four were enough to provide Japan with supernatural protection, but it was now weakened by Akio's greed.

Desperate men do desperate things and Akio used all of his skills of cunning, deception and concealment. He spotted a small rug seller's panel van. The window was wound down and a coat was draped over the seat. He knew that the coat would serve as a disguise. As he put it on, he naturally placed his hands into the pockets. Surprisingly, he found the ignition key. He couldn't believe his luck. Without hesitation, he hurried to bury the swords inside a rug. He hid the small knife in his new coat pocket, then the soldier hoped that his disguise would work.

In just three days he travelled north to Wakkanai, the most northern point of Japan and the shortest distance to Russia. Although the port was heavily fortified, he was able to find an unscrupulous captain of a fishing boat that would provide safe passage for one man and a rug, for the cost of a van full of rugs.

On the morning of 6th August 1945, Akio jumped from the boat and swam 100 yards in the freezing water. As he stepped onto a bleak, deserted Russian beach, at exactly 15 minutes and 15 seconds after 8 o'clock, Enola Gay's bomb bay doors snapped open, and Little Boy was freed from its restraining hook.   The command was given, "Bomb away." The nose of the *aircraft shimmered as it rose* ten feet and the gigantic A-bomb was released nearly six miles above Japan. The pilot immediately executed a sharp 155-degree turn to the right.

On the ground, the air raid siren called a feeble warning for almost a minute, before Little Boy explodes over the city of Hiroshima. At the time of the detonation, the *Enola Gay* was already eleven and a half miles away and Akio was oblivious to the devastation that he allowed to be unleashed.

Three days later, a similar attack took place in Nagasaki. Akio was still unaware, although if he had known, he would have failed to make the connection. He was now in Russia, enemy territory, but he would have less than a month before the war came to an end.

As the remaining half dozen Sixers gathered with Captain Hanson, they all felt battle-weary, although some could not understand why. They didn't feel as if they had been in a battle, yet their teammates had been taken from them, brutally slaughtered.

Hanson looked at Bekker uneasily, unsure what to think, then, he looked at the rest of the team and felt the same. "Any one of you could be the enemy."

"That particular enemy has gone. I think it acted alone, like an assassin. We can assume that we are safe for the time being", Ashia spoke to the remnant of her team but made sure that she focused most of her attention on the traumatised Hanson.

"You haven't been through what I've been through. I could feel that thing inside of me, it controlled me and there was nothing that I could do to stop it. Then for a moment, I thought that you were about to kill me, but you didn't. How did you get rid of it?"

She explained about the water and showed him the bottle, which had somehow magically been refilled to the top. She didn't want to take credit for her small victory and said, "Without the water, the knife, the Pneuma power and Gideon speaking to me, I never would have been able to release you."

All apart from Jeru, looked at her inquisitively, as if she needed to tell them more. Tommy Lopez was never afraid to speak out, "Boss, what do you mean, *'Gideon speaking to you'?* Your brother has been dead for over a year. How can that be?"

"I can't really explain that Tommy, in the same way, that none of us can explain the Pneuma power in us that makes us all Sixers. Somehow, I hear his voice. It's as if he's stood right next to me. I think that I'm the only one that can hear him."

She shared her story about the dream that might not have been a dream. She explained about Elafria, the river of life, the bottle, how she met her ancestors and even Meiyo.

Jeru smiled as he had heard the story before. Lopez didn't say much, simply, "That's unbelievable, yet I do believe you."

Bekker chipped in, "We all believe you", as she looked at the other two team members for confirmation. Yichen, of Chinese descent, nodded a single fast nod in agreement and looked at his Russian partner, Andrei. Built like a cross between an ox and a weightlifter, he was known for his brute strength and slow movements. His head moved up and down as if about to fall asleep, but they all knew him well enough to know that he also agreed. Then, in his deep Russian accent, he spoke, "Affirmative."

"OK, good. Now there is one other thing that I found out when I visited Elafria. I was told of someone called 'Elio', who made everything. I thought that they meant that he made Elafria, but I think that it's more than that. I believe that he made the earth and everything in it and that includes us.

You know I'm just working this out in my head, right? I think that he made the Elafrians, to serve him and look out for us. That's why Meiyo saved Masamune. We all know that the Pneuma is powerful and I think that this Elio is just as powerful, if not more so."

As she finished speaking, the room seemed to become brighter and the whole team gasped in shock as Gideon manifested next to his sister. She turned and smiled, but also shook her head, so much as to say, '*I'll never get used to this.*'

"Sorry I didn't mean to startle you", he joked.

Ashia looked at her team, "Can you all see him?"

They just nodded; stunned to see him and Gideon continued to talk. "Let me tell you all this. You are correct, Elio is powerful, in fact so powerful, that he is greater than any of the Erebusians and just the sound of his name will strike fear into them. His name is another weapon for you to use, you have the Pneuma in you; so, you can use his name with authority. My sister is right, Elio reigns as sovereign, not just in Elafria, but over the whole earth, both in the north and the south. For that reason, whenever you greet each other and especially anyone new, you must say the words, *'Elio reigns.'* Respond also with the same. No Erebusian or a human that is possessed by one will ever be able to say these words. This is how you will know if you are safe from them. Remember, they may be strong, but the power that you possess is even stronger and their weakness is that they cannot be everywhere or in everyone. Now, let me hear you all say, *'Elio reigns.'"*

The room erupted with the shout; and, as it did, Gideon disappeared. For the next few days, they talked about what they had seen and their expectations, but none of them could say where they would be directed after Japan.

The seas around Japan were also protected by the same invisible Pneuma shield and the submarine navigated its way under the ice that had barely melted in the last year. Once clear of the ice and the barrage raining down from above, they surfaced and headed for Sagami Bay.

Chapter Thirteen

When adversity strikes,
that's when you have to be the most calm.
Take a step back, stay strong,
stay grounded and press on.
LL Cool J

After Masamune made the Honour Blades, he sat upon a seat carved out of a huge protruding rock. As he looked out to sea, he contemplated what had just taken place. He puffed on a long clay pipe and wondered about the future, his own future. With his task over, he no longer had a purpose and already felt worthless.

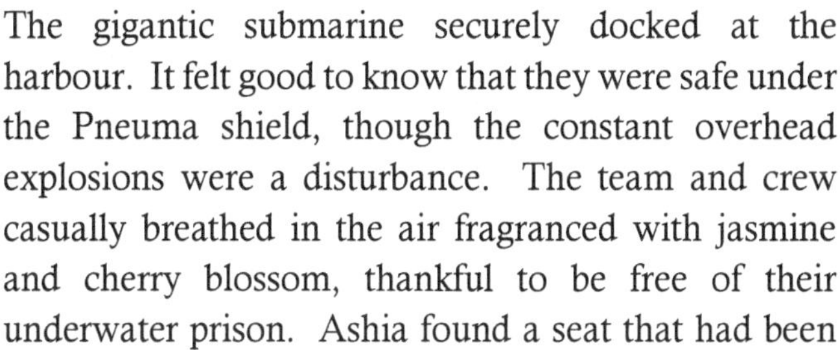

The gigantic submarine securely docked at the harbour. It felt good to know that they were safe under the Pneuma shield, though the constant overhead explosions were a disturbance. The team and crew casually breathed in the air fragranced with jasmine and cherry blossom, thankful to be free of their underwater prison. Ashia found a seat that had been carved out of the rock centuries earlier and enjoyed the early evening sun on her skin. Over the years the rock had been worn smooth and she pondered on the people of this land and all that had sat where she now rested. Something inside of her told her that she was home, although she had never previously set foot in this foreign land. This was her origin, where her family line had begun and she was anxious to meet the Japanese people.

Hanson walked up the gentle slope to chat and she stood to greet him, "Our orders are to stay here at your disposal, so whenever you know where you are heading next, we are ready."

"Thanks, Harry", after their experience, they had become good friends and she joked, "Sorry to have made such a mess of your ship."

"Ah, you mean 'boat'; submarines are referred to as 'boats', not ships."

"Ha, right, OK, I'll try to remember that."

They were interrupted by a man with an American accent and uniform, "Mam, welcome to the Kanagawa Prefecture, Japan. I'm Major Garcia and I've been assigned as your liaison officer during your time with us here."

"Thank you, Major, it's good to be here, but please don't call me 'Mam'."

"Sorry Mam, err sorry, I'm not sure how I should address you, Mam, oh sorry." He could feel himself begin to blush with confusion. He had expected someone in a military uniform, with designated rank and insignia. Ashia had accepted the mission, but as yet, not the commission, so as such she was technically, just a highly trained civilian contracted to carry out a task. Dressed from head to toe in black assault gear, like the rest of her team, now making their way to join her; Garcia was perplexed.

"My team just call me 'Boss', but 'Ashia' is just fine too."

"Ah, Ok Ashia it is then, we can head off as soon as the rest of your team are here."

"This is the rest of the team", she said and tilted her head toward the other five.

"But we were expecting ten of you?"

"Yes, I know, we ran into a little difficulty, this is it. So, let's get going."

Camp Zama appeared to be a miniature version of how America used to be before the current ice age. At the main gate, the guards checked paperwork before they allowed them to pass by. Once inside they noticed the cafeteria diner to the left, before the right turn down 5th avenue. Here they spotted the surf shop with an assortment of brightly decorated surfboards. At the end of the road, they took another right into East Street, which traced around the golf course to meet with Long Drive and eventually passed through Gate No.7 into the Sagamihara housing area. This would be their home for the duration of their stay. In comparison to their own African barracks, Camp Zama was like a small town.

The house was luxurious, with eight bedrooms, communal rooms, offices, a games room and a swimming pool. None of them had ever seen anything like it, but especially Ashia and Jeru, who had spent most of their lives fighting for survival. Ten minutes after their arrival they heard a knock at the door. Lopez opened it and grunted at a handsome young Japanese gentleman, well dressed in a pale linen suit. He had abundant confidence in him for someone so youthful. His short stature could deceive a person to think that he would be a pushover in a fight, however, the scar on his right cheek told a story that he had been in at least one and lived to tell the tale. He smiled warm and friendly at Lopez.

"I'm here to meet with Ashia."

Lopez was unsure how to treat him, so switched to the default of, "Err..um… Elio reigns."

"Elio reigns? What's that supposed to mean?"

"You're ok, you can come in."

The man thought it a very strange welcome and that perhaps it was a strange African greeting, but would later find out the significance. "My name is Haru Kurai and I need to speak with Ashia, please. It is urgent."

Lopez led the visitor into the communal meeting room where the rest of the team relaxed after being cooped up for eight days. "Boss, someone here to see you… Err, Harry something." Where Lopez lacked in manners or etiquette, he would make up for when his true skill set was required.

Lopez stepped to the side of the room and left their guest exposed as he faced the Sixers. With only two women to choose from, identification of Ashia was an easy task, as he recognised the oriental, Masamune likeness. "Hello Ashia, it really is wonderful to meet you at last. I've eagerly awaited your arrival and simply could not delay seeing you any longer."

He spoke perfect, fluent English, with a soft, gentle tone that poured gracefully from his wide smile. His mannerisms were such that he addressed royalty or a deity as if worshipping her and it made her feel uncomfortable. "Please, allow me to introduce myself. I am Master Haru Kurai, but you can call me Haru. I am so pleased to meet you at last."

"Yes, you've already said that. What can I do for you Harry er Haru? Spit it out." She was tired, impatient and in need of sleep in a good bed and this man currently prevented that.

"Haru, I'm Haru and no, no, it is I that am here to help you, I have so much to tell you and I am so excited. You are my '*Kankei*'." His over-enthusiastic mood suddenly made him revert back to his native Japanese tongue, so he corrected himself.

"Relative, sorry. <u>You</u> are *my* relative, we are related, very distant, but we are... We are related. Is there somewhere that we may talk in private?"

"Look ahh, Haru or whatever your name is, if you have something to say, you can say it to the rest of my team. Related you say? How can that be possible?"

"OK, please let me start by telling you that my middle name is Masamune and that every person in my family has had that same name for centuries. We can trace our family line all the way back to the great Gorō Nyūdō Masamune, the greatest swordsmith that ever lived, but of course, you already know of him. You have Honour, the '*Shuriken*', may you be so kind as to show it to me?"

Ashia was taken aback by the sudden request to see the knife and went on the defensive, "Hold on a sec, let's just back up a moment. Do you know that Elio reigns?"

"Ah… Well, yes, according to the kind gentleman that greeted me at the door, but I am afraid I do not understand this term, '*Elio reigns*.'"

"It's not a problem; if you can say it, you're ok." She continued to explain the expression and power that it has to reveal the Erebusian enemy. He told her that even though he had never heard of '*Erebusians*', he was well aware of a dark supernatural presence on the earth.

"I have so much to tell you", he continued. "My family name, Kurai, means darkness, but don't let it alarm you. The first Kurai was born from a concubine woman that our great ancestor, Masamune took soon after he made the Honour Blades. The story goes that he was beside himself, having killed his beautiful son, Ketsueki. He gave his life to Meiyo and the task that he agreed to carry out, but he never expected it to cause him so much grief and pain. So, he sought succour and comfort with another woman whose real name is unknown, but Masamune named her Kurai. This was in contrast to Meiyo, the Elafrian, who was a creature of light. Until recently, it was thought that the only line that survived was the Kurai and that the true '*Sishon*' were no more. So, you see it truly is an honour to meet with you at last." By the time he finished the story, his excitement had calmed down and she began to warm to him.

For his whole monologue, he stood, as six sets of eyes and ears observed, although he focused his attention on her and never allowed the lack of hospitality to affect him. Now she offered him a seat and introduced him to everyone else in the room and Lopez smiled at him as if they were old friends.

Once sat, he continued to talk but still aimed everything at her, "You have had a long journey and if you can, with the noise of all the bombs, you must get some sleep. Tomorrow you will know the Truth."

"Truth? What truth? Why can't you tell me the truth now? Are you telling me that all that you have said is a lie?" She seemed frustrated and angry; Jeru leaned forward to the edge of his seat as tension built within the room.

"No, no, please allow me to explain. Yes, everything that I have said is absolutely true, but the Katana, the Honour Blade that was found recently, its name is

'*Truth*.'   Tomorrow you will meet her, she is so beautiful. Have you ever held a Katana before?"

"Yes, we all have, we're all trained in a full mix of weaponry."

"In that case, I look forward to spar with you." She didn't answer as she didn't want to embarrass a relative that she had only just met. Instead, she thought to herself, '*You would never stand a chance against me or any of us, we all have the Pneuma, we're all Sixers. You're just a little man in a suit'*. She felt pride well up but thought nothing of it.

As he left, he turned and said, "When we meet tomorrow, I am sure that it will be a day of surprises."

Chapter Fourteen

While we celebrate our diversity,
what surprises me time and time again
as I travel around the constituency
is that we are far more united and
have far more in common with each other
than things that divide us.
Jo Cox

Joash wanted peace and to be released from her torment, but Mortemus gripped tight on her mind. Every so often, as she slept, she dreamed. Mortemus was aware of it yet unable to access her subconscious mind. Her dreams were reflections of childhood. She had struggled, as her children had, fought for her life and survived. Her dreams always ended at a point with her being plunged into darkness, whilst stood naked in the snow. This latest dream brought with it new distress and agony, with labour pains and childbirth. The dreams were now more frequent and she knew that they were her experiences, such as brutal rapes, physical punishments and abuse. During one such dream, she had a revelation. These things happened after the darkness, she was remembering and overcoming the power of the Mimics.

Sporadic bombs continued to fall throughout the night. She couldn't sleep with the noise, so walked to the window and looked up at the dark night sky. Lights flashed like lightning, shortly followed by the deadly and potentially destructive booms. Beyond the flashes, Ashia noticed the light of the waning moon. The image made her hopeful, despite not knowing where she was going or what would happen next. Nevertheless, the hope settled her mind into peace as she returned to her bed and slept a deep long sleep. When she eventually awoke, she felt invigorated and ready for whatever lay ahead.

The hot Japanese sun dazzled her through the window, as it was still low in the sky. The rest of the team had been up for some time but hadn't wanted to disturb her. The aroma of coffee and pancakes wafted through the house and she felt a sudden pang of hunger. Garcia and Haru had already arrived and both took advantage of the food on offer. People moved about, prepared for the day in silence, no words were necessary, as each face said, *'I'm anxious to know what happens next.'*

They didn't have to wait for long as Ashia tried to speak through the final remains of her last pancake, "Ok, let's go meet the *'Truth'*." To which Garcia raised his eyebrows and Haru smiled, the rest held onto their poker faces as they all clambered onto the minibus.

Garcia pulled the vehicle to a halt outside a large gymnasium building, with armed guards at every entrance. The foyer was as large as some small gyms and festooned with memorabilia, awards and photographs dating back more than a century. Haru led the way towards yet more armed guards standing next to an entrance. As he placed his palm on a blue panel, the electronic locks released and the door swung open.

Lights activated upon entry and they all stepped into the windowless room, built like a panic room. Ivory silk cloth was now all that stood between them and the Katana. Ashia felt tempted to just whip the cover off, but she had to respect Haru and whatever he had planned.

"Please, be seated. You are all our honourable guests and we are so privileged to have you with us. Before I introduce you to the '*Truth*' I would like to tell you a story." He told them about Akio and how the four blades were stolen and the serious consequences that followed. He explained that these blades were not just instruments of war and death, but that, when in their rightful place, they provide protection and deliverance from evil. He sensed some scepticism amongst some of the team. Even Ashia and Jeru had their doubts.

"Let me explain. My country is an ancient land and has been known by many names. Originally Cipangu, then Nihon and now as you now know it, Japan. This name literally means the centre, source or origin of the sun. Of course, our scientists now know that this isn't true, but we do know that Japan is a very significant country. This is why the Pneuma has chosen to protect it, out of all of the countries in the north. We know that Masamune was not just a great swordsmith, the greatest, he was also a holy man… which is why he was chosen."

He paused to allow his words to sink in.

"Obviously we have no proof, but we have the belief that this sword and the Nephilim power contained within, is what helps to sustain the protection currently over Japan. Whilst we know that it is imperative, that you, Ashia, the true 'Sishon' of Masamune take the blade and use it to find the lost Honour Blades, it will, unfortunately, leave Japan more exposed. There are some among us, small factions that believe the blade of *Truth* should not leave Japan, hence the security. However, the majority of people understand that we at times, need to make a sacrifice; it is written into our culture."

Heads nodded, knowing that each one of them was now ready to make the greatest sacrifice, as Gideon had done before them, should the need arise. "Good, then, without further ado, allow me to introduce The Honour Blade known as '*Truth*'." He threw the silk cloth into the air and before they had a chance to even glimpse at the sword, he demonstrated its effectiveness. With his left hand, he grabbed the sheath and immediately gripped the hilt in his right, drew the blade and held it underneath the floating silk. As the cloth fell and touched the blade; it parted into two and with the grace of a butterfly, glided to caress the floor.

Ashia clapped her hands in applause, but was tired of the show-boating, "Very impressive, a clever trick, but can you use it?"

"But of course, would you like to see it in action?" He sounded confident.

"Well, that's why we're here, so why not. Pick any member of my team and the challenge is on."

"In that case Ashia, my long lost relative, I choose you, Kurai versus Sishon."

A surge of pride filled her again, as she thought to herself, '*I'll do this for the team*', but Haru sensed her arrogance and so already knew that he had her at a disadvantage. Haru had trained all of his life for this moment; the darkness in him edged him on and taunted him, '*Take her head*'. He knew that he could and part of him feared that he might, yet he still stood confident. He knew that he could beat her, with this sword he would, without doubt, win the fight. He was, however, unsure if he could win the other battle that now raged in his mind.

They all made their way to the vast gymnasium big enough to contain 5,000 military personnel, where she chose from a selection of regular Katana. As he removed his jacket, the darkness in his head spoke to him again, '*Take her head*'. He smiled, bowed a traditional Japanese bow, with eyes fixed on his opponent and then attacked. His small form moved at the speed of a falcon, with such ease and agility. The blade moved like lightning, although these first opening moves were designed to draw out his opponent, to assess her capabilities, her strengths and her weaknesses. Ashia was unaware of any weaknesses, but he knew that her pride and smugness would be her undoing. He thought to himself, '*This so-called Honour Squad will soon need a new leader and the Kurai line will be supreme*'. The darkness within him could devour him if he wasn't careful.

Ashia taunted him, "Is that the best that you have? You will need to do better than that." More pride filled her, it slowly built a barrier between her and the Pneuma power within her. The more her pride manifested, the more he taunted her; teased her with superior swordsmanship. He was a Masamune of the

Kurai line and he knew that her pride would be her downfall.

He lunged; threw his body forward aggressively, a series of short jabs, swipes, and slashes, all well-coordinated with seamless focus. She twisted, evaded, parried and counter-attacked. With all the sustained pushbacks, her energy drained from her muscles and in a weakened state, she stumbled. He knew that it wouldn't be long and soon, it would all be over. He grasped the sword in both hands above his head, wrists close to his scalp; he extended his arms, shifted his hands, centred overhead then slashed down and sideways from left to right, controlled, precise and cut flesh, blood leaked from her arm.

He stepped back, stopped momentarily, tilted his head and raised his eyebrows in a taunting gesture as if to say, *'Is everything ok?'*

Jeru stood with a concerned look aimed at Garcia. The rest of her team sat on the edge of their seats as they shouted and encouraged, "Come on Boss, you've got this." Haru looked briefly in their direction and mocked with a brief laugh, "Ha."

In a slight display of concern for his wounded opponent, he asked, "Are you ok? Shall we continue?" The injury was a mere scratch, though her pride had yet again taken another blow that ignited another weakness, anger. He knew that pride combined with anger could be a deadly combination, especially for her, she was out of control and disconnected from the power of the Pneuma.

She lunged, violently, with infuriation and exasperation written all over her face. She knew that she was losing, but struggled to grasp why. Her mind raced, tried to ascertain control. *'If this was for real, I could die'*, she thought. Her efforts seemed vast, but his were slight and accurate. She defended, whilst he attacked, she fought like an amateur, whereas he was the professional.

As she slipped and staggered, he bent his left leg fully, dropped to a crouch position with his right leg fully extended and twisted into a whirling spin. *'Take her head, do it now'*, the darkness nagged at his brain. She tried to avoid his outstretched leg but her uncoordinated stagger became a trip and changed into a fall; she was down. His movement didn't stop, she tried to regain control, to jump back to her feet, but he was fast, too fast.

He moved in for the kill, his powerful stance over her, she felt humiliated and defeated, but he didn't stop. He continued, shifted his body weight, knees apart and slightly bent, prepared for an overhead cut. His blade above his head faced the ceiling and as it was swung downwards, it cut the air, on target for her neck.

'TAKE HER HEAD.'

"STOP." Jeru gave a strong, firm command and the blade stopped abruptly against her neck. He stared with concern and anticipation and the team gasped a sigh of relief, then he rushed forward as realisation dawned, thrust his fists into Haru's chest and pushed him violently backwards.

The short Japanese man steadied himself, placed the sword on the floor, looked at Jeru placed both hands together in a prayer stance and gently bowed at the waist. Then he stepped toward Ashia, as Jeru made an attempt to intervene, but she showed him her palm as if to say, *'Stop.'* Haru continued, took her outstretched arm and helped her to her feet.

"For a moment there, I honestly thought that you were going to kill me", she said jokingly.

"So, did I", said Jeru abruptly, "What were you playing at? What sort of demonstration is that?"

"You are angry", said Haru, "Please breathe, calm down, take a deep breath; anger is not good for you. You are right Ashia; I could have killed you and part of me wanted to. There is darkness in me and I hear it in my mind, it tempts me, tests me and tells me to do bad things. I am also Samurai. I have lived my life according to the old Samurai ways, the traditions and disciplines. It is those disciplines that allow me to stay in control and not allow the darkness to consume me. The thing is, we all have the potential for the darkness in each of us to consume us. You allowed your pride to take advantage of you and pride is a dark thing."

Jeru listened whilst he inspected her arm and made an unnecessary fuss. She turned more towards Haru and ignored her concerned friend. "You're right, my pride blinded me and I totally underestimated you."

"The first rule of any form of engagement is, *'never underestimate your enemy.'* To do so was your first weakness; pride was your next, then, you allowed it to give birth to anger and when that happened, you had already lost - it was simply a matter of time. Even with your Sixer abilities and Pneuma power, you were defenceless as you isolated yourself. You lost your power and if you allow these things to control you, the same could happen again. My power is the way of the Samurai, I can never be separated from that, it is who I am, what I am, my life, my culture. I used to say that it is *'my everything'*, but I no longer say that. I want… no I desire what you have, I long for the Pneuma to be in me."

The group of onlooking Sixers all reacted with comments of, *'Not possible, never going to happen, etc'.* Jeru, now calmed down and intrigued by his comment told him, "You can only have the Pneuma in you if you have gamma wave activity in your brain. Do you have that?"

"No, but… what if you are wrong and your scientists are wrong? What if it's the other way round? What if, you receive the gamma brainwave activity WHEN the Pneuma comes into you and *only* when the Pneuma comes into you. What if the power of the Pneuma is really available for everyone that wants it, for the whole of mankind? Until the Sixers, the Samurai were the greatest warriors to ever live, so why can't a Samurai become a Sixer?"

"Well, if that were true", said Ashia, "The world would be an incredible place, but honestly, what would it take for people to, first of all, understand that and then want that? So many are lost, the Mimics left them in a messed-up state and the reports that we have heard are that things are now a lot worse. Right now, though, it's my turn with this beautiful looking sword." She reached down and picked up the Katana and instantly felt connected as if she was in the presence of Masamune and Ketsueki once again and the power of the Pneuma filled her.

They fought again, a sensible fight and she learned how to use the blade. She watched his moves and countered into an attack; all the time she thought about his words and wondered, '*What if he is right?*'

By mid-afternoon 'Truth' had been passed around, handled and used by everyone but Garcia, then Haru spoke again, "I did tell you that it would be a day of surprises. The Katana was the obvious one, my ability to defeat you was another, but you have also discovered some things about yourself, your weaknesses. We still have more surprises to come. Please follow me and return the '*Truth*' blade for now."

Chapter Fifteen

Knowledge is power. Information is power.
The secreting or hoarding of knowledge or information
may be an act of tyranny camouflaged as humility.
Robin Morgan

Joash noticed that her dreams were more frequent and recurring, overcoming the power of the Mimics, being set free and freedom itself. She had experienced it briefly and it felt fearful. Night after night they repeated and she remembered standing in her office seeing her reflection for the first time and then the fear. Mortemus sensed her active memories so dug his talons in deeper and whispered seductive tones into her mind, *'I will take care of you. In me, you shall know no fear. All who follow me will spend eternity with me. I give you everlasting power and control. When you are in control, you have no fear. Without fear, there is no pain'.*

Whenever she awoke, she heard his soft, hypnotic, voice. She wanted to believe him, but her dreams told her another story. Her mind was in conflict and confusion. Gradually the tone of his voice morphed from seducer to tormentor, whilst the dreams became more lucid, colourful and real. The scenes evolved from memories into something new, different and abstract; they were beautiful and she wanted more. Every once in a while, she heard a faint, distant voice in her dream. She couldn't make out what it said, until eventually, after endless nights, through the muffled distortion, she understood one word, "Joash."

"I have a very special Samurai relic to give you. It was passed down the *'Sishon'* line for centuries, but at some point, it was placed into the care of the *'Kurai'* line. Over the years there's been rumour and speculation as to why this happened, but I believe it was a declaration and a statement of trust, it said, *'The Kurai is part of the Masamune family'*. Now I feel the need to pass it back to you, as you are 'Sishon'."

She waited as he paused. Though she had slept well, she woke full of anticipation. *'We still have more surprises to come'*, his words resonated in her mind as excitement grew. They were alone in a typically Japanese garden, with neatly raked miniature white stones. A large maroon Acer tree sheltered them from the morning sun, as they rested on a simple bench formed from an immaculate lacquered slab of thick cherry timber sat on top of two large carved white marble spheres. The faint, ambient sound of water trickled to fill the silence; as he once again paused for dramatic effect whilst the blossom scintillated her nasal cavities. She felt nervous and anxious, though relaxed. Then, his revelation made her gasp and took her breath away.

He reached around his neck to produce a triangular flask identical to the one that she had concealed around her own neck. "Somehow I think you may already know what this is", he said as he passed it to her with a glow on his face and a happy smile. As he set it into her open hand, he closed her fingers and wrapped his own hands around hers.

"This is the blood of Ketsueki, it was spilt to create the Honour Blades and it truly is my honour to restore it to the Sishon. Something tells me that you will know exactly what to do with this."

He allowed her hand to slip from his and said nothing as she reached for her flask that contained water. It was his turn to gasp, then, as she held one bottle in each hand, she said, "If I am right, this should be interesting." She brought the two glass vessels together to sense a slight warmth and vibration as the two became one, contents mingled and suddenly she felt a new level of energy; even the chains merged to form one stronger, thicker version."

"Wow", he exclaimed with uncontainable excitement, "That was far more than interesting than I thought it would be. It was incredible, I really didn't expect that. I wonder what will happen when you find the third one?"

"So, you know that there are three?" She thought to herself, '*Of course he does.*'

"Yes, naturally, I am '*Kurai*'; it is the legend of the '*Sanmiittai*', which translated means the Trinity. There is a final flask to be found that will most certainly fill the remaining space, but where do you think that may be?"

"I'm not entirely sure, but one thing that I now realise is that it will be revealed when the time is right. At present though, I just feel that we need to stay here until we know more. So, with that in mind, what more can we do to prepare? Do you have any more surprises?" She dropped the new chain around her neck and the reconfigured bottle under her shirt.

"Haha, this is an American army base in Japan, the land of high tech, gadgets and of course more surprises. Let's meet with the others and have some fun."

He never knew of the devastation that he had caused until sometime later and even then, failed to make the connection. His actions had wiped out hundreds of thousands of innocent lives; the cost of greed. Now, on the run, in a hostile land, he needed to keep out of sight and stay on the move. Akio travelled west under the cover of darkness and followed the setting sun. He moved like a mouse, from village to village and stole anything of use.

The first small township provided food and warm civilian clothing. At the next community, he took more food and a blanket. Before long, his load became heavy, so decided to steal a handcart, but an old, Russian peasant woman caught him in the act. First, he silenced her shout with a hand over her mouth, then, with his other hand he silenced her permanently with the stolen Shuriken.

He had never before killed a woman and for a brief moment, despised himself. Then, with no one to talk to he talked to himself to justify his actions, *'I didn't want to, but I had to. I had no choice. She would have raised the alarm. She had to die. It was me or her.'*

The further west that he journeyed, the more hostile it became, first from the people, then the land itself. The Katana remained hidden in the rug, although in order to be prepared for any trouble, he kept the Wakizashi close at hand. He fashioned a stolen goatskin into a dual back sheath, with each ornate hilt visible over his shoulders.

At first, he killed to protect himself and he could justify each life that he took. He was Japanese, they were at war with Russia or so he thought. During one such killing, as the warm, sticky blood of his victim sprayed his face; he naturally licked his lips and rather liked the taste. He had, of course, sucked on his own cut finger and tasted his own blood, but what he noticed now, or at least what he thought, was that the blood of others tasted sweeter. As his mind and actions devolved, he started to kill for fun. Darkness consumed him and eventually, he consumed everyone that he killed.

For months, he survived and hid in the Altai mountains, but he would venture down and into traveller's camps for fresh meat and gained a reputation as a fearful legend. As with most legends, he was given a name, the *'Zmey Gorynych'*, meaning dragon or snake of the mountain. After years of loneliness, so the folklore goes, he wanted company, someone that he could talk to for companionship. Deep down he wanted to change, so he made his way to a small mining town, Kosh-Agachsky. A battle raged in his mind, a struggle of good and evil and for a brief time, good won as guilt and remorse began to soothe the beast within.

With trimmed hair and beard, he sauntered into Kosh with genuine intent to change. No longer did he want to kill and wished to rid himself of the memories, so he sold the Wakizashi and the Shuriken blades, to be rid of the killing tools. The Katana had never been used by him and therefore, he simply regarded it as a trinket. An ore merchant heading west had paid him a handsome price, telling him that he would never return to Kosh, as the mine there was depleted as the seams had dried up. It was then, in a moment of impulse that he bought the old mine, but soon discovered a new load.

For a while, he felt at peace, although, every day a battle raged within his mind, still, he managed to live in this new community. On the outside, he did normal things, worked the mine, fell in love, married and had children, but even so, the battle raged and the beast called '*Snake*' could no longer be contained. He needed to kill, to eat human flesh once again.

After years of freedom, he squeezed the life out of his victim and, like an addict receiving a longed-for fix, it felt like ecstasy. The mine made a perfect fridge and kept the meat fresh. The legend goes on to say that he brought fresh cuts of meat home to feed his family and in doing so infected them with the same evil desires.

After Ashia revealed their latest weapon to the team, they all made their way a short distance around the far end of the golf course, along 3rd Avenue and stopped at a huge metallic box of an aircraft hangar, with a square white concrete tower alongside. A vast expanse of concrete, with a long strip of tarmac that stretched from it, informed them that they had arrived at an airfield. Heat and light radiated and glared from the late morning sun as it reflected off of the Kastner army airfield.

Their liaison, Garcia spoke out first, "Welcome to Kastner airfield. It's not much to look at from here, but it does hold a few surprises; please follow me."

Tommy Lopez quipped, "Ooooh more surprises, we do like your surprises don't we Boss?"

"Yeah, Tommy just as long as they don't plan to try to kill one of us again." She glanced back and smiled and her team smiled back, apart from Andrei, who never smiled.

Just inside the personnel door of the hangar, they were greeted by a Japanese woman who looked more like a man. She wore black-rimmed spectacles with thick glass lenses that over-exaggerated her eyes. Her cropped hair and flat chest removed any signs of femininity, but her soft American accent said, *'I might be a woman'*. The logo on her immaculate, white overall read '*SWAG*'.

"Hello and welcome", she bowed and touched her elegant fingers together. "I am Sara Sato, the lead engineer here at SWAG.”

Tommy butted in again, “SWAG? What does that mean… err… Mam… uh, Sara?”

Ashia scowled at her subordinate but knew that his manners would always let him down. “Yes, a good question, we are *‘Special Weapons and Gadgets’*, although technically it’s not our official name, it’s a nickname that kind of stuck, but it’s what we are known by nowadays.” As she talked, she also walked and they politely followed. In the corner of the hangar, they made their way into a gigantic metal structure, large enough to contain all manner of vehicles and once safely inside, a huge wall rose out of the floor to prevent their escape. Inner ear inertia informed them they were plummeting fast.

When they stopped and the door opened, they found themselves deep below the massive concrete expanse that they had previously driven over. The underground bunker was similar to the one that Jeru had seen with Gideon, whilst on the island of Madagascar; a small town of activity. “We have a very special piece of equipment that we hope you will all want to test for us. It works using a neural interface system, similar to the one that you, Jeru, used previously in the *‘Mechs’* that you used on the moon. So, you should find it quite easy to learn. Until now, we have only been able to use our own personnel, without great success. We believe that the hardware is all sound and that the problem lies in the pilot and their abilities. We now anticipate that your Sixer abilities with your gamma brainwaves is what is needed to make this project a success."

Having been singled out, Jeru was keen to know more and stepped forward, "You have my attention, what is it? Where is it, whatever it is?"

"Ah, Jeru, I am excited by your curiosity. We do hope that you will accept this wonderful opportunity? Please, everyone, walk this way."

They entered a darkened room with a series of spotlights along one wall. Each of the lights illuminated an intriguing matt black costume, as if on display in an exhibition. The back of each suit protruded slightly, with two large circular ports at waist height, facing the ground. Similar, yet smaller ports ran down each side of the moulded protrusion and yet more to the rear of each foot. Built into the left forearm appeared to be a control panel. The helmet and nerve centre, with black visor, completed the menacing-looking high tech outfit.

Sato seemed to stand taller in preparation for a proud announcement, "You are the first people outside of Japan to see this project, this is my life's work. Please allow me to introduce you to the *'PJP Battle Suit'*."

No one said a word, but the silence asked, '*What does that mean?*'

"PJP stands for Pulse Jet Pack or to be precise, it's a solar-powered sonic pulse thrust jet pack with a neural interface, built into a lightweight, power-assisted armoured suit. It should be capable of flying at speeds of up to 300kph and the batteries stay fully charged for 24 hours, so as long as the sun shines, you can fly continuously. What's more, when you wear it, you hardly notice, yet it protects you and makes you feel stronger. Well, what do you think, Jeru, would you like to go first?"

"Ah, you never said anything about flying before. How does it work and why have your previous pilots failed?"

"From what we can gather, from the pilots that survived, It's the interface. It's both a strength and a weakness; strong because there is very little to learn to be able to use the PJP and make it fly. Weak, well quite simply it's because of our own human weaknesses."

Ashia looked puzzled, "Can you explain what you mean by that? How have previous pilots failed and what do you mean by '*pilots that survived*'?"

"Yes, quite right", she continued, "You do need to

know why they failed. Some had some very good flights, albeit until they doubted themselves and the equipment. All of those that survived, say that prior to their crash, they believed that they were going to crash.”

“Well duh, hello, what sort of an explanation is that? If they are falling from the sky, of course, they think that they are going to crash?”

“No, no, it wasn’t like that. Everything was perfectly fine, then they lost faith, they thought that they would crash and so they did. Remember, it does whatever you think. If you think you want to be on top of a particular mountain, it will take you there in seconds. The problem is a normal human’s weaknesses and doubts, but none of you are normal, you have been given some form of supernatural ability and we think it is what is needed. So… Jeru… how about it?”

Chapter Sixteen

*I think our life is a journey, and we make mistakes,
and it's how we learn from those mistakes and
rebound from those mistakes that sets us
on the path that we're meant to be on.*
Jay Ellis

Joash squirmed as the messenger from Abaddon delivered his painful words, "Lord Abaddon is not happy with you Mortemus. You may have control of this mountain, the so-called *'seat of power'*, but you have achieved very little. The south is still free, Japan is also and your control over humanity is minute. You have been lazy…"

He paused to add his own words, "…And please do not harm me in any way or Abaddon will do far more to you." The lesser Erebusian sneered, taking pleasure in hiding behind the name of their supreme commander.

He reiterated and continued with his message, "You have not worked hard or smart enough and it is time to change strategy. You need to find the humans who already carry out the most evil and heinous acts, those who have been disconnected from their humanity, the ones already living in darkness. Use your troops to take control of these and it will be these '*people*' that will do our bidding for us and with us within them, we will be an unbeatable force. As for the disobedient humans, use your host to start disposing of them. If they cannot follow my laws, they will be executed. I only have one law, that they accept me, Abaddon, as their supreme ruler and certainly not this female that you currently possess. Now get it done."

Joash heard every word and for the first time since being controlled by Mortemus, she began to question what was really happening. She knew that he had used her and was still doing so, but she was unable to resist. She felt weak and wondered how long it would be before she was '*disposed of*'.

Mortemus had two things to do; first, he forced Joash to assemble her immediate world leaders. Most of these were normal human beings, loyal to her leadership and ruling as the President of the north. As Mortemus worked her body like a puppet, she explained that she is not the ultimate commander, that there is one even greater and that his name is Abaddon. Having issued the declaration, she then issued the decree, "Anyone failing to accept and acknowledge Abaddon as their Lord and Master will pay with their lives."

There were some that immediately protested, and questioned, "Who is this person, Abaddon?" To these challengers, she showed no mercy and responded immediately by ripping their voices out of their throats and their dead bodies slumped to the floor, which quelled the discord in an instant. Each of the remaining subjects returned quietly in fear to their respective regions with plans to set up death camps for the '*Refusers.*'

Mortemus next gathered with his trusted Generals. He needed to meet them as himself, the strong and respected Erebusian leader that they all feared. He knew that they would never take commands from a weak human woman. As the vile horde gathered, he took Joash to a bedroom, laid her down to sleep and for the first time since the defeat of the Mimics took his true form.

Jeru found a battle armour suitable for his body and was now fully equipped, ready to go. "Are you sure about this Jeru?" Ashia tried to hide her signs of concern. As his commander, she knew he always did the right thing for the team and their mission, but as something more than a friend, she was anxious for him.

"Don't worry, I won't crash and so long as I keep thinking that, I'll be fine, no matter what." He had been briefed and synced the neural interface. He smiled at her and with his right finger, pressed the launch icon on the touch screen, situated on his arm. A helmet grew in layers from the top of the suit, and the visor immediately closed, but nothing else happened.

Some of the team started to make witty remarks about it perhaps being, *'broken, a dud, disappointing, etc'*.

Sato scowled at them, "Shush, everyone, please be quiet. Jeru focus, just relax and think about direction, trajectory, speed, whatever you feel."

He thought out loud, "How about for starters, I just go a mile straight up?"

Still, nothing happened and more sarcastic remarks were forthcoming. "Jeru, the PJP hasn't responded to you because you asked a question and it doesn't know what you want yet. Your thoughts need to be directives, like a command and don't worry, it's been a few days since a suit exploded on take-off." Now it was her turn to joke, although for a few seconds they all thought that she was serious.

"OK, let's go a mile straight up." In the blink of an eye, he was gone. A slight whoosh, like a sudden gust of wind, announced his departure and everyone craned their necks to identify the small dot in the sky. Suddenly he found himself very close to the bombardment on the shield overhead; too close for comfort. The speed of ascent had also freaked him out, as he had no idea what it would feel like. This time he decided not to vocalise the command, so he simply thought. *'Freefall to 300 metres above the ground, then slow my fall and stop 10 metres above Ashia.'*

As soon as he thought the command, the thrusters cut and he dropped. He spread his arms and legs as he hurtled closer to the ground. After 450 metres he reached terminal velocity and fell at 195 km/hr. His mind raced as he tried to think, trying not to panic, *'What was I thinking? I could be killed? No, I won't... I won't... Come on Jeru, pull yourself together.'*

Adrenalin rushed through his veins, as it prepared him for the natural fight or flight response. "I will not die – I will not die." He shouted it out, repeated it over and over until the indicator on his wrist told him that he was 600 metres above the ground. "I WILL NOT DIE – I WILL LIVE – PLEASE ELIO, LET ME LIVE."

At 300 metres he breathed a long, audible sigh of relief, "I did it – I'm alive – Thank you – Thank you Elio – I'm alive." The thrusters cut in exactly where they needed to and straightened his body to an upright position. He still muttered to himself when he came to a hover and halted above Ashia, 'I'm alive, I'm alive…"

He looked down at his friends and his visor opened, "I'm alive, I did it and it was amazing." He felt connected, almost at one with the machine and it reminded him of his mission on the moon. "OK, let's see what this thing can do", he said and instantly flew into a variety of intricate manoeuvres. If he liked a particular move, he gave it a name and memorised it for future use. Very quickly he was able to fly in complex patterns, with the thought of two words, *'pattern Gideon, pattern Cowboy, pattern Xander, etc.'* He had lost so many good friends, he wondered if he would ever run out of names for these evasive manoeuvres.

The connection to the interface, the concentration of thinking and the exhilaration of flying had exhausted him. After an hour in the air, he landed to cheers from the rest of the team. "Who's next?" He asked, with a slight tremor in his voice and a jelly sensation in his legs. They all responded positively and stepped forward.

"Maybe first, you should debrief and share with us how it felt, what you learnt and your thoughts on how it could be improved?" Sato was right and Ashia agreed with her. After just a few days, they could all fly and were used to the mental energy required. They all did as Jeru had done, asked Elio to keep them alive and they all felt safe.

As Joash slept peacefully, Mortemus gathered with his Generals in a large meeting room, deep inside the rock of Mont Blanc. He knew that the longer he physically separated from her, the harder it would be to reconnect, so he managed to maintain a weak psychic link. Stood tall, as their esteemed leader and number two to Abaddon, they all feared him. Each of the Generals also brought with them their own fearful qualities of death, destruction, plague, pain and all types of evil. Within the riotous atmosphere, of hate, bitterness and mistrust, Mortemus demanded their attention. "Right, shut up you wonder, repulsive, hideous and repugnant sight for sore eyes. It's so good to see you all and your combined stench reminds me of home. Erebus, our home, where Abaddon lies in wait and becomes impatient. It's time for a new strategy. The humans that we do not control seriously outnumber us and we will never be able to possess them all at the same time; so, we will now target those that have already fallen to the darkness, the most insidious and evil ones. If just one of us can possess these fallen, we will be able to use them and their influence to cause others to fall."

He told them about the extermination plans and the

death camps that were currently being put into play. "Every day we hear reports of more humans leaving the north for the protection in the south. We need to act fast, implement our new plans, gain control over the whole of the north, then we will be powerful enough to take the south."

They all agreed and flew off to spread the word and bring about a new level of destruction, with their increased motivation. As they departed, the sky seemed to turn slightly darker, yet in the next room, for the first time in ages, Joash slept peacefully. Her eyelids moved rapidly, as a still quiet voice repeated her name over and over, *'Joash… Joash… Joash…'*

The voice persisted, tried to break through and take advantage of the time that Mortemus had given her. His psychic link was strong and the voice battled to be heard, fought for her reaction. She would never awake from the connection and power of Mortemus, but her subconscious mind was free. She heard it again, although the voice was like an old radio set tuning in and out of signal, *'Joash… Joash… Joash…'*

In her sleep state, she answered, *'Who is it? Who are you?'*

'I… I… (static, crackle), I… I am… I am…'

'I am? I am? I am who or what?'

'I am… I am Elio.' The signal seemed stronger, clearer and for the first time ever in her life, she felt peace. The peace overwhelmed and she started to cry. She no longer felt the need to ask any more questions, as the peace brought with it a fresh comfort and understanding. Although she had never before heard this voice or this name, it seemed familiar.

'Joash… Why do you persecute me? You are weak and unable to control yourself, but to be free will not be easy. Your pain can end, but you must be willing. You will know what to do when the time is right.'

As the connection severed and the radio in her mind was smashed, Mortemus returned. His talons pierced her brain, as he once again took control of her body.

<hr>

Haru longed to be like the Sixers, he spent the day watching them, now confidently flying with the jet packs. He compared them to the many test pilots that he had seen fail and plummet to their deaths. He too wanted to fly and have their skill. He wanted to be one of them, to go with them, wherever they were told to go next. He knew that he had special skills, but also knew that he wasn't *'good enough.'* Not that anyone had ever said as much, but he just felt that is what they thought.

Now in the privacy of his own quarters, he began to mutter to himself. "Why… Why can't I be one… Be like them… Like Ashia and Jeru… Why?" Soon he stumbled around as he sobbed, searched and questioned, '*Why*'? He trembled as every muscle in his body went into spasm and his heart pounded on his chest wall. He continued in this manner until exhaustion overpowered him. At an unknown point, his questioning changed from '*Why*' to '*Please can I?*'

In his brokenness, he cried out, "Elio, please show me favour, show me your power, show me mercy and forgive me for being dissatisfied and inadequate. Forgive my arrogance and impatience; use me however you wish, I just want to do your will. Please, Elio, give me a chance." During his exhausting rant, he failed to notice the sun go down, he now sat in darkness. Suddenly he felt something warm touch him. In the dark, he was uncertain what it might be, but he was not afraid. The warmth moved all over his skin, sensually touched and caressed, like a healing hug. Then he realised that the sensory feeling was no longer on the outside, it was inside his body and it felt incredible – He felt incredible. The room became clearer and he wasn't sure if someone had turned a light on, so he looked around the room. Everything seemed clearer and the thought occurred to him, '*Is this what the power of the Pneuma feels like? Am I a Sixer?*'

In his excitement, he ran to Sara Sato and asked her to scan his brain activity; she confirmed the presence of gamma brainwaves, he was a Sixer and his power increased as she scanned. The next day he flew with the others and when they all landed, Jeru looked at him, smiled and said, "It seems you were right about the Pneuma and the gamma waves, maybe the Pneuma and Elio is for everyone, the whole of mankind? Anyway, welcome to the team, it's good to have you with us. Will you come with us when we leave, wherever that may lead?"

"Yes, yes", he said, "This is my heart's desire."

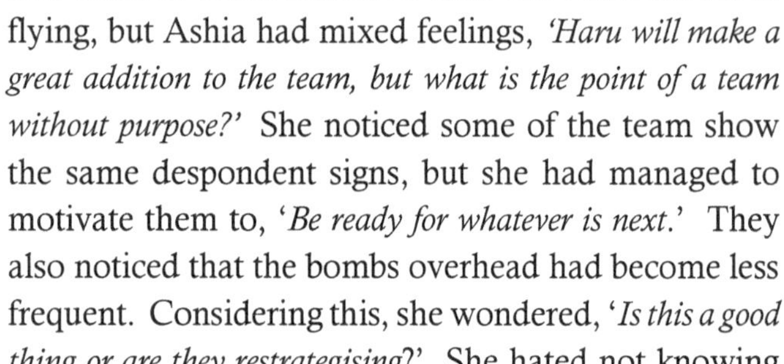

The team of seven mastered their suits and the art of flying, but Ashia had mixed feelings, *'Haru will make a great addition to the team, but what is the point of a team without purpose?'* She noticed some of the team show the same despondent signs, but she had managed to motivate them to, *'Be ready for whatever is next.'* They also noticed that the bombs overhead had become less frequent. Considering this, she wondered, *'Is this a good thing or are they restrategising?'* She hated not knowing and realised that she needed to learn to be more patient.

Her pride and anger had been tested; now this realisation of how impatient she is told her that she had other weaknesses. It had been a few hours since everyone had turned in for the night, but sleep seemed elusive. Her mind churned her thoughts round and round in circles. Disbelief crept in, with self-doubt leading to imposter syndrome. Then she realised this was another weakness.

Lying on her bed, trying to relax, she took a deep breath in and slowly released it. As she did so, she recognised that she wasn't alone. "How long have you been sat there?" She asked the dark figure.

"Sorry, I didn't want to startle you. I've been here long enough to know what you are thinking. I've always known. I even knew when you were dragged out of the cage for your enlightenment; I knew what you were planning. You need to believe in yourself, Sis. There will always be times of uncertainty, but you must have faith and trust the Pneuma in you. You know your weaknesses, but you also know that the Pneuma can turn any weakness into strength and opportunity." As Gideon talked, he seemed to make himself more visible and she felt comforted to see him.

"I still can't get used to this, you just popping up. It is good to see you again Gideon, but we really need to know what is next. We are ready. We may have suffered some losses and that did affect all of us, but it made us realise that we are all vulnerable and that we face a strong enemy." She stopped as once again doubt crept in with a new thought, '*Are they too strong?*'

"You're doing it again. Stop doubting yourself. You are ready and the waiting will soon be over, have a little more patience. Now sleep."

She didn't remember him leaving or falling asleep, but her dream was vivid. The motion in her ears told her that she was flying and she looked down to see where she was. It was cold, freezing cold. Ice covered the mountains and everything she could see below. A voice told her to, '*Look closely, this place has no justice, but it has 'Justice''*. As she puzzled at the scene, faint red lines began to appear in the shape of what looked like a giant letter '*X*'. She had seen maps with this symbol drawn on to mark certain locations, but this '*X*' was huge and the lines uneven, not straight. The voice spoke again, *''Justice' is with 'Sin-a-bar' near the 'Four Corners.'*

Chapter Seventeen

Man is an animal that makes bargains:
no other animal does this –
no dog exchanges bones with another.
Adam Smith

History always records the most heinous and atrocious of acts and Mortemus knew it. Instead of the random, haphazard selection of targets, he now strategically searched the archives. His search had taken him back 141 years to World War Two. He admired the works of Adolf Hitler and his Third Reich, knowing that his Erebusian brothers had also played their part to write this history.

He already knew of the *'Little Boy'* bombs that were dropped on Japan, but accidentally stumbled across some information about a young deserter soldier, who had stolen from the Imperial War Museum. Akio had escaped capture with some priceless Samurai swords. Mortemus had prowled the earth for centuries and knew of the legend of the *'Honour Blades'*. He knew of their power and the whereabouts of the Wakizashi, but he also knew that the five blades would never be reunited. He wondered if the Akio bloodline still living as Cannibals in Siberia, might still possess the Katana.

He had a hunch that he would find the missing blade with the Akio family, a bloodline drenched in evil. His type of people. He wanted them and the power that he believed they had in their possession.

The sound of the heavily armed Mil Mi26 '*Halo*' helicopter, approached from the north. It could be heard long before it arrived. The occupants had no intention of a stealth approach. Before they fire one bullet or launch any missiles, fear would be their first weapon of choice. Their second weapon was reputation and theirs had earned them the title of 'Dark *Demons.*'

A year earlier, as the gateway started to open, three Erebusian scouts were deployed to wait patiently in the city of Kemerovo and to be ready to strike. With the defeat of the Mimics, they had rushed in to fill the void of panic. During the Mimic occupation, the city was fortified to protect the nearby weather modification machine. The Commissar General and his second in command were easy, soft targets and to control them gave control to the entire armed forces of Kemerovo. Penthos and Agonia now commanded their puppets, whilst Chaos remained in his ethereal form. He caused havoc as he searched for a suitable host.

Word of their deeds spread across the land and with it the stories of horror and dread.

Akiono Musuko recognised the familiar sound of the Halo, it had passed over his small mining town on previous missions, but usually at a much higher altitude. He knew that his defences were inferior compared to cannons, missiles and machine guns. The helicopter would either land or attack, either way, he anticipated things going sideways, so gave the command for his wife and young son to hide in a secret part of the mine. Tsuma ran with her child, a well-rehearsed procedure. As she entered the mine, she turned to witness the first of the explosions and her friends being cut down. As the gunners fired the machine guns and the co-pilot deployed the missiles, the pilot manoeuvred the craft to avoid being hit. He maintained a calm exterior, whilst inside his heart was broken at the scene of human carnage before his eyes. He wanted to scream, to tell everyone to stop, but he couldn't; if he did, he would die.

Tsuma remained in her hiding place until she felt safe. When she surfaced, she searched for her husband amongst the dead.

The voice repeated, reinforced, imprinted on her brain until she awoke, sat upright in bed and shouted, "'Justice', is with 'Sin-a-bar' near the 'Four Corners'." She didn't understand it, yet she believed it and kept repeating it. The brain imprint was working, now all that she had to do was work out what it meant. She told the others she was going for a run, but her destination was SWAG and Sato.

As soon as she awoke, she had written down what she had seen and heard, then carried with her a page from her notebook. Next to the scribbly, wobbly 'X', she had written, *'Justice' is with 'Sin-a-bar' near the 'Four Corners'.*

The tension of the wait for their next destination had all been too much for Ashia. Her lack of patience made it difficult to tolerate and now she was about to burst with excitement. Like a child on Christmas morning, she raced to unwrap her present, the gift of her dream.

Sato instantly shared her excitement, "We know that 'Justice' is the name of the missing Katana, so we need to find the 'Four Corners' that this refers to."

Ashia in her impatience wanted to know everything, "Yes, and find out who this *Sin-a-bar'* is and what about the wobbly 'X'?"

"All in good time", she said and slid her fingers over a

computer panel to bring images up on a large screen. "Is this the 'X' in your dream?"

The map was labelled with a name that she recognised, 'United States of America'. Two straight lines intersected to form a cross, a point where the states of Utah, Colorado, New Mexico and Arizona meet. "This is a place known as *'Four Corners',* does this look familiar?"

Ashia shook her head, frustration fuelled her impatience, "No, no, nothing like that."

Sato did the same with a map of Canada and showed her the point where the states of Saskatchewan, Manitoba, Northwest Territories and Nunavut, all meet. Once again, the lines were straight and nothing as she had seen. Ashia paced the room like a trapped animal, her impatience now more visible.

"Let's try a little closer to home", Sato said, "although strictly speaking, it isn't really an 'X'." She swiped the screen a few more times and brought up a map showing the mountainous terrain of *'Altai'* and Ashia stopped in her tracks. The image had a familiarity, but then one mountain can appear to look like any other. As Sato zoomed in, boundary lines became visible and weaved their way throughout the mountains. A wonky line traced from east to west for a very short distance, before it split into two. From a distance, the lines appeared as a wonky 'X'. She zoomed in closer and names of countries started to appear; China, Mongolia, Kazakhstan and Russia.

"That's it", she exclaimed, "that's what I saw in my dream." With both hands on the desk in front of her, she focused, leaned forward and waited for more answers. Sato allowed her to soak up the image, just to ensure that she wasn't mistaken. Ashia felt her impatience again as if someone had stopped her unwrapping her Christmas present; not that she had ever experienced a Christmas. "It's going to be like trying to find a snowflake in a snow storm. Where do we start? Where do we find this '*Sin-a-bar*' person?"

"Ah, this is where it is interesting and, in some respects, quite easy. At first, your writing misled me, you see it's not '*Sin-a-bar*', it is C-I-N-N-A-B-A-R and it's not a person, it's a precious red ore." The Chief Engineer became side-tracked briefly, as she explained what ore was and that this particular ore was red and used to make mercury as well as jewellery. Ashia showed her impatience again, which reminded her of the purpose of the conversation.

"You see, the only place where Cinnabar is mined in this area is a small town called 'Kosh-Agachsky'. I think this is where you will find your sword."

Ashia let out a long sigh of relief, "Yes, yes, at last, we

can move on. Don't get me wrong, Japan is a great country and it's been great being here, but not knowing where we are meant to be has been difficult and tense. At last, we can see a goal."

Sato nodded deep in thought then said, "Ashia, it has been good to work with you and to get to know you. You are a very strong woman, but as you know, you also have weaknesses. I've seen them in you. I know that you are anxious to move on, but you have to realise, that there will always be times when you can't move and you may feel trapped. The scientist in me knows that I have to be patient and that I can always learn more. I would like to think that your time in Japan has taught you some things about yourself. Now go and find that sword."

They parted company with a traditional Japanese bow and Ashia continued her run back to her accommodation. After she briefed the team, Garcia sent a message to Captain Hanson to make ready for departure and plan a course for Russia.

They were heading back into the cold and it would be the first time that Ashia had returned since being released from the Mimics. They were issued the latest SWAG, electronic regulated, thermal bodysuit, designed to electronically regulate their temperature when not wearing their combat attire.

As they made preparations, she had a thought. At first, she wasn't sure if it was her own thought. She had experienced crazy moments of her brother appearing from nowhere, gained great knowledge from dreams and been transformed by her visit to Elafria. These events and her own life experiences had incubated yet another gift within; the gift of '*Wisdom*'. It was her own wisdom that now prompted her to provide the team with special protection.

"Listen up", she spoke with authority and everyone stopped what they were doing. "We all have the Pneuma power in us, we are Sixers. We know that the Pneuma will protect us, but I want to make sure we're all protected as much as possible. We don't fight a battle of flesh and blood; this is a spiritual battle. We know where we are headed next, but after that, we don't know where we will end up. We all need faith that we will be led on the right journey, but I also feel that we need extra protection. We lost four good friends to just one of these Erebus things and we don't want to lose any more. I've seen the power of the water in this bottle around my neck and I believe that with the blood, it's even more powerful. So, before we do anything else, I think it wise *(she liked the sound of that)* to anoint each of you with the blood and water."

They all agreed and the six men and one woman lined up as she worked her way along the line. She touched her finger to the liquid in the neck of the flask, then, used it to mark a cross on each of their heads saying, "By the blood of Ketsueki and the water of life, may you be protected and filled with the Pneuma."

She repeated the same words for each person and they each sensed a new sensation; a renewed, fresh vigour. Finally, Jeru said the same words and painted the same crimson mark on her forehead. As he did so, she felt what seemed to be an electrical charge surge through her body. Her fingers and toes tingled; she felt a warmth grow inside and for a moment thought that her bodysuit might have a technical problem. Finally, she sensed a release as the things that she struggled with, her weaknesses, left her. Anger left, replaced by a steady, calm, peace. Self-pride left as the metaphoric scales fell from her eyes and allowed her to see her team members in a new light. She was proud of who each of them is, proud to call them her friends. Eventually, she had a new understanding. *I may be the leader of this team, but I'm not ultimately in control. I know that there is a time for everything and that everything has a purpose. I can't force things and make things happen.'* She now understood the importance of patience.

The huge Russian strike force rapidly overpowered the inhabitants of Kosh. Many fled in panic and headed to the mountains; they knew they would never survive the attack. They would return later when the danger had gone and fresh food needed to be gathered. The invasion force searched the town and the mine but failed to secure the sword. Survivors were tortured but knew nothing of where the trophy could be. They all died agonising deaths, which was Agonia's specialism.

Akiono Musuko fought but failed. The battered and bruised man had not yet disclosed the whereabouts of the family secret, the blade of '*Justice*'. He never would tell them what they wished to know. He would rather die than discredit the honour of his Japanese ancestor. Despite being riddled with evil, he nonetheless had an unbreakable bond with his family. His name had survived the presence of the Mimics, when many lost their identity. His name had been handed down through six generations, Akiono Musuko, meaning son of Akio.

Bundled into the back of the Halo, Agonia and Penthos now stood before him as the victors and headed north. Though they appeared as average Russian officials, Akiono sensed more to them than meets the eye. The evil within him recognised a dominant presence. He also noticed something else, even though it was still daytime, he noticed that the further north they travelled, the darker it became. He was being transported to their lair, a stronghold of wickedness and power. His life was about to change and then it would only be a matter of time before they discovered the location of the sword.

A black ominous vapour hovered over the three characters. It gradually became thicker and heavier. It sank to the floor in front of Akiono and then grew taller. It transformed into a pillar, which changed into '*Chaos*' in his true form. Muscles of iron bulged through the creature's black scaled skin. He craned his thick, bulging neck to fit into the confines of the helicopter and peered down at their captor. His ruby red eyes against the black of his face spoke '*menace*'. Horns sprouted from his head. They were also black and polished, twisting upwards into a corkscrew. Thick saliva dripped from his fangs and landed on the terrified man's face. As he opened his mouth a stench filled the aircraft and the voice that emerged was deep and forceful. "Son of Akio, at last - we meet. I have sought after someone like you. I've longed to find a man with a black heart, full of evil desires. I have searched endlessly for a man who takes what he wants and gives only pain and heartache. You think that you are strong and powerful, yet look at you now. Where is your power? You have something that I want and you will tell me where it is."

"I have nothing for you, whatever you are. It would seem that you have already taken everything that I owned, all that was precious to me." Akiono believed that it was only a matter of time before they killed him, so taunted the beast, to urge him on with it.

"You have two things; the sword and your life. So, which one will you give me first?"

"I know nothing about a sword and as for my life…if you intend to kill me, just get on and do it." Despite his young age of 33, he considered that he had had his life and he was ready to die. He knew that his name would live on in his son.

Chaos responded with a softer tone in his voice, "Oh no my friend, you are mistaken, I have no intention to kill you. In fact, I wish to offer you an alliance. You can have more power than you could possibly imagine. Just accept my hand of friendship. This is all that I ask." He reached out his large, powerful fist and uncurled it ready to take the man's hand. Chaos no longer showed any interest in the sword, he knew that once he possessed this man, he would eventually know everything that was in his mind. Though Akiono was strong and his mind would take longer to break than his body, but he would eventually know the hiding place of the powerful blade.

Akiono considered his options; die or accept this partnership, or 'friendship' of sorts. He chose to live, shook hands and by doing so, relinquished control of his own body.

Chapter Eighteen

*Being the first to cross the finish line makes
you a winner in only one phase of life.
It's what you do after you cross the line that really counts.*
Ralph Boston

As HMS Trenchant broke through the ice on the eastern Russian coast, the Halo helicopter had touched down in Kemerovo. Chaos fed off of the evil within Akiono, whilst Ashia and her team made ready to launch with fresh concern. Although it was still daytime, the sun seemed weak and, in the north, it already seemed to be night time. She sensed the presence of evil and though she could not see the enemy, she knew that they were close.

The Honour Squad stood as a line of shadows along the freezing metal deck. Ashia in the middle with three others on either side. "Everyone ready? Check your comms?" Another gift from Japan had been micro-in-ear, fully integrated communication devices. Various radio checks and weapon checks, followed by head nods and a simple thought, they were airborne.

'Head to Tunkinsky National Park, maximum speed, fly below radar, but high enough not to be seen from the ground.' Within seconds they were at 6,000 feet above the ground and visible as just seven small dots in the sky. Hanson, in the meantime, would head further north, out of sight beneath the ice and skirt around the Russian coast and wait for any commands. At times he felt like nothing but an elaborate taxi driver. Then he would remind himself of the vast arsenal of firepower that he had available at his command, including the impressive Tomahawk cruise missiles, which had already been primed for launch.

With their cosy, thermally regulated base layer of clothing, it was a comfortable ride and some even managed to catch a few hours of sleep. After 15 hours though, they were thankful to set up a temporary shelter, well hidden in the national park. Haru had a concern, "Boss", he had quickly picked up and used her title, "I'm concerned that our suits might not charge enough for us and we could become stranded?"

She had thought the same, but wanted to remain positive, "It should be ok, we still have nine hours of charge. We'll leave at sunrise and they will charge as we fly. Hopefully, the charge won't drop much lower."

The rest of the team listened in and agreed that it was nothing to tworry about. Jeru made a comment, "Did anyone notice the small town that we flew over during our approach?"

They all confirmed with a yes, but Andrei asked the question in his thick Russian accent, "Did you see all of those cross structures? What do you think they were? Russia was, one time, very religious country, but those crosses were not on church buildings."

"Whatever they are, I have a strong feeling that we will soon find out, but for now, let's all get some rest and sleep. I'll take first watch." Ashia didn't feel tired due to the adrenalin rush, but it kept her alert, calm and focused.

As they slept, innocent people died. The death camps had been established throughout the northern hemisphere. Great consideration had been given to the best method of execution. The French guillotine was considered an impressive piece of engineering but rejected because death was instant and therefore too humane. The mass-extermination method of gas chambers, as used by the 'Nazis' against the Jews, received a high vote, but was rejected because it was all done in secret.

Abaddon wanted mankind to worship him, to acknowledge him as Lord, but he didn't want to kill them all, only the '*Refusers*'. Their deaths must be slow, painful and very public. Each execution needed to inject fear into the minds of the witnesses and so the chosen procedure was the ancient Roman method of crucifixion, although with the addition of some even more barbaric enhancements from the dark ages.

Special, giant steel crosses had been hastily welded together, each with a series of 10mm holes drilled at equal distances along the crossbar. With the cross lying on the ground, each victim was placed in the centre, arms stretch out, pulling at the joints before a sharp steel spike was driven into their hands or wrists and into one of the holes. Agonising screams built even more fear into the awaiting '*Refusers*', knowing what they had to face.

Most victims of crucifixion died very slowly from suffocation, as the weight of their bodies, hung on their arms and gradually made it impossible to breathe. The Roman crucifixion cross included a small footrest, to which the victim's feet were also nailed and enabled the accused to momentarily lift their body weight, which also further prolonged death. The Erebusians chose not to use a footrest; instead, they tied the victim's ankles together with a chain and hooked a heavy weight onto it. This form of torture was similar to the medieval rack and eventually pulled limbs from their sockets.

In every camp across the world, every day was spent

torturing people and nailing them to the crosses. Then as night fell, the bodies were doused with oil and set fire to. This combined yet another form of Roman execution, the *'Roman Candle'*.

As the team slumbered, high up in the national park, the flaming crosses in the town below filled the air with the stench of burning flesh. From her guard position, Ashia looked down at the flames and realised what those crosses were for. Then she knew that none of them could allow themselves to be captured alive.

As Tsuma searched among the dead, the survivors started to return to help and as her husband's body could not be found, they all assumed that he was dead. Tsuma and young Akiono were not convinced. In her heart, she knew that he was still alive and that she would give anything to be able to see him again.

Now, as the group of seven dropped from the sky, she became even more hopeful. Their means of transportation and superior weapons told her that they could be a match for the *'Dark Demons'*, but would they be willing to risk their own lives? A crowd rushed to greet them, as was customary. This place had developed a culture of welcome, acceptance, and then win the trust of its visitors. However, then they would kill and eat them. Tsuma signalled to the crowd to stand down and let her talk, "Welcome, you are all welcome, such an unusual way to travel. We've never met your kind before, have you travelled far?"

Ashia allowed Jeru to talk, "Yes, quite a way, but it would seem we are a little too late and we missed the party." He looked around at the remaining bodies still being moved and the smouldering remains of burnt-out buildings and the fearful survivors. "Who did this?" He asked.

"It wasn't as you call it, '*a party*', it was a massacre. What you see before you is the work of the '*Dark Demons*'. Until now, they have always ignored us and left us in peace. They took Akiono Musuko, my husband."

"He's likely dead by now", one of the survivors shouted out.

"No, I don't believe that he is. I would feel it if he was dead. If they wanted to kill him, they would have just done it here, but they didn't they took him. As if they have a need for him." Tsuma reached for her son's hand and looked with a plea, "We need him; we really need him back."

As she scanned their faces, she recognised that Haru was Japanese and he questioned her, "Your husband is called Akiono Musuko, '*Son of Akio*'?" She nodded her head and Haru looked at Ashia, so much as to say, *'We are in the right place'*.

"We haven't been properly introduced, my name is Ashia and this is my team. Now, what is your name?"

"It's Tsuma and this is my 12-year-old son, also known as Akiono Musuko."

The Sixer continued, "Tsuma, I'm pleased to meet you and I am sorry that it's not under better circumstances. You are correct, we have travelled a very long way and we came especially to find your husband. Well, actually it was to find something that he may possess."

The inhabitants of Kosh-Agachsky had always told visitors that they had very little, but that they are welcome, so she did the same. "We are a poor people and have very little, so you must be mistaken."

Ashia paused before she answered, using her new found patience, she waited for wisdom to tell her what to say. She reflected back to her dream, *'Justice' is with 'Sin-a-bar' near the 'Four Corners'.* She knew that they were currently just north of the *'Four Corners',* so planned to ask the obvious question. "Your mine, it produces Cinnabar." Instead of a question, it was a statement, which received the response that she expected.

"Yes, but how do you know that? Cinnabar is so rare; most people assume that it is gold or silver. How could you possibly guess that we mine Cinnabar?"

"Tsuma, it's not a guess, you see, we knew." Ashia used her right hand to pull down on a cord that ran diagonally from her left shoulder down to her waist. In doing so, the hilt of the 'Truth' Katana, moved from her back, down and into her hand. Her left hand gripped the sheath and separated it from the blade. "We also believe that you possess a sword just like this one and maybe even some other smaller swords. We would like to see them."

Her face confirmed what Ashia already knew, "Please follow me", she said, "Let's go somewhere more comfortable. They headed for the biggest building at the head of the stone track. Upon entering, they could see that she was far from poor. Lavish textiles, perfumes and ornaments adorned the large room. Each item with its own story of how it arrived there – stolen from a visitor passing through, who no longer had any need for it once they became a food supply.

Once safely indoors, she turned to them and spoke with a new voice, a strong, powerful, assertive voice. "You don't just want to 'see' my sword, you 'want' my sword, don't you? I've seen enough people come here and they nearly always want something, usually, it's gold. None have ever asked to see the sword, because none have ever known about it. Only the direct descendants of Akio know about it. So how do you know and where did you find one like it?”

She spoke in singular and Ashia had already deduced that she must only have the one sword, the Katana. She has '*Justice*'. '*Justice is with Cinnabar*'.

Ashia waited for the wisdom to answer, buying time as she returned her Katana to the sheath and her back, “To answer your questions is a very long story, but I can tell you that your sword is needed for the protection of mankind. The creatures that you know as the '*Dark Demons*', are just a small fraction of an enemy that wants to enslave the world. We know them as the Erebus and have witnessed their power. Your sword has a power that we need to be able to stop them, but you only have the Katana? What happened to the other swords?”

“That sword has been with my family for 141 years. It is priceless, I would never sell it.” She stopped speaking briefly, looked around the room then continued, “you’re not here to buy it, are you? You’re strong enough and powerful enough to just take it, but you will never find it. It’s well hidden and no one else knows where it is. As for the other blades, we believe our ancestor, Akio, sold them to be able to buy the mine.”

A thought rolled around in Ashia's mind, '*Do something for her*'. "We don't wish to force you, but what would it take for you to give us the sword? You say that we would never find it, you don't know that for sure, but let's try to do this in a civilised manner."

Tsuma thought about the question and about her kidnapped husband. "Bring him back to me, bring my husband back. If you find Akiono Musuko and return him safely, the sword is yours. We'd rather have him than an old sword and well, if what you say is true, we will be doing our bit to save the world. That would be a first."

The two women smiled in agreement, then, Ashia looked around the room for team approval. With nods of heads and comments of affirmation, Ashia reached out a hand and said, "It's a deal. We need to rest here first, whilst our suits fully recharge, then we will leave to find your husband." Tsuma gripped her hand and shook it.

Chapter Nineteen

I like these calm little moments before the storm,
it reminds me of Beethoven.
Gary Oldman

Their battle suits charged while the team rested and slept in shifts. They were the first visitors to the town in decades, well at least ones that had not been dished up on a plate. The cannibals could not be trusted, even though Tsuma had given her word, they were all on edge. The inhabitants had all previously been controlled by the Mimics and therefore none had any knowledge of the area in the darkened north. After being freed from the Mimics, Akiono Musuko discovered a cryptic clue, which had led him to the hidden bunker, the sword and its significance.

With a few finger swipes on the screen of her wrist device, she brought up a topographic map of the area to the north. Siberia had been a bleak terrain long before the Mimic ice age and now it was mostly barren, until about 1,000km north of their position. She discovered two cities that were just 250km apart, Kemerovo and *Novosibirsk. She zoomed in and identified military bases and Novosibirsk seemed to be the main force, with a smaller outpost at Kemerovo.*

"He's probably being held captive on one of the military bases, in one of those cities. The question is which one?" Ashia chatted casually to Jeru and Haru.

"We need intel Boss; we can't just launch an attack without knowing. It'll only take three hours each way, another hour to go between the cities and not long to recon the military presence. Say eight hours and the two of us could be back with a plan." Jeru finished talking and Haru looked at him with concern. It was a risky mission and he was not as experienced as Jeru.

Ashia remained quiet, deep in thought, and used her newfound wisdom again, but Jeru was insistent, "Come on Haru, we can do this, we stay high, map the bases, determine their strengths and weaknesses, then hopefully, we'll find out where our target is. Boss, what do you reckon? For some reason our suits seem to have the most charge, we should leave ASAP."

"No", she eventually replied.

"No, what does that mean? Come on Ashia, we need the intel." Jeru was a little irritated but tried not to show it. He had been on more missions than her; this was her first mission, so he had more experience.

She continued, "No, we don't recon both cities, just the one, Kemerovo. Don't ask me why, because I don't think that I could explain, I just feel that is where they took him, plus it's the smaller of the two and less defended."

"You feel?" Asked, Haru.

"No, I know; I know that he is in Kemerovo. I just know, so go and check it out."

Chaos continued to suck, feed and probe into his host's brain. He absorbed and devoured information, he knew that it would not be much longer before he broke Akiono. He would know the location of the sword that would give him even more power. He would naturally give the sword to Mortemus, who would in turn destroy it. The clock was ticking and time was running out.

As they flew into the darkness, it crept forward to consume them. Engulfed within the black envelope, they immediately sensed an oppressive presence and headed directly to the location of the airport. The air was dense with plumes of thick black smoke. Between the raging spirals, they noticed what appeared to be hundreds of intense bonfires.

From their safe height of 6,000 feet, they observed a quiet airport. No aircraft landed or took off and they both hovered to scan, plot and record the area. Within seconds their visors mapped the entire airport and stored the information for later use. They identified and highlighted both known and unknown potential assets and threats. With the exception of some outer machine guns and guard posts, defences were low.

Haru saw something which looked very interesting and so zoomed in for a closer look at the potential high-level asset. His powerful technology identified the Cessna Citation-X+, which was a private jet, capable of Mach 0.935, almost the speed of sound.

Scattered around the perimeter of the airport, Jeru spotted more of the strange bonfires, so he decided to take a closer look. Each bonfire was in the shape of a tall cross. He made out movement on the ground and as the wind parted the smoke, he took a sharp intake of breath. The people on the ground were setting fire to other people that had been hung on crosses.

They regrouped quickly, synced data and continued north. From the same high vantage point, they surveyed the military base, paying particular attention to the large mysterious building in the centre of the compound. Thermal imaging revealed troop locations, with the majority being in the barracks at the northwest corner. With all key installations logged and mapped, they both had the same thought, '*Time to rendezvous with the rest of the team.*'

Ashia was pleased to see them both return safely but more excited to see Jeru again. It was the first time that they had been separated since their reunion on the harbourside, back in Angola. She had reflected back on that moment when they had both been targeted by an assassin. Now, even though she had all confidence in his abilities and he was only gone a short while, she realised how much she missed him. She cared about him and her memory reminded her of what he had told her, '*Absence makes the heart grow fonder.*' She compared her feelings now, to the harbourside and her mind questioned, '*Did she love him?*'

Akiono Musuko held on to his family secret, his knowledge of the bunker and the sword; that part of his mind was a cerebral bunker. Chaos hammered persistently on the theoretical fortress and persevered in his efforts. Both man and beast knew that the walls would soon crumble and Chaos would possess the power of the '*Honour Blade*'.

Ashia was no stranger to danger. In the camps she fought for survival, in Africa, she killed her would-be assassin and most recently, she dispatched a hideous beast that had taken control of Harry Hanson. As they made their final preparations before departure, she reflected on each incident and realised that she had never, before now, intentionally placed herself in the line of danger. Her mind raced with thoughts, '*Why am I doing this? Is this mission a distraction? It's the sword we came for, not to rescue a bloodthirsty cannibal, who has no respect for human life. Why are we doing this?*'

'*Because I want you to*', a new thought entered her mind, but it wasn't her thought. She recognised the voice, as it reinforced, '*Because I want you to and I need you to.*' As she mulled the thoughts over, she began to realise that we sometimes have to do the difficult thing, the right thing, even though we are unable to see the reason why; that we simply need to have a little faith. "We need faith in Elio and the Pneuma power, she mumbled under her breath with her head down."

"What's that Boss? What are you mumbling about?" Tommy Lopez, being his usual rude self, had exposed her. She wanted to ignore him, to pretend it didn't happen, but she couldn't really do that.

She spoke out loud so that everyone could hear and addressed her squad as many commanders had done so throughout history, on the eve of a battle. "I said that we need to have an extra measure of faith in Elio, and the Pneuma power that is in each one of us. We cannot succeed in our own strength, we have good recon intel and we all know our roles, but there is much that we don't know. We don't even know for sure if Akiono will be there, but if he is, we will find him and bring him back here. I also feel… No, I know, that there is more to this mission than meets the eye. This battle is bigger than us, we simply have to be obedient to Elio and I believe that this is all part of his bigger plan. So, lock and load people, helmets on and let's be gone."

She concluded with "Elio reigns" and they all responded with the same. As they departed, she heard the voice in her head again, '*Try to spare all human life. Dispatch the Erebusians, but spare the hosts*.' She spread the word over the in-ear transceiver and then remained in radio silence.

As they approached the city, they were shocked to see the number of people below that had been tortured by crucifixion and were now burned as a warning to others that refuse to recognise Abaddon as Lord. She zoomed in with her HUD (Head-Up Display) and saw more people being spiked to torturous steel crosses, their faces screamed out in agony. She wanted to fly down to rescue them, but she resisted the temptation and reminded herself to remain engaged. '*Stay focused, stay on mission*', she thought over and over.

Each of the Honour Squad had a personal side-arm on their thigh, a 10mm Glock 20, with a choice of clips, red or blue. Red contained lethal Parabellum rounds, whereas the blue contained non-lethal, human electro-incapacitation (HEMI) rounds. In addition to their handguns, each member carried a personal weapon of choice. Bekker carried a SIG Sauer Cross long gun, as the designated Sniper. She was the first to enter the military camp.

In the southeast corner, the furthest point from the barracks stood the overwatch post. This was stage one of the assault. Ashia had given the green light to secure this target, protruding from the mountain forest below. It provided the perfect vantage point for someone with Bekker's skills.

Her instrument panel indicated four white lights, the presence of four warm bodies, two on each side of the tower. A fifth, unknown heat source was also nearby. She descended almost silently, with a slight wind-like pulse; she held the element of surprise. She aimed the Glock, THUMP, THUMP, twist re-aim, THUMP, THUMP. The HEMI rounds successfully stunned the inhabitants of the viewing platform in seconds and she had them gagged and bound before the kettle finished boiling. She thrust her handgun into the holster and set up the SIG, then gave a hand signal, '*Overwatch secure.*'

More hand signals from Ashia and phase two was initiated. Lopez, Yichen and Andrei, advanced in a small 'V' formation; Lopez took the lead. As they passed the Overwatch post, Bekker swiftly eliminated the guards on the roof of the mysterious building. Lopez headed north, whilst the other two went east to take up positions above their designated targets and waited for the signal.

Ready, another signal and Lopez dropped to the ground inside the generator compound. Casually he threw the large leaver on each of the four generators and destroyed the circuit breakers. One by one the four quarters of the camp plunged into darkness and Lopez flew out of the generator compound. Yichen landed on the armoury roof, whilst Andrei took up position on top of the helicopter hangar.

From the tower, Bekker saw them in her rifle scope as she switched to heat signature. The two blue lights on her instrument panel confirmed that they were friendly and the third one, Lopez, now waited on the flat roof of the large, mysterious building. So-far-so-good, though a maintenance truck was already en route to investigate the power outage, while Ashia, Jeru and Haru, joined Lopez in the forward position.

Tommy Lopez had already laser cut through the lock of the roof access point and now took up his tactical position on the north of the building, with a clear sight of the barracks. On top of his jet pack sat an additional box which gave him a unique look. A flexible chain feed attached to the box and dropped down to Tommy's personal weapon of choice, the lightweight, titanium, 'Metal Storm' – M134 minigun, capable of firing a million rounds in a minute.

The rest of the team had opted for the standard FN P90 machine guns; except for Ashia, who carried an Uzi PRO sub-machine gun, plus the Katana.

With everyone in position, phase three commenced and the retrieval team opened the hatch, then disappeared into the depths of the building. Their tech had already scanned and created the building's schematics and they identified two floors plus a basement. Each floor indicated numerous white heat signatures. Most of them chased around in a state of confusion and any that came too close in the dark were greeted with a HEMI round. The blue glow from multiple HEMI rounds attached to slain bodies scattered the floor. With their target location technology and HUD visors in night vision mode, they had a clear advantage. They checked the identity of every victim against an image of Akiono on their screens. All negative, so they pressed on.

Outside, the maintenance men lay unconscious next to their truck, where Bekker shot them. From their rooftop vantage points, Yichen and Andrei took silent potshots at personnel and removed anyone that would become a problem.

At some point, the alarm sounded and multiple white dots appeared on Lopez's screen as they scurried from within the barracks. He didn't shoot immediately but waited for his moment. As the flow of troops from the open doors slowed and the wave advanced wave directly below him, he opened fire. Like a fireman with a hose, he sprayed the unsuspecting, uncoordinated rabble. Thousands of blue lights lit up the darkness, and made contact with multiple electrical discharges on almost 200 unconscious and temporarily paralysed soldiers.

None made it inside the building and any lucky enough to escape the Lopez onslaught were picked off by the rear guard of Bekker, Andrei and Yichen.

On the basement level, each of them identified a central room with three warm bodies that didn't move. "They're either asleep, unconscious or waiting for us", Jeru deduced.

"Let's assume the latter", Haru responded.

"Just be ready to grab and make a run to that helicopter", Ashia spoke with authority. She tried to remain strong, though she knew the plan wasn't perfect. With a passenger in tow, they needed to secure alternative transport. Fortunately, there were a couple of helicopters on the landing pads outside and Haru had informed them that he could fly anything. The question still remained, *'Would they find Akiono'?*

At the top of a staircase, they paused, assessed, counted numerous heat sources on the level below and then dropped a HEMI grenade down the stairs into the passageway.

The stairs brought them down halfway along the corridor, which ran around the outside of the square, central room, with smaller rooms on the outer side. Stunned bodies scattered the passageway, but none were their target. They noted a high presence of more heat signatures, strategically spaced as they lay in ambush in the other corridors. "We need to split up. I'll go left, you two go right and use your HEMI grenades if you need to." Jeru nodded to Ashia for approval of what he had said and she put her thumb up.

As they made it to the end of the passageway and the corner they stopped. The two men checked that the other was ready. Ashia raised her left hand in the air, then dropped it fast and the grenades were away. As soon as the electrical discharge had died down and it was safe, they ventured down their corridors, picking off more attackers as they fired from the side rooms. Each of the outer rooms was checked and cleared as they passed by. The sound of battle was all about, the pops of their suppressed machine guns, mixed with the deafening and deadly sound of real bullets. Their battle armour protected them, but every so often they dived into an empty room for cover, before another advance.

With the sides cleared, only one more corridor remained. They would meet in the middle, as they attacked from each end, then enter the doorway into the central stronghold. After their fiercest resistance, the three regrouped at the room entrance. The three white dots on their monitors still waited, with a sense of power and arrogance.

Outside, all was quiet as Andrei lowered himself from the rooftop to assess the inside of the hangar. Yichen did the same with the armoury. In the pitch of night, with their matt black suits, they drifted like spectres. In almost silence, the helicopter ground crew that remained were eliminated, all but one. Andrei identified the heat signature of someone concealed behind a pile of steel drums. He also had another indication. This time it wasn't his technology that informed him, it was his own senses, his sixth sense. He could sense another Sixer. His Russian accent boomed, "Come out show yourself, I know you are there."

In the armoury, Yichen had successfully eliminated any threats and the whole camp, with a few exceptions, were now unconscious, as if they were under a wicked spell. He now set to work to gather the explosives that they required. An adequate C4 charge was set and he dragged his slain victims clear of the blast radius, then headed toward the hangar. He arrived at the same time as Andrei's prisoner emerged with his hands in the air.

Chapter Twenty

*The greater danger for most of us lies
not in setting our aim too high and falling short;
but in setting our aim too low, and achieving our mark.*
Michelangelo

The three gathered momentarily outside the door. Ashia felt her heart pound like a galloping horse and it reminded her that she was alive. They had moved at such speed and cut threw the enemy in a matter of minutes, but knew that the real enemy was most likely behind this door. Fear tried desperately to gnaw at her mind, to sow seeds of doubt and rob her of any confidence, but she pushed it aside. "Elio reigns", she said.

The men repeated her words with a nod and a, "Let's do this."

As the more experienced, Jeru took the lead he was surprised to find the door unlocked. He lobbed in his last HEMI grenade and thought to himself, *"This is going to be too easy."*

He closed the door and waited for the electrical charge to subside, then entered the room with Ashia and Haru close behind. In a nano-second they assessed the situation; two men in Russian military uniforms lay unconscious on the floor on either side of a desk, stunned from the grenade. Two fierce-looking Erebusians towered over them, with long, gangly arms and legs equipped with razor-like talons. In the centre stood an even taller, bigger, stronger looking specimen, even more ferocious. The beasts stood with confidence and an air of menace; savage eyes bulged from their sockets.

A smell of death, their smell, filled the room.

It was the first encounter for Jeru and Haru with an Erebusian and in that same nano-second they froze; shocked. Ashia used the brief moment of time to evaluate and determine that their target, Akiono, could be unconscious beneath the desk. Then finally the nano-second ran out, as Chaos simply lifted his hand, thrust it toward her and an invisible power threw the three of them back out of the room. Their feet lifted from the floor, as they launched and crashed against the wall, then slumped to the floor. Without their battle suits, they would already be dead and for a few seconds, none of them moved as they lay stunned.

Chaos screamed, "You have the insolence to come in here and think that you can beat me? Who do you think that you are? You disrespect your masters and you think that your toys will destroy us. You will worship us and declare Abaddon as your Lord, or suffer the consequences."

Jeru, coming to his senses said, "Never going to happen", as his main thrusters fired and he flew at the beast. Like a human bullet, his helmet smashed into the revolting face of Chaos and the force caused him to stumble momentarily. Jeru continued his manoeuvre, as he took advantage of the tottering tower, swung around behind him and wrapped his head into a power-assisted headlock. He knew that he couldn't kill him, or at least, that is what he thought, so he decided to just hold onto him.

Agonia and Penthos instantaneously reacted to defend their superior and lunged toward Ashia and Haru. Ashia was ahead of Haru, with her Katana already drawn, Agonia found himself skewered through by the blade. As she was about to withdraw the weapon, her prey vanished into a black vapour; sent back to Erebus. She also had the same thought, *'That was easy.'*

Chaos saw what had happened to his subordinate, witnessed the blade of *'Truth'* in action and panicked, as he too changed his form to vapour and escaped to the west, in the direction of Mont Blanc. She thought again, *'That was too easy.'*

Penthos was too focused to see what had happened to his companions, as he kicked, flailed with his talons, snarled and bit with his fangs. Haru had hold, but his grip weakened. The energy in the beast became a relentless frenzy and he would never give up. His purpose was to bring about mourning, his objective to kill and his aim to continue until death. The pair moved fast, too fast to determine where to place the blade, so Ashia whispered, "Elio, please guide me." Jeru looked on with uncertainty.

She advanced near to the frenzy, touched the edge of the blade toward them and waited. She felt contact as the blade slid across the tough shell of Haru's battle suit. Contact again, but nothing. She closed her eyes and waited and then she felt the slice of the blade into hard, bony flesh. When she opened her eyes, she laughed at Haru, who still wrestled on the floor and wondered where his assailant had gone. Before she had a chance to speak, she heard the voice inside her head, *I will deliver my enemies unto you, but it will require sacrifice.* She thought about what that could mean, then allowed it to pass from her mind as she said, "Well, that was easy, I beat him with my eyes closed." Pride was never too far away and she allowed it to creep back in.

"Hey guys, I'm on your side, don't shoot." The

prisoner looked a little out of place, not at all like your average Russian, apart from the standard thick black beard, that obliterated half of his face. His dark, black hair, deep brown eyes and skin, indicated that he was of possible Indian origin. "I'm one of you, I'm a Sixer."

"Who are you and what are you doing here?" Yichen asked the question in his rapid Chinese manner and demanded an answer even faster.

"My name is Deepak, I'm part of the Southern United Resistance Force, you know guys, SURF, that is who you are, isn't it?

Yichen thrust the barrel of his assault weapon under Deepak's chin and even though it was loaded with HEMI rounds, Yichen still thought it intimidating. Deepak just laughed and said, "What do you think you are going to do, electrocute meet as well? I may not have your fancy suit, but I'm SURF, I'm Deepak Masih and I'm here undercover."

Andrei accessed the SURF database on his wrist panel and confirmed in a few seconds. "He is who he says he is, served with Gideon on Apateon operation. He's genuine. What are you doing here?"

"Well, it's a long story, which, when we have time, I might just tell you. Right now, I need to get one of these birds ready to leave. I take it you're waiting for the rest of your team?"

"Are you a pilot?" Yichen asked as Deepak ran to the closest helicopter.

"Yes, I fly anything that flies, that is with the exception of those crazy suits that you're wearing." He shouted back as he ran.

"Well don't touch that one you're going for, it's rigged to blow." Yichen smiled and continued, "I can blow up anything.

Jeru checked the bodies on the floor and determined that Akiono was unconscious beneath the desk. "You two make a sweep of this place for any useful intel, while I leave a quick message for the Commissar General, here", said Ashia.

Jeru started to check through cabinets and cupboards, whilst Haru extracted a data transfer lead from his suit, opened his visor and started to download the computer hard drive. During their preoccupation, neither of them noticed Akiono stir. Beneath the desk, he peered up at the underside above him and spotted a loaded, concealed, sawn-off shotgun. His natural survival instinct kicked in and he reached, grabbed and pointed it up. Haru looked down directly at the barrels and it was the last thing that he saw, as the blood-thirsty murderer blew his face off.

Jeru fired his side-arm, planted another HEMI on him and he passed out again, as Ashia ran to check on her cousin. She had only known him for a short while, but he was more like a brother. No one would ever replace Gideon, but Haru was the closest that she had, he was the same blood. With her visor now open, she stared down in disbelieve into the helmet of her cousin. Where his face had been, she saw a mass of blood, flesh and bone, which made him unrecognisable. She had seen death before, was brought up on it, but this made her wretch and puke, then she screamed, "WHY… How did this happen?" Then she remembered, '*it will require sacrifice.*'

Jeru tried to calm and console her, but she was distraught and losing grip of the situation. "Ashia… Boss… We need to go, there's nothing here for us, apart from Akiono… Ashia, do you hear me?"

On her knees, she sobbed, oblivious to the threat of the Russians that could also wake soon. He grabbed her head, opened his visor, turned her to him and said, "Time to go soldier, remember the mission, grieve later, ask questions later, right now we survive, move and get out of here."

They embraced for a moment, before she said, "You grab Akiono, I'll take point."

"But Ashia, who is going to fly the chopper?"

"Hopefully, you can carry his weight and fly, let's go."

As they made their way out of the building, each of them took care of any hostiles that were recovered and they soon found themselves in the open. Ashia immediately took off to an elevated, defensive position above Jeru, but he was stuck to the ground, too heavy for flight, so he ran.

Lopez and Bekker kept watch as the other four regrouped at the helicopter. Yichen and Andrei looked puzzled and asked where Haru was. Ashia couldn't answer, so Jeru spoke, "He's gone, so we have a problem."

As experienced soldiers, they knew that they need not ask anymore, Haru was dead. There would be time for a debrief and explanations later, but right now they needed a plan of escape. As Ashia and Jeru were busy trying to work out if they could carry Akiono between them, Deepak stepped out from behind the helicopter. Their reaction was to drop the unconscious man and aim their weapons at the strange-looking man in Russian uniform. "Jeru, my old friend it's good to see you again, but let's not talk here, get on board now."

Jeru looked him over and tried to determine who he was. He recognised the voice, but the beard confused him for a moment, before responding, "Deepak, what the heck are you doing here."

"It's a long story my friend, but first let's get out of here." He jumped up into the pilot's seat.

"What you fly now?"

"I can fly anything. Now come on."

The whole encounter had been less than a minute. They were in the air in the next minute and in the third minute, Yichen pressed the detonation button which rendered the Russians flightless and with seriously depleted defences; they were vulnerable. As the explosions lit up the night sky, Lopez and Bekker joined them, flying alongside as escorts.

The Commissar General recovered, he felt dazed. He could recall doing things that he had been unable to control; some despicable things to innocent civilians and he puked in the same place as Ashia had done earlier. In his hand, he found an electronic recording device, placed there by Ashia. He pressed the playback button and heard Andrei's voice speak in his native tongue. The message explained everything and also apologised for the mess. He ran from the room to find his comrades all recovered and not one of them dead. Agonia had been inside of him for over a year and he now had a sense of freedom. He also knew that the infiltrators of his base were on the side of good.

He didn't pursue them, instead, he instructed that all executions are to cease. He also knew that, in the next 30 minutes, troops would arrive from the nearby town of Novosibirsk. The leaders will no doubt be possessed in the same way that he was and would plan to take control. He could not let that happen, he would not allow it and he made plans to fight against his own countrymen.

Chapter Twenty-One

I don't believe the world's a particularly beautiful place,
but I do believe in redemption.
Colum McCann

During the three-hour return flight to Kosh, Jeru kept his sidearm pointed at Akiono. The man had recovered and remembered firing the shotgun. He had tried to apologise, but no one listened to him. "You rescue me, I thank you. I sorry about your friend... I sorry... I not mean it... I sorry."

His main language was Japanese, though during the short time that Chaos had been in his head, he had picked up bits of Russian and English, enough to get by. As they approached Kosh, his thoughts changed. "I been bad man... done bad things... you should have left me."

Ashia had been deep in thought for the entire journey and now felt the need to speak. "We came because of your wife, she must love you, although I really can't see why."

Ashia watched with slight envy as Akiono reunited with his family. She thought about her family, her losses, Gideon and now Haru. She felt the envy turn into bitterness, anger and hate. She wanted to kill, thought that Akiono deserved to die, so, she hatched a plan, to retrieve the *'Justice'* Katana, and then kill him.

Tsuma explained to her husband about the deal that she had made for his life, but she was quite surprised when he took them to the old mine and recovered the precious sword. The man that she knew would never do that. Once back above ground, Ashia confronted the cannibal with all of her pent-up anger and hate, "What is to stop me from killing you now? Why shouldn't I just kill you, blow your face off, the same way that you did to my brother?"

Jeru looked at her with a shocked expression, he never realised how she felt about the Japanese man that they had only recently met. He had not seen her in this way since the death of Gideon and he wanted to reach out and hug her but did nothing in his confusion.

"Please, I am sorry", responded Akiono. "I understand… you want to kill me? Do that. You can take my life, I deserve it. Not just for killing your brother. I have killed many before. I am evil, done many evil things, but all of that is nothing like the evil I have just tasted. I have seen my destiny if I stay on my path now. I must die or change. I want to change, but if not; then it would be better all-around if I was dead. I don't deserve to live."

Ashia sensed a genuine sorrow in his voice, they all heard it, but she also sensed something else, an increased presence of the Pneuma. She looked toward Akiono and realised that the presence was in him, another battle took place before their eyes, as the man's mind transformed. He dropped to his knees and awaited his execution, as the tears rolled down his face. Remorse, compassion and repentance filled his heart and he sucked air deep into his lungs. He felt like he breathed for the first time; that he had been dead and was now alive. He sobbed, deep cries of pain, emotional pain and he looked up into her eyes.

What she witnessed was a miracle, as his eyes had changed along with every other facial feature. He had somehow been transformed, become a new creation. As he now spoke, his voice sounded softer and concerned, "I have knowledge, information about the creature that controlled me. He was in my brain, but I was also in his. This is how I can speak your language, but it is also how I know where he fled. He headed west, to Mont Blanc, he went to report to someone called Mortemus, another creature, his superior."

Deepak observed the scene before him, "What he says is true, Mont Blanc is the seat of power in the north and all commands come from someone called Joash."

Jeru looked at Ashia with astonishment, "We know of Joash and have experienced her wrath."

Ashia reacted in defence, "Yes, we do know her, but we were all different then, Jeru. She was under the control of the Mimics. I know what that is like, you don't so let's not make assumptions. She is probably being controlled by an Erebusian, maybe even this Mortemus?"

Akiono remembered more, "Mortemus, he also wants my sword… err your sword, both of them."

"Well in that case, maybe I should go and give him them?" She looked serious. "We need to get to Mont Blanc, wherever that is, and get there fast. Let's not forget that Japan is still being attacked and without the swords, is vulnerable. Trenchant is still on standby awaiting our return or my command to unleash her firepower on a designated target."

Jeru chipped in again, "If Mont Blanc is their centre of operations, we need to let Hanson know, give him the location and a deadline to destroy it."

Deepak had an idea, "If we head back to Kemerovo, we could steal the Cessna Citation that is sat on the runway, fuelled and ready to go. It'll take three hours to reach the plane, five and a half to reach Geneva and allow another hour to seize the mountain. In the event that we fail, Hanson will need to launch his nukes to hit the mountain ten hours after we leave here. Find out where he is and confirm he can do this now."

Deepak suddenly sounded as if he was in charge, but he had been in charge of his own actions for over a year behind enemy lines, so it was only natural. Jeru smiled, pleased to see his old friend and how he had grown in skills and abilities.

Ashia nodded at him, looked down at Akiono and as she walked away, said, "Get up, you are forgiven."

She returned five minutes later with the plan confirmed. "HMS Trenchant is currently in the Barents Sea and will soon be off the coast of Murmansk. From there a Cruise missile flight time to Switzerland is two and a half hours. They will have to launch when we are still en route. If we succeed…"

"When we succeed", Deepak piped up.

Her look told him he had overstepped the mark and she continued. "When we succeed, the call sign to call off the nukes is, '*Javelin Down.*'

The engine of their stolen helicopter barely had a chance to cool down and the six remaining members of the '*Honour Squad*' were back on board. Deepak climbed into the pilot seat, with Jeru by his side, ready on the weapons systems. They were fully armed and anticipated trouble. "No HEMIs this time people, this will be a hot zone. News will have travelled and we can expect to face multiple hostiles." Jeru spoke through the comms and turned his head into the space behind.

Ashia agreed with the more experienced combat veteran and they settled down for another three-hour flight.

Mortemus grinned with delight at the news from Chaos but was also irritated at the news that two more of his warriors had been dispatched back to Erebus. "You have done well Chaos. This is indeed good news. What of our helpful cannibal friend? Did you show him what he needed to know?"

"Yes, my master and he will certainly tell the puny humans that he thinks have rescued him. None of them is aware that it was all part of your great plan. I saw the ancient relic, the sword in the hand of the Sishon girl. I witnessed the power of the blade, but it is insignificant in comparison to your power and cunningness, oh great one."

"NEVER underestimate the power that we are up

against", Mortemus spat the words back at his underling.

He continued, "Even the humans fail to grasp how powerful the so-called, *'Honour Blades'* are. When I destroyed the two swords they foolishly named, *'Sure and Steadfast'*, the gateway to our kingdom opened more. When the others are destroyed, the gateway will be fully open and we will establish Erebus here on earth. Abaddon will, at last, join us and reign over mankind. Even without the swords, we will still win with our greatest weapon, FEAR."

During the seven decades of Mimic rule, the human race was enslaved, oppressed and subdued, unaware of anything. That lack of awareness removed any form of fear and in doing so, removed the power of Erebus over the human race. For decades Mortemus waited impatiently, biding his time, getting ready for his moment, for the void that he could rush into. Fear now consumed the human race, mankind had almost entirely succumbed and the gateway continued to open, as it was fed by that same fear. The shield over Japan had weakened, but it wasn't the bombs, fear had done it. He knew that it would be less than a day, before his Lord and Master, Abaddon would stand on Mount Osore and that mankind would bow down to worship him.

Chapter Twenty-Two

The One who is greater than us is near –
nearer than we could measure.
Amy Layne Litzelman

"We should time our approach to be under the cover of darkness", said Jeru.

"That place is always in darkness", said Ashia. "The evil in that place is so strong that we can use it to our advantage. We leave now."

Their flight to Kemerovo was different in many ways compared to their previous mission. Sat within the bowels of the enormous helicopter, each one contemplated in silence. They had previously caught the Russians off-guard, with the element of surprise, but now their presence was known. Their pulse jets allowed them to approach in silence, but now, the deafening thwock, thwock, thwock of the rotor blades, would clearly announce their arrival. Loaded with lethal ammunition, their solemn faces betrayed their pain and anguish; they could be about to take lives. Crazy Tommy Lopez was different, he smiled a psychotic grin, like an addict about to get a hit. They all knew that he was crazy and they were glad that he was their crazy.

Ashia observed the sky through the small window, clouds rushed by and the sun shone brighter than usual. She knew that it would start to dim soon, as it had done before, but it didn't. Jeru noticed her concern, "It's not getting dark", he stated. The rest of the team glanced toward the sky, and then looked towards her in trepidation.

"Deepak, hold at 50 clicks from the target, if we all go steaming in, we're a single, noisy target. We'll jump out at that point and go on ahead with a stealth approach. We don't know why it's not dark, but something must have happened. Jeru, stay with Deepak to assist him with weapons; something tells me that we're going to need them. Remember, our primary aim is to secure that plane and get the heck out of here."

An initial, small recognisance team from Novosibirsk had arrived in two helicopters and landed at the base in Kemerovo. The scene was peaceful at first, as the Commissar and his assistant greeted them. The leader of the team had queried about the distress call that had been sent earlier.

"All is ok now", said the Commissar. "We are all fine, we had an accident, but there's no need for you to be here, we can deal with this ourselves thank you."

The other man looked at the scene before him, the destruction of the helicopter and the armoury. He deduced that the Commissar was lying and his instincts told him to treat him as hostile. As he drew his sidearm and aimed it at the lying man's head, he started to speak, "Tell me the truth, what happened here?"

At the mention of the word 'truth', the Commissar folded his arms; it was a signal. As the man said, 'happened', the shot from the over-watch tower rang out and the bullet shattered the man's skull. Before his body hit the ground, the rest of his team was also neutralised, but not before the chopper pilot sent a distress signal.

An hour later, a full strike force arrived and over-powered their comrades, who had earlier been delivered from evil. The good that was in them fought a ferocious battle, but evil endured. Evil once again had control of the base and a shroud of darkness already began to encapsulate the entire site. The forces of good fled to the south and regrouped at the airport, which they now held firm, although it would only be a matter of time before they were yet again overrun.

The Commissar had a plan of his own. He had tasted evil as it dwelt within him, he still sensed the stench that lingered, but most of all, he had the knowledge. He knew where he needed to go, in order to strike the enemy at its heart. Mont Blanc was his destination and the jet that was fuelled and ready; it would be his transport. He also knew that if he and all of his men were to jump on the plane, it would be instantly shot out of the sky. So, his only current option was to fight and wait for a window of opportunity or a miracle.

Deepak hovered, as the Honour Squad exited the aircraft. "Give us a five-minute start before following up our rear", Ashia shouted to Deepak, who nodded.

Jeru remained silent, but the look on his face said, *'Take care of yourself out there.'* He wanted to tell her how much he loved her, to tell her not to go. He wanted to take her as far away from danger as possible, but he knew that she had to fulfil her destiny, whatever that may be.

As they moved into the distance he spoke to the whole team through the comms, "Keep it tight and follow the light. May the power of the Pneuma and Elio be with you guys."

Deepak looked at him and laughed, "Keep it tight and

follow the light? Very poetic Jeru, where did that come from?”

“I really don’t know”, he said, “it just came out without thinking.”

“Well, I like it”, said Deepak with a friendly smile. Instead of two soldiers on the brink of battle, they were just a couple of old friends having a laugh together.

Each burning crucifix around the perimeter of the airport had been extinguished and Ashia looked down at the charred and smouldering remains of people. Any who refused to bow down and worship Abaddon paid the ultimate price. She could see the jet at the end of the runway, with the pilot visible in the cockpit. To the northwest, at a short distance from the airport, a battle could be seen. She used her HUD screen and zoomed in for a closer look to assess the situation. She saw Russians killing Russians, a small force, held back a much larger force. The small force provided a barrier of protection and made it possible for them to just swoop down behind, and then seize the plane that they had come for, their primary target. Their way was clear and looked like they could do it without a fight. She was about to give the command, then she saw him.

The Commissar and a handful of his men held back the larger force. They were a barrier of good that prevented the flood of approaching evil, but they would soon be overrun. She calculated in her mind and realised that, if they went straight to the plane, the Commissar would be defeated before Deepak and Jeru arrived. Then the advancing evil would target them and the plane. She couldn't allow that to happen.

"Yichen, you head for the plane, take control, keep it secure and wait for us. The rest of you, let's even up this fight a little." She barked the order as if she were a seasoned veteran and they all obeyed. Crazy Tommy Lopez, flew into the lead and soared out of the sky, hosing down bodies in his path. The other three, Ashia, Bekker and Andrei fell in behind and fanned out to the flanks of the enemy, then moved swiftly in for the kill.

Yichen crept, soft-footed, like a cat up the steps of the jet and found himself at the rear of the cockpit. He met no resistance, but now the pilot stared at him through the open door, like two cats in a stand-off. Yichen pointed his gun gently towards the pilot, who shouted at him in Russian. As Yichen shouted back in Mandarin, it sounded as if the two cats were fighting. Very gradually the noise quietened and Yichen felt that all was calm.

The Russian pilot had a sense that the person in the strange suit, didn't really want to kill him, if he did, he would have done it by now. Confidence grew in the Russian as Yichen lowered the gun and his guard; then he sprung. Like a gazelle, he flew from his seat and made a beeline for the gun. The shock took Yichen by surprise, the gun flew out of his hand and slid underneath a seat. As he grabbed for his assault rifle, the pilot grabbed hold of Yichen, the best that he could.

Yichen reacted in the way that he had been trained all of his life, his martial arts skills kicked in as he dropped to a crouch position. Face to face, the pilot tried to hold tight but fell forward onto Yichen, who smoothly progressed into a backward roll. At the precise moment, his right foot thrust upward from a bent position into the gut of the Russian. He had learnt the 'Tomigachi' judo move as a child and favoured it. With the additional power-assisted suit, his assailant was thrown to the rear of the fuselage.

He landed in a crumpled heap but recovered quick. The former gazelle now transformed into a crazed bull and charged. As he charged the Sixer had the thought of planting a HEMI round on his chest, instead, he threw his rifle to the floor, not out of foolishness, but in admiration of the determined Russian.

He shifted into the Xuan Ji Bu stance, one foot planted on the floor, the other bent at the knee and raised towards his chest, like a crane. His arms positioned for balance, elbows bent, he was ready and waited, confident, strong and amused, but did not smile. His serious expression said, 'Please stop, I don't want to hurt you, but I will if I have to.'

He calculated the precise time in his head and when the moment was right, in less than a second, pivoted his standing foot. He followed the subtle movement with a rotation in his hips, leading with his knee, then drove his shin from horizontal to diagonal. The swift move finished as the elevated leg snapped straight and kicked through his target. His target was the man's head and it hit him with such force that, the 'roundhouse kick' knocked him sideways and he tumbled down the steps, to snap his neck on the frozen tarmac.

Yichen stood in the doorway, looked down the steps and spoke to the corpse, "It didn't have to be like this."

The plane was his to protect and as he sat, he thought about the life he had just taken and wondered how the rest of the team was coping.

In the space of two minutes, bullets flew and bodies fell. Lopez screamed; his eyes bulged as he stared into the threat of evil. The other three couldn't watch as human beings were slaughtered, they didn't have to look. Their sixth sense, the Pneuma in them, directed their shots, as the supernatural power guided and protected them.

With most of their force wiped out in a burst of fury, the hostile force from the north turned and ran, but it wouldn't be long before they returned with reinforcements. They would have no choice, they either fight or burn.

The Commissar looked up and beckoned their newfound allies to come down. Ashia gave the command to Bekker and Lopez to stand fast, as she and Andrei dived to land beside him.

The Commissar spoke and Andrei interpreted, "Thank you, that's twice you have saved me now. We all owe you our lives, but I'm afraid we don't have long. They will be back and will never stop. We need to reach that plane, it's our only way to escape, but we will never take off before they are back and they will stop us." He spoke fast and Andrei relayed what he said.

He continued, "Will you hold them back, whilst we escape? You are stronger than us." As he posed the question the huge Milo helicopter could be heard in the distance.

"I have a better idea", said Ashia, "we give you the chopper, I assume you still have a pilot?" He nodded, affirmative.

"Then, you protect us as we make it out of here. We need to get to Switzerland asap and only we can end this madness, but we can only do it with your help." She paused, unsure how to say the next part, "It will almost certainly mean your sacrifice."

Her eyes looked deep into his battle-worn eyes. He looked back and saw something that he had no memory of ever seeing before; he saw love and sincerity; he saw human kindness and he saw sense. He somehow knew that what she suggested was the best option and he shook her hand as Deepak landed the helicopter.

"Boss, I wish to stay here, to fight alongside my countrymen." Andrei looked at her with the same sincere look that she had just shown. He continued, "We are the 'Honour Squad' and this would be an honourable thing for me to do."

She didn't want to agree, to say yes and send her friend to certain doom. She also needed him and his skills but respected his wish for honour. She didn't speak, slowly closed her eyes then opened them again and as she did so, shook his hand.

As the darkness moved in again from the north, Jeru and Ashia stood on either side of Deepak, grabbed his arms and flew with him to the Cessna Citation jet.

Lopez had a sense of loss as the battle was over, but knew that there would soon be more, as they headed deeper into danger with every minute that passed.

Chapter Twenty-Three

Hours of crisis often call for sacrifice.
In matters of consequence, when have doubt
and fear given the best advice?
Why not heed faith, courage and honour?
Brandon Mull

With the team, minus Andrei, onboard, Deepak put the headset on and commenced his taxi to the runway. An angry Russian voice in his ears shouted, but Deepak ignored the abuse that he heard and switched it off.

Andrei listened to a different type of message in his ear, "You arc without doubt one of the bravest men that I have ever known. I'm proud to know you as a soldier, a Sixer and my friend. Andrei, it is an honourable thing that you now do and we all respect you. We will all, always remember the sacrifice that you now make. May the Pneuma strengthen you and Elio shine his light on you. Now, give 'em all you've got soldier." Ashia held back the tears as she spoke and thought about the sacrifice that her own brother had made in order to save others. The rest of the team listened in.

Jeru sat next to her and placed a gentle hand on her shoulder, they all felt as she did, though they hid it well.

The ice-covered, Siberian runway made the plane difficult and dangerous to control. "Everyone, strap in and hold on", shouted Deepak, "this will be tricky."

The luxury jet slid into position and aimed up the runway, whilst two helicopters approached from the north. The lead craft released a missile. His sighting computer told him that it was on target for the Cessna, though at the last minute, the deadly projectile veered off and destroyed the hangar to the rear of the jet. Deepak reacted with a push of the throttle as much as he dared and the powerful, twin jet engines thrust the aircraft down the runway. They narrowly escaped the explosive blast and debris, but the persistent helicopter pilot readied for another shot, whilst in pursuit.

The pilot now seated in the gifted, stolen helicopter, retaliated and chased with guns ablaze. His quarry was good, evasive, and hard to hit, but the rookie pilot continued to fire in the general direction. He knew that one lucky round was all that he needed.

The enemy helicopter closed in on the jet as it hurtled over the ice and gained speed. The skilled pilot swerved, dived, and attempted to lock a missile onto his prey. Lock, no-lock, lock, the screen blipped on and off; never enough time to fire between blips.

The rookie on the chase breathed a sigh of relief, as one lucky bullet managed to make contact with the main rotor blade drive. Sparks flew, smoke spewed from the stricken motor, which slowed to stop. The helicopter spun out of control and the experienced pilot attempted to land and stay in control. On any other surface he would have been successful, however, on ice, his spin continued once he was on the ground. Unable to avoid the landing lights transformer housing, he smashed into it. More sparks flew, ignited the fuel and the chase ended in an abrupt fireball.

The jet was safe and the rookie turned his chopper to return to the main battle. As he turned the jet left the ice-covered tarmac and shot upwards out of reach and too fast to follow. The pilot, pleased with his effort smiled but before he managed to finish his turn, a second enemy helicopter was upon him, shot a missile and took him down.

Andrei glanced away from the oncoming horde and noticed the carnage behind him. He was the only air support that remained and he felt the need to retaliate with an as-yet unused weapon. Each battle suit contained two MHTK's (Miniature Hit-To-Kill) missiles. In his head, the Russian thought, *'Missile hit that helicopter'*. In an instant, an upright, tubular moulding on his back opened and a missile shot into the air, then redirected. Direct hit followed by a spectacular mid-air fireball.

The sight inspired the failing troops on the ground, who were rapidly being overwhelmed. They fought back harder and Andrei flew over the melee to shower them with bullets. An armoured vehicle of some kind appeared with a machine gun turret on top and joined the fray. As his newfound allies scattered, he fired his second missile which eliminated the immediate threat, only to be replaced by another.

Soon Andrei realised that he had another problem. His suit was losing power and he gradually sank to the ground; then ran for shelter. Fallen bodies littered his escape route and he stumbled over one. He fell and landed to see the eyes of the dead Commissar stare up at him. All of his ammunition was spent, he'd even used the last of his HEMIs, but they were defeated. Survivors raised their hands in surrender but later… they would wish that they hadn't.

The jet shot through the air at almost the speed of sound and Ashia took time to relax and reflect. She had left Africa with a team of ten, lost four before they arrived in Japan, where she had learnt so much about herself. She had discovered her weaknesses but also gained so much. She had the blood flask and the revelation that the Pneuma and therefore, Elio, is available to everyone. Haru taught her so much and in a short space of time, she began to love him like a brother. Now, in the stillness of the plane, she grieved for him. It was the first time that she had slowed down enough for the reality to affect her and her eyes welled up.

She glanced around the luxurious cabin, the team rested around a thick glass coffee table, on white, soft leather seats. No one spoke a word, each sat in contemplation, except Lopez, who was already asleep. Bekker cleaned her long gun, after doing the same to her sidearm. She needed to stay busy to think. Yichen sat with his head rolled back, eyes half-open. Every so often he shook his head, his mind wondered if he could have secured the plane without loss of life. She looked toward the open cockpit door at Deepak, a friend and brother-in-arms of Gideon and Jeru. She wondered what they would have done if he hadn't been there. She mused at how fate had caused their paths to intersect and again considered her destiny. She was meant to meet Deepak, but what now? What would happen at Mont Blanc?

Finally, she looked at Jeru, deep into his dark brown eyes and he returned the stare. They remained silent, with no need for words between them; they were so close. They each knew the thoughts of the other, simply from eye movements and facial expressions.

Jeru dipped his head slightly, raised his forehead and nodded. It meant, *'Are you ok?'*

She raised a smile briefly, then dropped it and looked down. He could see her struggle and he knew that no one can ever be mentally prepared enough for war. He coughed to regain her attention, then looked at her in a way that she had longed to see, the look said, *'I love you more than you know'* and she mirrored his expression.

She felt the need to speak, "There's six of us left, but Deepak needs to fly the plane. The five of us will bail out and freefall over Mont Blanc. Deepak, you will have to land at Geneva, tell them that you were hijacked, but we parachuted out. We need to storm Mont Blanc stronghold and seize the swords if they are there."

When she finished, they each heard a crackle followed by Andrei's whispered voice, "Boss, we are defeated. They're executing all survivors. Make sure that you find those swords and somehow, wipe out this evil." He stopped talking, but kept his comm channel open and they heard the tortured screams of the prisoners.

A voice shouted at him in Russian, "Who are you talking to?" His de-charged battle suit had since been stripped from him and the guard punched him in the stomach. Two more guards grabbed him either side by the arms, whilst another yanked his head back from behind. The first guard now stood in front of him, smashed his rifle butt into his face and said, "We'll make sure that you can't ever speak again."

Andrei, dazed and staggered, was unsure of what was about to happen. He sensed the hard tug on his beard and a hand in his mouth. He wanted to bite it, but the smash in the face left him numb and unable to do so. He didn't feel the slice of the knife, but instead tasted the blood as the warm sticky liquid filled his mouth and mingled into his beard. The sadistic Russian smiled and said, "Another little trinket for my necklace", as he held up Andrei's tongue with pride and Andrei noticed the man's necklace of tongues, then he realised what had just happened. He coughed, gagged and choked as the blood ran down the back of his throat. The sadistic guard leaned forward, placed his face inches from Andrei's and screamed, "A wise monkey speaks no evil."

He paused for a moment, whilst the other three held their victim even tighter. Then the first guard thrust his dirty, long fingernails into Andrei's eye sockets and gouged out both of his eyeballs. The tortured man let out a gargled scream, as the guard continued to shriek, "Now you will see no evil."

Andrei was well aware of the three-wise-monkeys expression of, 'see no evil, speak no evil and hear no evil and he tried to struggle, but he was already too weak. He felt like a lamb in a slaughterhouse and wondered how much more torture he could take. Now, the guards on either side of him took their knives and simultaneously sliced off both ears.

Simultaneously, the team listened to all that had happened in horror, then they were plunged into silence, as the earpiece communication device was temporarily swamped in blood. The guard knew that Andrei was in communication with his comrades and purposefully provided a full commentary, as a form of sport. Deepak had translated the Russian words and Ashia puked on the deep-pile carpet, at the sound of a friend's torture and being mocked; then she instantly felt embarrassed. Andrei had reached his limit and collapsed into a crumpled heap, so the guards now moved on to torture the next in line and would return to Andrei once he had recovered; if he recovered.

The sounds had been too much for Deepak, who had been made to witness this form of torture and execution numerous times. Even after all those first hand encounters, he had not in any way become desensitised and could now picture the scene. Guilt gnawed away at him, as he had watched and done nothing. In doing nothing, he now felt that he had accepted the power and dominance of Abaddon. He had rebuked the Pneuma, denied what he believed in order to protect himself. Guilt, shame and remorse now consumed him.   He regretted being alive, survivor's guilt gnawed at his conscience. He wanted to make amends, he needed some form of atonement. He knew what he had to do and what his destiny would be.

Chapter Twenty-Four

Life is a race against disappearing time.
Sunday Adelaja

Just over halfway into their flight, Trenchant had already arrived off the coast of Murmansk and the nuclear missile then launched. The clock ticked down with 225 minutes before impact; time was running out fast.

Back at the airport, they had fled from, it was still daytime, though darkness had fallen, both physically and spiritually. Evil had re-established its dominance and Andrei slowly regained consciousness. A guard wandered nearby and checked the tortured people that were sprawled out on the ground as a macabre spectacle. Any who had been fortunate enough to die from their wounds were subsequently carted off and thrown onto a huge bonfire of corpses.

Andrei found the strength to sit up to see what was happening, then remembered that he was blind. He made an attempt to listen but failed to hear the roar of the flames each time a fresh body was added to the pile. He just heard a muffled sound. As the wind changed direction and filled his lungs with black smoke, he instantly recognised the stench of burnt flesh and choked. He touched his hands to his face to feel what he had become, then breathed a sharp breath in shock. Pain filled his head, but at least he was alive.

His ear canal had filled with dried blood and he dug his fingernail into it, in an attempt to restore at least some hearing. He struggled through the pain and his guard watched with intrigue; he had never before now, seen anyone attempt this. Three of Andrei's natural senses, sight, taste and hearing had been taken from him, now his sixth sense drove him on to survive. He thought hearing would give him more chance to endure what was to come next.

As he dug deeper through the pain, he began to regret doing so, because now he could hear the screams of those he had earlier fought alongside. Mixed into the screams, he noticed the sound of hammers hitting steel, as it pierced through flesh, muscle and bone. A cacophony of wicked laughter completed the barbaric soundscape and Andrei knew what he could hear; he was aware of his fate.

In his sat-up position, the guard placed an abrupt kick into his stomach to stun him. "Come on", he said,

"It's party time for you", then he dragged him to his feet. Andrei staggered, felt weak and realised that the Pneuma power was no longer with him. For a moment, he felt alone, abandoned, then he heard more screams and felt a sudden peace.

As Andrei had cleared his earpiece, his friends in the aeroplane could once again hear everything as it happened in the frozen Siberian landscape. Deepak didn't want to listen. He knew what was about to happen and he couldn't stop his mind as it flashed back to visualise the image. No one said a word, as a sombre mood fell within the cabin.

Andrei knew that his time had come, he knew it when he volunteered to stay behind and he was ready. As the Pneuma departed from him, the fight in him had also left. He did not struggle, despite how he was oppressed and treated so harshly. Still, he never said a word. He was led like a lamb to the slaughter and as a sheep is silent before the shearers, he did not open his mouth.

They were about to force him down onto the cold steel cross but stopped to marvel at a scene they had never before witnessed. Although he couldn't see, he felt the location of the cross with his feet. Then, with a calm and serene motion, he lowered himself onto the instrument of execution, stretched out his arms and waited. The guards looked on, astonished by the will and strength of the man before them, but the stillness didn't last.

"Who do you think you are? Nobody ever does that; it takes all the fun out of killing you. Why don't you fight like all the others?" The guard whined like a child that had lost a favourite toy, but still, Andrei remained silent.

Another guard approached and asked, "This is your last chance to rebuke your old ways, worship Abaddon and save yourself. Will you yield to our Lord and Master?"

Still, the stricken Sixer said nothing and the guard nodded to the other who waited with hammer and spike. He placed the spike on the palm of the upturned hand, then waited again. Still, Andrei did not open his mouth and with another nod, the hammer fell hard and fast onto the spike and ripped through flesh like a hot knife through butter. It continued on through into the hole drilled in the steel.

Andrei gritted his teeth and winced, but still made no sound. His hand felt numb and he tried to move it, but it was impossible. Whilst he contemplated his skewered hand, two more guards brutally stretched out his other arm, pulled until they heard the pop of his shoulder dislocate, then drove a spike through the other hand. They secured a chain around his ankles, attached a large weight and then pressed a button on a nearby control panel.

The sound of hydraulic oil hissed through pipes and the gigantic, metallic cross lifted into a standing position. The weight on the chain dropped as it was designed to do and the sudden jolt on his already broken body caused even more injury, as his other shoulder and both hips dislocated. More pain shot through his body like a shockwave, but even so, he did not scream out. He suffered in silence and waited patiently for death to bring him peace.

He seemed to hang for hours and as he felt the last of his life leave his body, he cried out, "I forgive you, for you know not what you do." The guards would usually have set fire to him whilst he was still alive, but they had never seen anyone behave in such a way, with such dignity and humility. Instead, to make sure that he was dead before ignition, a guard thrust a knife into his side, then hit another button on the deadly killing machine.

Immediately a valve at the top of the cross opened and spewed oil over his head. Simultaneously, a gas valve at the foot of the cross ignited. The oil continued to flow and anoint the corpse until there was enough to reach the flame, then combust into a human candle. The fire shone brightly into the darkness, a symbol of fear and tyranny, but the guards that witnessed the unusual behaviour of Andrei saw something different. They could not identify it, but it gave them hope.

At 15,000 feet above Mont Blanc, the jet circled in a holding pattern. The cabin door opened and the five members of the Honour Squad waited for Deepak's signal. Once again, Ashia felt the need to motivate her team, "We do this for our fallen friends, for Big Al, Cowboy, Chuck and Xander, who we lost so quickly. For Haru, whom we'd only just met, he was like family. For Andrei, who sacrificed himself, so that we could survive and fight another day. He has given us a chance to finish this mission, for the whole of mankind; who now depend on our success."

The team were roused by the mention of their dead friends and Jeru chipped in, "And for Gideon and all of Elafria, may Elio and the light of Elafria shine on us all."

As he finished, a cheer went up and Deepak shouted over the comms, "We're almost in position, may the Pneuma fill you, Elio reigns; now get off of this plane." Deepak managed to sound composed over the radio, but none of them saw his tears of brokenness.

Ashia, smiled at his words, as he tried to make a desperate situation humorous; then she jumped. The other four soon caught up with her, they joined hands in a circle and plummeted toward the monument of rock and ice, the appearance of which, would soon be changed forever.

They had all free fallen before but now, as they dropped like stones their hearts thumped like a runaway steam train. The missile had already passed Stockholm; they needed to hurry. They stopped at a safe distance to the west of the mountain and accessed the situation. The glass dome that once glistened in the sunlight, looked dull under the darkened sky. On a helipad above the dome, cut out of the mountain like a shelf, sat two Apache helicopters, armed and ready to roll out. On another shelf further above, a sophisticated multiple-launch missile system loomed out of the shadows. On a small terraced area in front of the dome, they noted two automated gun turrets. Gun-crazed, Lopez, inspected them through his HUD and looked concerned. "Boss, I know those turrets, they're deadly. They'll cut us to shreds as soon as we're within 3 clicks. Our missiles have a 3.2Km range, so we will need to be pretty close to be able to take them out."

A plan formulated in Ashia's mind, "Bekker, establish

an over-watch at a safe distance, be ready to pick off stragglers. We've got ten missiles between us, the choppers, missile launchers and turrets will take half of them and I guess that dome is bulletproof, so will also require a missile. Jeru, Yichen and Lopez, you'll use your missiles; choose two targets each and on my command, unleash the wrath of Elio upon them."

Chapter Twenty-Five

People don't run out of dreams,
People just run out of time.
Glenn Frey

Deepak kept his eye on the fuel gauge, there was plenty for what he knew he would have to do. He knew the mountain well as he'd been here before, his role as a pilot required him to deliver high-level personnel to the dome. Although he had never stepped beyond the glass temple, he had seen the door into the depths of the mountain and knew that none of the team possessed the means to open that door, but he did.

For now, he waited from a safe height, monitored the comm chat and knew that it wouldn't be long. More tears trickled down his cheek as he thought of Andrei and how he had suffered. It would soon be time for him to repent for the previous times that he had stood by and done nothing at previous executions. In the past, he had reasoned with himself and believed he had done no wrong. He had not actually executed any innocent people, although he had supported the executioners with anything that they needed. The guilt would soon be gone, he would soon be gone; he would soon meet his destiny.

<hr>

With everyone in position, she screamed the command, "EXECUTE, wait for impact and move in."

From three different locations, six missiles shot up into the gloom, acquired their targets, redirected and seconds later, the mountainside erupted. The scene was similar to a volcano that spewed out its deadly contents, although this was not nature, it was man-made destruction. Secondary explosions from fuel tanks, missile stores and other ordnance added to the spectacle. The dome shattered as the missile came into contact and Bekker took out any survivors in a matter of seconds.

"Move in, MOVE IN." Ashia flew forward straight toward the temple, whilst the others skirted around the outer perimeter. They were shocked at the devastation of the miniature missiles and once again proved that Sato's Japanese tech, with the combination of the Pneuma power, was a tour de force.

The squad moved fast, reinforcements would soon arrive and they would be sitting ducks. They all watched from a safe distance as Bekker released her missiles at the doorway that blocked their way into the mountain. Unfortunately, they simply scorched the surface. Ashia moved in to take her best shot with their last two missiles. Lopez tried to tell her that it was doubtful and a waste of ammo, then she stopped.

The voice in her ear warned them to take cover. "Boss, get out of the way… You all move now. This is the only way… I was going to bale out, but the autopilot was damaged when we took off in a warzone." As Deepak talked, his voice became calm. He had flown out to the west, turned and redirected the plane at the temple. He knew that at Mach speed, those doors would have no chance against his battering-ram bomb. No one could possibly hit such a small target, with a plane at such speed, but the Pneuma filled him, focused all of his senses and prepared him for his repentance.

The calm Indian accent in their ears continued, as they responded to his warning. "I've done many bad things… Things that I am ashamed to mention… This is the only way… This is me paying for my mistakes… Farewell, my friends… Knock, knock, her I come… BOOM."

The fuel in the wings ignited on contact and debris flew in every direction. Anyone immediately behind the door was instantly killed, incinerated as the aviation fuel poured into the tunnel. The five team members looked on in horror as they watched yet another life sacrificed in the fight against evil. With the protection of their battle suits, they now raced toward the heat. The tail of the luxury jet was blown out in the explosion and now provided access. Ashia took point, with the two missiles that remained and the sword of 'Truth'. Lopez went next, with his superior minigun, followed by Jeru. Yichen and Bekker took up the rear.

The fuselage served well as a tunnel and they soon found the charred remains of people that would have given them a fight. The fire-suppression system had triggered soon after the explosion and extinguished the threat, but not before the fireball had forced its way into the bowels of the mountain.

The chard tunnel was wide, like a road and they walked in pairs, side by side. Tommy Lopez disposed of the slight resistance, in the same way, that an exterminator sprays disinfectant on cockroaches. He laughed as the pleasure centres of his brain triggered. IIc had often joked that, if it wasn't for the Pneuma in him, he would probably be a serial killer, as he seemed to take so much pleasure in it. His laughter came to an abrupt end as one of the 'cockroaches' spawned into black smoke.

At first, with the smoke from the fire, it was hard to tell the difference, until the plume gathered into a thick mass and became a creature. A giant black, scaled fist smashed Lopez in the chest, which pushed on his back down the tunnel. Jeru rushed to the front and stood alongside Ashia, both with swords drawn, they waited. It wasn't long before more claws, teeth and eyes formed in the smoke. Ashia, gripped the Shuriken and the Katana, one in each hand. She knew that just a slight scratch from either blade would send these grotesque creatures back to Erebus, but there were too many.

Jeru had the '*Justice*' blade by her side and they slashed, hacked, thrust and parried. Heads rolled, arms lopped and chopped, but still, they didn't stop. The scene was reminiscent of Masamune fighting in battle alongside Meyo. Back-to-back they fought, protecting their three friends behind them. They knew that bullets would not touch this hideous enemy, only the Honour Blades could win, or so they thought.

The pair had been through so much together, survived the camps and escaped, but doubt now filled their minds. Doubt brought weakness and they both staggered then regained their balance. They struck one after the other, but it seemed that the over-whelming numbers, would mean an inevitable defeat. They knew it, sensed it and expected it, even though they had given it their best shot. Mortemus cackled to himself, within his inner sanctum, as he sensed the taste of victory. The last of the so-called, Honour Blades were being brought to him as a gift, the human fear had increased around the northern hemisphere and the gateway opened more.

"Ashia, you must fight, you have to fight."

She glanced towards Jeru, but he just shook his head, so much as to say, *'I heard it, but it wasn't me.'* She heard the call again and recognised her brother, "Gideon, is that you?" She cried out, "Gideon, they are too much for us."

Dressed in white, her brother appeared alongside her within a glow of white light. The light wrapped around her and Jeru and filled the tunnel. The frightened Erebusians ceased their attack and backed away, unable to see. Gideon spoke with serenity, "I can't hold this form for long. As soon as I go, you will be back in the fight, but you all have another weapon yet to be used. There is power in the name of Elio. These enemies of Elafria will flee at the sound of his name. Just shout it out as a united force."

She gave Jeru a puzzled look, turned back and Gideon was gone. The light returned to normal and the Erebusians rushed their position for one final assault. She shouted at the top of her voice, "Stop in the name of Elio." The horde hesitated enough for their leader to step forward.

"Who are you to tell us what to do? I am Legion, commander of thousands and we will finish you all now. Who do you think you are to use that name? We will crush you." The bigger-than-average Erebusian had half stepped, half slithered from within the crowd of wickedness and stood before her as a taunt.

Without fear, she stepped toward the mocker, stood her ground and spoke with authority. "I am Ashia of the Sishon. My name means life and hope and that is what I bring. I command you all to GO NOW… LEAVE… In the name of Elio. By the power of the Pneuma, in Elio's name, I tell you, you have no power, SO LEAVE THIS PLACE NOW. Tell them Sixers."

The Sixers responded with the same conviction and were a little surprised that they could command this demonic horde and they would run. They shouted and most obeyed, with the exception of the bigger ones, which were dispatched with the honour blades.

The battle took time, far too much time as they now only had 28 minutes until the nuclear strike. They needed to find the swords, quickly. As far as they were concerned, that was the reason why they were there. The swords were the mission at all cost.

Outside of the mountain, with the exception of the troops gathered to retake Mont Blanc, not one person knew of the small victory that had just taken place.

Their win had no effect on the gateway. The rest of the northern hemisphere still lived in fear, aware that if they didn't worship Abaddon, they would all die a long painful death. The crucifixions were broadcast to the population; causing panic, terror and dread to increase. Fear washed away all hope in every country, with the exception of Japan. Japan would fight back and they made ready.

Strange phenomena appeared over Mount Osore. The gateway opened more with each minute as another race against time had begun.

Chapter Twenty-Six

Will you walk into my parlour?"
said a spider to a fly.
Mary Howitt

From the safe confines of his sanctuary, Mortemus watched the scene play out on his monitor. He had ordered his horde into battle, along with his lieutenants and generals; but he grimaced as he saw them turn and run. He was momentarily alone, although he knew that it would not be for long.

The task force, scrambled from Geneva, now assembled at the entrance to the tunnel, where the burnt-out aircraft smouldered. Mortemus gloated, as he waited patiently behind the same type of security door that his pursuers would never open. It had taken a high-powered, kamikaze jet aircraft to smash down the outside door and he knew that they would never be able to use the same technique again.

He also knew that the human task force would not run at the name of a deity. They had found a weakness in the weaker Erebusians, but his human rescue force, driven by fear, would not turn and run and neither would the much stronger force that was about to invade Japan.

<hr>

Bekker, Yichen and Lopez found cover and took up defensive positions, though they already felt a sense of hopelessness. They were low on ammunition and it was only a matter of time before they would be defeated. The question in their minds was, '*Would it be before the nuclear strike?*'

With just 21 minutes until detonation, the first of the strike force appeared round the bend in the tunnel and opened fire on them. Ashia and Jeru retaliated with their three friends, then Jeru had an idea. He spotted the retina scanner next to the sealed door. He could tell from the bloody remains on the panel, that it had a booby-trap defensive device, but he also knew that they were out of options.

"Ashia, do you remember anything from your time here as Apateon?" He asked the question, but already knew what she would answer.

"Of course not, I have no memory of that time, why?" She felt frustrated by his question and didn't realise he was really trying to remind her that she was here before and that she was in power.

"Well, I assume you had security clearance at the highest level. The retina scan might still work for you… but…" trying to continue, he pointed to the panel as she interrupted,

"Why didn't you mention that earlier? It's worth a shot." She was about to jump up to test his theory, but he stopped her.

"No, don't. This system has a defence mechanism. I've seen it before on Mimic installations. If you're no longer in the system with clearance, it will kill you.

"The clock is ticking, with 19 minutes left and we're out of options. Hold on." As she finished her sentence, she launched a mini-missile down the tunnel to slow down the attack. As the explosion blasted a fireball down the tunnel, she jumped to her feet.

Stood in front of the panel, she took a deep breath and waited. The enemy regrouped and advanced through the bloody, charred remains of their fallen companions, spurred on by fear. She opened her visor but kept her eyes closed. Jeru stood by her side, anxious about his suggestion.

As the attack recommenced, she opened her eyes, the door also opened, so she grabbed Jeru and dragged him through the open door, simultaneously she fired her last missile, in order to buy her friends some more time and the door closed behind them.

They had 17 minutes left to find the swords, 17 minutes left to live and no means of escape. They expected to face more resistance, but instead, they were greeted by a familiar face.

"YOU, so you *are* here?" Jeru recognised Joash in an instant. He had vivid memories of the pain he had suffered, that she had caused him and others like him.

Ashia tried to remember the name of the person who stood before her. She appeared to be no threat, but she had to think through the fog of her time as Apateon, to reawaken her regressed memories. She allowed the image of this person to filter into her conscious memory. She last remembered seeing her whilst standing semi-naked in the snow, at the altar. "Joash? You are Joash, *is* it you?"

She stood before them expressionless, under the control of Mortemus, who now released her enough to do the things that he knew she would do. She had held the thought ever since Mortemus revealed it to her. Her emotions had grown but been quelled now, like the release of a sluice-gate of a dam, her words gushed forth. "Ashia, I'm your mother. You are my daughter."

She removed her helmet and responded, "You… But you're the one that persecuted us, you abused us and used us as slaves. I have no mother, I have no need of a mother, as far as I'm concerned, if you're in here, you must be the enemy. We're here for one thing and one thing only, the Samauri swords, where are they?"

"Ashia, you must realise that I was also a slave of the Mimics. Like you I was used and to answer your question," looking at Jeru, "I am still being used. Your lives are in great danger being here talking to me, he has allowed me to speak as myself for some reason, but I don't know why."

The statement of lives being in danger caused her to check the time, 16 minutes left, they needed to hurry. "Where are the swords?" She demanded.

"I believe the swords that you seek have been destroyed, Mortemus melted them down in a furnace and he wants to destroy the ones that you now carry." Mortemus dug his talons in deeper as she revealed his plan. He didn't expect her to be so strong, so free with her words. She reacted in physical pain, and clutched at her head, which now drooped forward.

Ashia suddenly felt sorrow for her as her mind raced back to the Angolan harbourside and the dancing man assassin. She thought about Harry Hanson and the pain that he had been in, whilst under the control of an

Erebusian killer. She could see that something was inside of her and controlled her but still took a step closer with a thought to help, then stopped suddenly. It might be a trap.

Joash fought through the pain and regained her composure, "I can prove that I'm your mother. Your tattoo, on your arm, will be a very similar number to mine."

In the same way as a Jew that had been in a Nazi concentration, could recall the number, tattooed on their arm, Ashia could do the same. She stepped forward again and said, "Show me."

Mortemus sensed his prey being lured into his trap, as she moved closer. Joash, pulled up her sleeve to reveal the number and Ashia gasped with the realisation that it was true. "You are my mother, but how can that be?"

On a large screen behind Joash, the scene in the tunnel played out before them.

The task force team leader grew impatient, he had lost too many good soldiers, especially to two deadly missiles and was irritated by the fact that bullets just seemed to bounce off of the three targets that they attempted to eliminate. Now, it was his turn to use the same tactic.

Lopez, Bekker and Yichen did their best to hold off the enemy, but they had nothing left to give. One by one their ammunition depleted and the scene on the screen became calm. Surrender was their only option, but after they had listened to how Andrei was treated, they now longed for a quick end.

The three stood to their feet, side by side, hands raised as a sign of surrender. At the bend in the tunnel, three of the enemy appeared in a similar row, like a mocking reflection. Each of the enemy soldiers carried with them a Law M27 Rocket Launcher and they waited for instructions. Their leader took great joy and grinned as he gave the command. "Ready, aim… FIRE."

The three triggers pulled simultaneously and a microsecond later the three rockets exploded, one on each battle suit. Ashia and Jeru, watched in horror as the screen became engulfed in fire and then turned black. They had witnessed the certain death of three more of the Honour Squad.

Ashia and Jeru, looked at each other with the same thought, *'It's just the two of us now, but in 14 minutes we all die.'*

Mortemus made Joash step forward to close the gap between them and placed the words into her mouth, "I'm sorry about your friends." The tone was low and flat, without emotion and the Pneuma power in them instantly discerned the threat.

Joash fought back and managed to speak, the contrast in the voice was noticeable, it was that of a mother protecting her child. "GET BACK. He wants to kill you."

Ashia reacted with three moves in one seamless manoeuvre. Her instinct told her to do exactly as her mother had instructed and as she stepped back on the balls of her feet the Katana raised to point towards her. With her free hand, she had already released the lid of the flask that hung on the chain and flicked its contents at Joash. As soon as one drop of liquid made contact, Mortemus was revealed.

Jeru had also reacted and raised his sword, "Whoa, you're an ugly one, aren't you?"

Mortemus responded to the insult and lashed out with his fist, which knocked Jeru back and smashed him into the closed steel door. Before Ashia had a chance to move, Mortemus had overcome the power of the liquid and returned to the safety of Joash's body. Ashia shouted at Joash, but directed her words at Mortemus,

"Stop hiding, come out and fight, in the name of Elio, I command you."

The expression on Joash's face transformed; eyes enflamed, bulged in their sockets with rage. Her nostrils flared wide, whilst her teeth snapped and snarled. Her voice changed to a deeper tone, with evil menace and threat. "Who do you think that you are to command me and to try your magic tricks on me? You will relinquish your sword to me or I will take it, along with your life."

As Joash screamed, she made a dash to where Jeru had landed and retrieved his sword. Jeru stirred, but was still dazed and watched as the two women fought frantically with the Honour Blades. "I see that you are puzzled and wondering why your magic didn't work", said the voice of Mortemus.

"You are clearly different to the rest of your minions", said Ashia, "But I will still defeat you. Why don't you come out and face me like a… like a… well whatever you are?"

"I am Mortemus, the 'Bringer of Death' and you are about to meet yours. Your mother told you the truth, the Wakizashi blades that you pitifully refer to as 'Sure & Steadfast' are no more. When I destroy these two blades the gateway will open fully. I will then rule alongside my master Lord Abaddon. I answer only to him, not to the likes of you."

The blades clashed and flashed and Ashia held Mortemus back, but she was reluctant to strike. She felt the Pneuma power fill her and knew that she could easily end the conflict, but at the cost of her mother's life. She had to tease the beast out into open conflict, so she taunted him. "You are nothing like your Erebusian brothers that we have previously encountered, apart from being ugly, as Jeru pointed out, you are a coward. You hide in the body of a frail woman. The others faced us openly, but you are weak."

Although Ashia couldn't see it, her taunts affected Mortemus and he tried to scream back at her. He opened Joash's mouth, but the voice that came out wasn't his. Joash fought to restore control of her body; her body was also full of Masamune blood, she too was a Nephilim and Sishon and fought with her daughter to break free. She spoke with a gentle, calm voice, "Ashia… Ashia listen to me… This is your mother speaking. Mortemus will never free me, he will not come out to face you in the open. You will have to kill me… Kill me and kill him."

"RAAAARGH", Mortemus regained full control and fought back hard. The blade sliced diagonally down Ashia's face, from ear to mouth and the hot blood flowed freely. Mortemus sensed the aroma of blood in his nasal passages and laughed, "Pahaha, you had your chance now it's time for you to die."

It is said that a mother will fight harder to protect her child, especially when danger is imminent and Joash sensed that danger now. In one final effort to break through to her daughter, she screamed, "Ashia, you must kill me now… KILL ME NOW or you will both die."

All of a sudden, the Pneuma in her also spoke into her heart and said, "You know that she is right, DO IT NOW."

Ashia parried the blade away, spun her body into a counter move and ended with a thrust into her mother's belly. Joash collapsed, smiled, and then spoke her last words, "I'm sorry for all that I have done to you, please forgive me. Thank you for my freedom."

As she spoke, a thick, black smoke emanated from the dying body, but Ashia was too distraught to notice. The smoke changed, as Mortemus, had only one option left, to take his true form.

Jeru eventually staggered to his feet and watched. He knew that he had to move to the sword that now lay beside Joash's open hand. As he thought it, the suit knew what he wanted and moved his body. He transformed from a stagger to a flying dive, rolled up and jumped into a spring with agility. As he planted one foot on the ground, he swivelled and slashed the sword through the shoulder of Mortemus, then continued on through his body in a diagonal cut into the centre of his chest, before he disappeared.

Chapter Twenty-Seven

The end of the world is on people's minds.
We have the power to destroy or save ourselves,
but the question is what do you do with that responsibility?
Nicholas Cage

Mortemus was defeated, however, the opening gateway only slowed for a brief moment, then continued to open, as fear continued to fuel its growth. Erebusian foot soldiers waited to pour into Japan, to wreak havoc. Soon Abaddon would stand on Mount Osore and declare the earth as his kingdom.

Jeru checked the countdown, "We have 7 minutes left Ashia and there is something that I need to tell you." He paused, as he searched for the courage, "I love you more than I have ever loved anyone. I've loved you forever, for as long as I've known you, but have struggled to tell you. Gideon was like a brother, so you were like my sister and it just seemed so strange, almost surreal. I'm sorry, but I can't help the way that I feel." He knelt down beside her as she hugged her dead mother's body and they kissed.

Death was no stranger to either of them, but to see Joash laying in a pool of crimson liquid triggered something in both of them. Ashia wept, as she wrapped her free arm around him and said, "Jeru, don't be sorry. I love you too and not like a brother. I love you like a lover and I want to lay with you, but now it's too late."

They both cried and their tears poured down over the corpse beneath them. "Seven minutes you say, well we had better make the most of it. The fight is over, we lost. Just hold me."

They embraced but were interrupted by a voice that Ashia recognised, yet it was new to Jeru, "Actually you only have five minutes now, so you'd better hurry."

They looked around, toward the sound of the voice to see Meiyo stood before them with the final trinity flask. She breathed into the flask and handed it to Ashia, "I told you that we would meet again. You know what to do with this, quick now."

Jeru, looked on, mesmerised by the shimmering glow of the Elafrian. The same glow shone out from the flask as it joined with the other two and Meiyo gave another instruction, "Pour the contents into your mother's mouth, so that she may drink."

"But she's dead?" Ashia questioned the futility of such an act.

"No, she isn't dead", insisted Meiyo, "She's only asleep."

Ashia stooped down to her mother, cupped her head in her right hand and forced the open bottle between her limp lips. Once the bottle was empty, Ashia stroked the back of her hand down her mother's cheek. She then felt the sting of pain in her own cheek and put a finger to the wound. "Don't worry, we can take care of that, right now we need to leave this place."

Although she had only just met her mother, the thought of leaving her behind was unbearable and she began to sob again. Soon, she felt a hand on her arm, it comforted and reassured, her as a familiar voice said to her, "Don't cry my daughter, I am with you."

She looked down into the open eyes of her mother. They were deep longing eyes that reassured her. She tightly gripped her hand and Ashia spoke, "I only wish that I had time to get to know you more, but it's too late now. Goodbye Joash, my mother." Jeru knelt down with the two women and placed his arm around Ashia's shoulders.

As time ran out, the room filled with a bright white

light and they were gone. Hanson had followed his orders and come through. Mont Blanc was destroyed whilst another mountain would soon become the new seat of power; Mount Osore.

The battle for Japan would soon be underway, with a powerful military presence in place. Monks from each of the five temples on the mountain gathered in the Bodai-Ji Temple with a military liaison officer. The officer did his best to reassure them that the military presence was for their protection as well as the protection of the country.

"We have no idea what this phenomena is. It could be a gateway to another world and… we need to be ready, in case any… err, if any threats come through." Major Garcia continued to bluff his way with them, but it seemed that they were more knowledgeable than he appeared to be. A spokesman for the monks presented their concern.

"Please Major, do not insult us with your offer of theories as to what this event might be. We have waited for this occurrence for centuries. Ever since our Master Masamune forged the five Honour Blades. You see, Osore is the only place in Japan, where you can find the Mamushi snake. As you may know, the venom from these snakes was said to be used to quench the blades."

Garcia interrupted, "I'm sorry, I don't wish to be rude, but how is this relevant?"

The Monk stomped his foot in disgust, "Osore is relevant. It is said to be the place where the gateway to hell will open and the five blades are the only thing that can stop it. Our temples were built to house the blades, one blade in each temple, but without any of the blades, we will not prevail. You see, it is not a matter of 'if' any threats come through, as you say, it's a matter of 'when'. Something or someone is coming and all of your military might will not stop it. We need the blades and we need them now. Do you have any idea where they might be?"

Garcia pretended to mull over what he had heard, but none of it was a surprise to him. He knew that Ashia and her team left almost two weeks ago with the Katana called *'Truth'* and the Shuriken known as *'Honour'*. He now wished that he had not allowed them to leave the country. He wondered if the two blades would have slowed down the process and bought them some time. He had been in radio contact with Captain Hanson, who had confirmed that the team found the second Katana and were headed to Mont Blanc. Unfortunately, that was the last they had been heard of and after the nuclear strike, they were all assumed dead.

"No, I'm afraid I don't know where the swords might be, but we have a team in the field that is currently looking for them", he tried his best to bluff the monks, but they sensed his unease.

"Well, it would seem the only thing that we can do now Major, is pray. If you are a praying man, you had better start to pray for your own soul. We are nearly out of time."

Chapter Twenty-Eight

*It is during our darkest moments
that we must focus to see the light.*
Aristotle

As the bright light dimmed, Ashia, Jeru and Joash rubbed their eyes. They looked at each other, they were dressed in white robes and scrambled to their feet. All around was white. Ashia knew where she was, she had been here before. Joash looked around calmly and she sensed the peace of wherever she was.

Jeru seemed guarded, his eyes darted around and looked for his weapons, "Where are we? Is this the after-life? Are we… are we dead?"

"No, this is Elafria. I think Meiyo just saved us… Either that or we are dead and have been transported here." Ashia was uncertain but made an effort not to show it.

"None of you are dead, not yet, although death for all of you may not be far away. The earth and the whole of humanity are in peril. The Erebusians could be victorious." She paused to compose herself. Ashia could see that she was concerned and upset and she tried to reach out to her, but Meiyo stepped away.

"We need to be strong", she continued, "Your team has fought well, but they still have one final battle, the battle for Osore. It will be a difficult fight, you saw how powerful Mortemus was, just imagine an army like him. Until now, mankind has been terrorised by mere foot soldiers and a few generals, when the main force breaks through, they will be impossible to beat. Abaddon will then establish Erebus on earth."

Ashia tried to stop her so that she could ask a question, but Meiyo seemed anxious. She rambled, which was not her nature and the words just spilt out. As she stopped to breathe, Ashia jumped in, "Sorry, I have a question. What do you mean?"

She didn't feel right questioning a spiritual being, "Err… What do you mean, my team still has one final battle? The two of us are all that's left and for a moment there, we thought we were goners as well. Our team is dead."

"Ah, well, the word that you use, 'dead' is a very strange one. It implies that it is the end of life, but your soul and your spirit are what give you life. Your body is simply a vessel to hold that life. As each of your companions died, their true being, their spiritual being, was brought here. I brought them here. I told you that I would be with you on your quest and even though you faced the loss, I saved them."

At first, Ashia and Jeru were in shock and disbelief, as they tried to take her words in. They had grieved, faced the pain of guilt and denial. They had not had the chance to fully mourn. The anger of grief had not yet made itself known, but it did now. In her rage, she forgot where she was and flew at Meiyo, her fists bunched up and reached up to plant them into her chest.

Jeru had frozen on the spot. Meiyo sidestepped, grabbed Ashia into her arms and held her tight. She looked down at Ashia and whispered, "I'm sorry that you suffered loss, I really am, but they are all safe. Would you like to meet them?"

Ashia gathered her emotions and looked up at Meiyo, "Well, yes, of course. I'm so sorry for that. Does that mean all of them?"

"Yes, but they may seem slightly different. Despite having all been here since their… err, death, they have only just received their new bodies. Look over there." Meiyo gestured with her hand into the whiteness and as she did so, a scene opened up before them. Ashia recognised it immediately as the river of life and when her vision cleared, she saw people in the water. They too were dressed in white robes and stepped out of the river. As they came into focus, she saw Bekker, Lopez and Yichen, closely followed by Deepak. They all looked more shocked than she felt, as they inspected their bodies, their new bodies. Jeru ran to meet his old friend Deepak, he said a few words and then did the same with the others.

Andrei came next and they all stopped to look at him. He looked immaculate and strolled casually up to Ashia, "Hello, Boss, it's good to see you. That's a nice scar."

Ashia touched her finger to her cheek and realised that her wound had completely healed. She turned to Meiyo and mouthed a silent, "Thank you."

Haru came next and her heart leapt, as she now ran to greet him. His face was completely restored and looked even more handsome than before. She remembered the scene in the Commissar's office and felt a sudden release of joy. As the tears flowed down her cheeks and they embraced, she had another memory, *'Jeru'*. She turned, ran towards her lover and didn't stop until her lips met his. They kissed passionately and held each other tight.

Jeru broke off the kiss and came up for air, "There could be more", he said, and there was. The four that they lost on the submarine, finally came out of the water. Big Al, Cowboy, Xander and Chuck completed the team and each of them started to catch up, share stories and marvel at the place where they now found themselves.

As their leader, Ashia felt compelled to say a few words to the team, but she was unsure of what to say. "I ah… I'm lost for words… We lost you… We lost you all, but now you are found."

Andrei shouted out, "I was blind, but now I see."

"Ha-ha, yes, my big Russian friend, it is good to see you, to see you all. You were dead, but now you are all alive. I am so proud to have fought alongside you, but my friends, we still have more to do…" She stopped in mid-flow, as she noticed their faces. They were in awe of something and she knew that it wasn't her. When she turned, she stepped back with the same look of wonder and admiration.

It was as if they had all been transported back to 13th century Japan, as the four Samauri warriors suddenly appeared. Each one in turn removed their helmet, to reveal their identity. The tallest went first, it was Meiyo and she made a gentle bow but kept her eyes on all of them. The next two unveiled together and Ashia recognised and acknowledged Master Masamune and his son Ketsueki. Ashia bowed to honour them and they both bowed back.

When the final mask was removed, she lost all honour and dignity, ran forward and wrapped her arms around her brother. The rest of the team recognised him and saluted the hero that had delivered them from the Mimics.

"Please don't salute me", he said, "I am not worthy. I'm just an ordinary man that did an extraordinary thing, because of the Pneuma power. Welcome everyone to Elafria. These are my friends", he introduced each by name.

"Some of you may wonder how you came to be here. I did the same when I died, but you need to know that you were all chosen; chosen not to die. The Pneuma power in you brought each one of you here for a purpose. That purpose is upon us now. Whilst there is no time here in Elafria and you could stay and rest as long as you wish, you will need to go back to the time that you came from. When you return, it will be as if you hadn't left. The earth will be facing the most serious threat that it has ever known. It's more serious than the Mimics and you will be in the most important battle of your now, eternal lives. Yes, you heard me, your true dwelling place is now here, in Elafria, where Elio truly does reign. You have all bathed and drank in the river of life and that life is eternal.

Gideon looked to Meiyo, as if to say, you take it from

here, "Gideon is right, we will go head-to-head with evil. You Sixers are powerful, you wouldn't be here if you weren't, but we four are even more powerful. We will lead the attack. You will have the three remaining Honour Blades when you return, she looked at Ashia and Jeru, but our Katanas are even more powerful. We fight with swords of light, Elafrian steel, these swords are more than just a sword, they carry within, the power of Elio and with them, we will vanquish our foe, our common enemy the bringers of evil, the Erebus horde. We have one purpose, one united goal. Our aim is to close the portal, the gateway to Erebus.

We can slay the army that comes through the portal, but it will keep coming unless we can extinguish the fear that has consumed humanity. Hope can destroy fear and the more of the enemy that we destroy, the more hope will be restored. I will be honest with you all, this will not be easy and we may not succeed with this approach. However, there is another way, a method that is guaranteed success, but it's costly and we have to hope that it will not be needed."

She stopped talking, not really wanting to say any more, but she could tell that they wanted to know. They were all trained soldiers and needed to know every eventuality before a battle; options, strategy and information. Apart from the Pneuma in them, good intel is what gave them confidence.

Meiyo hesitated, then told them enough to satisfy their needs, "We call the process, *'Ketsueki Gisei'*, named after my friend here. I will make it known during the battle if we need to use the *'Ketsueki Gisei'* ceremony. She pointed toward Ketsueki and no one needed to know anymore, they were all aware of the history of the Honour Blades.

Chapter Twenty-Nine

Being deeply loved by someone gives you strength,
while loving someone deeply gives you courage.
Lao Tzu

Submerged within the peaceful tranquillity of Elafria, the team relaxed and regained their energy and yet, after just a few hours, they were restless once more. The fate of the world was on their shoulders and currently on hold until they decide to return; it made them uneasy and uncomfortable. Ashia struggled to know what to do. The rest of the team would return to Elafria after the conflict, regardless of the outcome. Now she wondered what would happen to her, Jeru and Joash.

She was tired of fighting and her mind flashed back to the time when she was in a cage with Gideon, when she had told him that she just wanted to give up. He had told her to use her knife then, but she had given in to the power of the Mimics. Now, they faced a far more ruthless enemy and she felt a sickness in the pit of her stomach. She knew from experience, that adrenalin would shift the feeling and that it would rush into her body when she needed it. She anxiously waited for someone else to push her into the decision.

Joash sat down beside her and distracted her thoughts, "Wouldn't it be good to stay here? There's no rush, right? I've only just found you and I would like to know you more before you put yourself in harm's way again."

"No, Joash, err em, I mean mother, we have a duty… I have a duty. I don't expect you to understand, so let me try to explain. You were a slave to the Mimics, like me, then a slave to Mortemus. You have only just tasted freedom for the first time ever. Freedom has a price all the same. It comes through duty and sacrifice. We have to do what is right so that others can have freedom. When the time is right, we will go back and we will fight for that freedom."

Jeru looked around at the team, his friends, the people with whom he had built a deep sense of relationship and understanding. He combined this knowledge with his experience of battle and the signs told him that they needed to move. He whispered in Ashia's ear, "Look at them, they want closure. We all need to know how this ends. I've seen soldiers anxious on the eve of battle and I'm seeing it now, but it's your call Boss."

She smiled a sigh of relief as if she had been given permission to go to a party and shouted out, "Listen up! We can't wait here any longer! We need to end this once and for all. I don't want to make it an order, but who is with me, who wants to go back now?"

Loudmouth, Tommy Lopez responded first, "Ready when you are Boss. Count me in." Echoes of agreement followed and every hand went into the air. Gideon listened and waited nearby. He already knew that they wouldn't be able to wait for long.

Gideon spoke, "We're going back to Japan, to Mount Osore. There are 16 of us and Joash. We'll be outnumbered by at least 100 to one, but we have the Pneuma. You will all have your battle suits and other gear when you return. You will return to the Bodai-Ji temple, where some of you will meet some familiar faces and you can all replenish your ammo. Now go with Elio's blessing."

The evil incursion arrived in the middle of the day, yet an oppressive darkness covered the land. On the ground, searchlights lit up the sky, as they moved in arc patterns. Floodlights illuminated the five temples and surrounding areas. Men and machinery moved into strategic defensive positions, in readiness for the unexpected.

The whole Japanese army had been mobilised two

days earlier, as soon as the circle of flames appeared in the sky directly above the Osore summit. The initial reaction, to fire a volley of missiles into the gateway, had only helped to increase the size. The monks advised the military that it feeds off of fear and that everyone needs to remain calm. Despite that advice, fear had already gained a foothold.

Rumour spread among the troops that they faced another alien invasion and as the first wave of black spewed from the portal, panic set in, then *everyone* opened fire. The black mass separated into black dots and each one grew into a creature, which then targeted a soldier. Once in control of a soldier, they turned the soldier 'puppets' upon each other. The natural chaos of spontaneous civil war grew and pandemonium swallowed minds. Abaddon watched his plan unfold and waited for his moment to make a grand, spectacular entrance.

The force of 16 appeared like aliens beamed in from outer space, directly into the temple command centre. The guards reacted in a hostile manner. Meiyo put them at ease, raised her hands before them and spoke, "Do not be afraid. We are here to help, stand down your men. You will not win this war with bombs and bullets. This is not a battle of flesh and blood."

Garcia and Sato stepped forward, "We know and we have been waiting for you. We never gave up", Garcia said as he glanced a smile towards Ashia. "Do you have the Honour Blades? We need them now."

Ashia shook her head, "Only three Major."

Meiyo forcefully reiterated her command, "Stand down your men! They are only making the situation worse. We will take the lead. Ashia, I believe Sato has your ammunition? Lock and load and follow up the rear with your team."

A pompous Japanese General questioned, "I am in charge here. Garcia is simply a liaison officer. How do you expect to fight these creatures in your Samauri party costumes and fancy swords?"

"We don't have time for this", said Meiyo as she raised a hand again and silenced the General, "Let's go!"

The uncanny sight of four ancient Samauri warriors, took the soldiers by surprise, as they stepped onto a modern warfare battlefield. The demonic presence in each of the soldiers recognised the Samauri, so one by one they slowly ceased fire in fear. A glow of bright light radiated out from each Samauri and each drew a shiny bright Katana, but instead of using it to fight, they tilted the blades toward the light. The blades magnified the light as it intensified and shone across the darkened battlefield. As it hit each soldier, the Erebusian beasts released their human hosts and flew to the skies.

Ashia smiled with amusement at the frozen General and turned to Sato, "What do you have for us, Sato?"

"Well, some very special ammunition for each of you. This is special Sixer's ammo, which we kept aside, in the hope that you would return in time. We know that Nephilim blood is powerful and you may recall that when you were with us, you gave us a litre of your blood to study. Well, we concluded that physically, it's just the same as any human blood, but as an experiment, we have weaponised it. We don't know if it will work, but it's worth a try." She produced the ammunition; each round had a red tip of blood.

They grinned at each other and Ashia gave the order to lock and load. "The two of us don't need these bullets", said Jeru. "We have 'Honour', 'Truth' and 'Justice' and we will prevail.

Ashia replied, "We also have the name of Elio and we know what happened the last time we used that. Come on!"

Sato and her team had managed to hack into the northern hemisphere broadcast transmission system. The giant screens had been used to show the continuous stream of crucifixions and stir up fear. A nearby film crew now captured events as they unfolded on Osore and broadcast it to the people. The populace watched the Samauri fight with hope. As the hope of deliverance rose, the gateway growth paused but never diminished. Fear still held onto the people.

Joash stood by, uncertain how to behave or what she should do. She didn't know if she could fight, it had only been a few hours since she was released from a life of slavery. During that time, she had talked with her daughter, heard the story of Gideon and fallen into her new role as 'mother'. For the first time ever in her life, she watched her daughter with a sense of pride. The kind of pride that any parent has when they watch their child perform. Though this was not a school play or a poetry recital, this was war.

"Spread out and make every shot count!" Jeru commanded as they exited the temple. For a moment they stopped and stared in awe at the sight before them. The four Samauri warriors were in the thick of battle and although they couldn't fly, apart from Meiyo, they could leap great heights. Ashia watched with pride, as Gideon projected himself into the gloom of darkness. As he shot into the air, he managed to spin his whole body with the blade flashing and slashing.

The Japanese army stood down, but wave after wave poured from the portal. Ashia shouted, "Aim for the flanks and anything that manages to breakthrough. Let the Samauri take the centre." They did as she commanded and cheered when the first of their special bullets worked and sent the enemy back through the portal.

The fight continued with no let-up, "I send you back in the name of Elio", could be heard from the 16 and it worked, so at first, they sensed a weakened foe. However, with each wave, the Erebusians seemed to grow stronger, they to be able to resist the command.

"They're growing stronger because mankind is growing weaker. Fear is growing out of control and it's only a matter of time before they overpower us. Abaddon will come forth and there will be no stopping him!" Meiyo screamed her own worries towards Ashia.

"We are still strong! We aren't giving up yet!" Ashia shouted back, as she slashed and swiped the demonic beasts.

"You are strong, Ashia, you are the Sishon, but the rest of your team is weakened, their energy is spent. Even when they use the name Elio, they lack authority. Their spirits may be willing, but their bodies are weak", Meiyo had a tone of urgency in her voice as she continued.

"This horde will not stop unless we close the portal. As soon as we dispatch them back to where they came from, they simply return again. We can't kill them, just send them back, over and over. The Sishon ammunition will soon run out and then we will then be over-ran. It's only a matter of time. I have an idea. Give me the Trinity flask."

Ashia tossed it to her and Meiyo grabbed it, fought her way forward through the horde and lobbed it into the gateway. For a moment the horde ceased to fight as they waited to be sucked back into the fiery gate. They watched the gate close slightly for a few seconds, only to restore again… as the power of world fear fuelled it.

"What now? What's our options?" Ashia asked.

"We only have one I am sorry to say, it's time for the *'Ketsueki Gisei'* ceremony. You and Jeru will need to make your way back to the temple. I'll meet you there but hurry. I sense that Abaddon will be here soon." Meiyo looked at Gideon with sorrow in her eyes and he looked back and gave a nod of acceptance.

As Gideon continued to make blow after blow on his enemy, he marvelled at the fact that he fought alongside Masamune and his beloved son, Ketsueki. He reflected back over the many fights that he had been in as a young man. He lost count of the times that he had protected his sister. He recalled the giant named Gath that he killed with a catapult and a knife. Pictures of the mission to capture Apateon flashed into his mind and the tough decision that he made when he realised that Apateon was his sister. He had paid the ultimate price to eventually set her free, as he gladly died in order to defeat the Mimics.

His memories drove him to fight harder and he screamed at the others in battle alongside him, "Come on, we **can** stop them! Send them back in the name of Elio. Fight harder!"

The Pneuma in all of them pushed them forward and they gained ground, "Yes, come on, we can do it." Tears began to fill his eyes and he felt as if he had been kicked in the heart by one of the monsters, but none had come near. Masamune and Ketsueki sensed his pain.

"We are with you Gideon and we will be with you until the end", shouted the father and son.

The end came nearer and as each of the Sixers ran out of the blood bullets, they made a hasty retreat back to the temple. As the Erebusians regained control, the Japanese civil war restarted and man continued to kill man. Soon, it was just the three exhausted Samauri left in the battle and the gateway became fully open.

"Quick, get to the temple, we will be safe in there", Gideon shouted the command with regret. He was regretful of their inability to win, but he had even bigger regrets about what was to follow.

Chapter Thirty

I am the resurrection and the life.
The one who believes in me will live,
even though they die.
Jesus the Christ

Once inside the temple, the Samauri generated a field of protection and the white light shrouded the building, "We're safe in here for now", said Meiyo, "but we don't know how long for."

As billions watched the TV stream, fear grew; so too did the portal and the people became even more fearful. Meiyo dived back outside to drag the film crew inside the temple, but it was too late. The damage was done. Fire rained down from the portal and engulfed the mountain. With heat more intense than any volcano or nuclear explosion, all human life on Osore was extinguished in the blink of an eye. The four, unprotected temples disintegrated in the multi-mega-tonne blast and were no more.

The Mimics had slowly and subtly terra-formed the northern hemisphere to suit their needs and it had taken decades. The Erebusians now transformed the mountain to suit their needs in an instant. Erebus had been established on earth and would soon spread. Osore acted as a bridgehead to the rest of the world, including the south and soon there would be no escape. Darkness and desolation began to engulf the rest of Japan and the atmosphere shifted. In preparation for Abaddon, the air changed, as **the elements nitrogen, oxygen and argon** decreased, whilst carbon dioxide, hydrogen, helium, methane, sulphur and ammonia increased.

Dark clouds rolled in and brought with them lightning which ignited the flammable gases, then the acid rain poured to wash the cremated human remains away. Multitudes of repugnant, hideous beasts prowled around on the ground and in the air. They moved with an air of superiority and arrogance; victory was theirs and soon they would celebrate. Before long, Abaddon would usher in a new rule, his dominion was nigh.

The beasts waited at a safe distance from the only hope that remained on Osore. The only hope for the world. Within the bright light of the **Bodai-Ji** temple, fear now also grew and Meiyo tried to bring a sense of serenity. Nevertheless, the temple was occupied by ordinary human beings, who simply couldn't understand. As far as they were concerned, they were defeated and this was the end of the world.

"We need to surrender, to submit to them and their leader", a man shouted with panic. He ripped off his white shirt to wave as a flag of surrender and ran, semi-naked from the sanctuary of the temple. The crowd looked on, half in expectation, half in shock from within the temple, but as the man stepped from light into darkness, he collapsed and screamed in agony, as his lungs burst. The rain drenched his skin and it blistered, then fell in sheets from his muscles. The flow of blood and body fluids stifled his gargled cry, then he was dead.

His actions gave birth to yet more panic and the film crew captured the mayhem that now filled the temple. Around the northern world, fear was now enough to drive many to suicide.

Abaddon now made his way to the gateway.

"STOP…Listen to me", commanded Meiyo.

"Why should we listen to you?" A shout came back. "You're not one of us. For all we know you brought this upon us. Look what you did to the General. Who put you in charge?"

Meiyo knew that dissension among humans could spread fast; if she didn't act quickly, she would have another fight on her hands. So, she held out her hand to the General and released him. "You have it wrong", she said, "We are here to help. You too would all be dead now if it wasn't for the four of us in our…How did you put it? Samauri, party costumes."

She stopped and smiled at the General, please remember your history, the word 'Samauri' means to serve and that is why we are here; to serve you. Yes, the battle looks like it is lost, but the war is about to start. We will have the victory, but you must believe, have faith. The more that you doubt and panic, the stronger the enemy will become. We do have a solution. It's a sure way to stop them, but it will take a willing sacrifice. One will have to give their life for the sake of many."

"Not me", shouted a voice from the crowd. "Me neither", came another. "Who is it, who must die?" They wanted an answer.

Jeru shouted and changed the atmosphere, "I'll do it, I'll gladly die if it means to put an end to this evil. Let it be my destiny." Ashia ran to him, took both of his hands and looked him in the face, then she knew that he was serious.

Haru stepped up, "No, let it be me. May my death

bring a spring of light to the world." One by one, each of the Honour Squad offered to die for the sake of the world and the crowd gradually calmed down. Never before had they seen so many people willing to do an unselfish act and it filled them with hope.

Ashia and Joash remained silent throughout. Joash had done so out of confusion, as she still struggled with her newfound freedom and questioned in her mind if she should give it up. Ashia remained silent because she knew that it was her, she was the only one. She had learned from Ketsueki that his name meant 'blood' and Masamune had told her that Gisei meant 'sacrifice'. She knew what was involved in the original Ketsueki, blood sacrifice. Before they had even left Elafria, she realised that this could be her destiny.

Eventually, she spoke, "I know that it's me. I've always known. This is my destiny and I'm sorry Jeru." She squeezed his hands tighter and didn't want to release him. He made an attempt to protest, but she prevented his cry with a kiss and he felt his heart melt.

He turned as he felt an arm of comfort around his shoulders, it was Masamune. He said no words, but his expression told him that he understood his pain; he too had been through it. Then he spoke, "Take courage, my friend, take courage."

Masamune had been a brief distraction and Jeru failed

to notice that Ashia had released his hands. When he turned his attention back to her, she had already removed her battle suit and turned to Meiyo, "How do we do this?"

A sinister voice bellowed from the fiery circle above, "Behold, all bow down, worship your Lord. All hail, our glorious Master, the illustrious, Abaddon."

Each of the beasts that surrounded the temple bowed down in fear and awe. None dared to look, but the assembled group in the temple peered up to the gateway. Two gigantic, cloven-hoofed feet appeared first, like those of a bull. Muscular legs followed, adorned with crimson red hair to match the rest of his body. Bony, skeletal spikes protruded from his shins and thighs. His powerful torso like iron narrowed to support a colossal barrel of a chest. His equally muscular arms, with yet more bony spikes, stretched out to reveal bat-like wings, which caught the air in readiness. As with all Erebusians, his hands were embellished with razor-like talons.

He dropped from the portal and swooped into a dive. In defiance, he aimed for the temple but veered off at the last second to avoid the light. The sound of wind rushed through his wings until the sound changed to a flap, and then he lifted high into the darkness. Like a god, he came to rest on his throne of Mount Osore and allowed the flickering light of the fire to reveal his enormous head. Spiral, polished, black horns like a ram, protruded in place of a crown. His large, pointed ears, flared wide open, alert and captured every sound, every whisper. A pair of bright amber coloured eyes, with black slit type pupils, pierced through the darkness and assessed the scene before him. He slowly opened his mouth to reveal ferocious teeth and elongated fangs, then drooled into his thick-set, black, goat-like beard.

"Welcome, my fellow subjects…Welcome to a brave new world…A new Erebus…At last, we are FREE…You have all fought well and I am pleased, but we still have one small problem to be rid of…The Elafrian interference…We will snuff out their light like a candle…Mortemus tells me that they do not have the five swords and even if they did their temples are destroyed…They have no temple to place them into."

A deafening, blood-curdling cheer rang out from the assembly of beasts, and Abaddon bathed in his own glory before he continued. "The Elafrians are fools, they forget that I was once like them, I was once one of them, but I found a new more formidable power. They will not hold us off for much longer and their light will fade. Then we will rush in and crush them.

Ashia looked at Meiyo with concern, "Yes, he speaks the truth", said Meiyo, "He was one of us, but he was consumed by pride. He thought himself better than the rest of us, even better than Elio himself. So, left with no choice, Elio banished him. He is powerful and took many of our brothers and sisters with him, as he poisoned them with power."

"What about what he said about the light? Will it fade? Will we be in danger?" Ashia asked.

"Yes, but he is wrong about the five temples, we only need one and we have that right here", Meiyo hesitated.

Ashia pressed for more, "Yes, the Bodai-Ji."

"No, Ashia, your body is the temple. You know that you are the blood sacrifice and that is the only way. The three remaining blades will need to be placed into your body; your body is the temple. You do realise that, don't you?"

"Oh yes, of course… sorry. I… I am ready…but can we do it quickly? I've accepted this as my destiny, so please, just do it now." She tried to sound strong, but her tears revealed her true feelings. Jeru stood next to her and held her hand, as he tried not to cry.

"I'm sorry Ashia, no Elafrian could ever harm a human being. Remember, Masamune had to sacrifice his son…"

Joash interrupted Meiyo, "Does that mean I have to do it? I couldn't possibly do it; I've only just found her. I can't just throw her away like that."

Meiyo continued. "No Joash, Masamune loved his son, but you haven't yet had time for a deep sense of love to develop. It must be someone who loves you deeply Ashia and from what I can see, that is you Jeru."

To kill the woman that he loved is not what he expected or wanted to hear. To lose her was bad enough, but to be her executioner came as a shock. Jeru dropped to his knees and wept. "Please could you take this task from me? There must be another way. We *all* love her."

"No one here loves her greater than you do Jeru. You are our best opportunity and the two of you are the hope of the world." As Meiyo paused, she realised the film crew was still in action and the majority of the world watched with hope. As she finished her sentence, Abaddon also sensed it and felt a tremor in his legs.

"Quickly Jeru, Ashia is ready, you must be also."

Masamune spoke softly, he understood and held Jeru's hand as he sobbed.

Ashia was already on her knees in front of Jeru and she handed him her sword and knife. He ignored the blades, dropped to his knees, wrapped his arms around her and wept deeply into her chest. "I don't want to do this… I can't do this."

"I know that you don't want to, but you have to. Please… do it now, I'm ready. I do love you Jeru and you love me. It's time." Tears now poured down her face as she thought of the life that they could never have together and he grabbed the Shuriken and told Masamune to hold it for him.

With a Katana in each hand, he staggered to stand, every muscle in his body trembled as everyone present in the temple and around the world cried. Even Lopez was on his knees in tears. She placed the two blades onto her chest, said the words, "Goodbye my love" and then nodded her head. At the nod, he thrust forward as if on autopilot. History repeated; as they had done so centuries earlier, the blades travelled through her chest and broke through her back. She exhaled her last breath and died instantly, as she had placed both blades over her heart. She was dead, but nothing happened. Jeru felt as if he had been tricked and that she died for no reason.

Chapter Thirty-One

We asked for God's help; and now,
in this shining outcome,
in this magnificent triumph of good over evil,
we should thank God.
George H W Bush

"Quick Jeru, she must die with 'Honour'", Masamune urged as he passed him the Shuriken. He took it and plunged it deep into her chest, still, nothing happened.

In a state of shock, Jeru calmly removed the three blades and laid out her body as if she was asleep, then anger hit him. He jumped up from the floor to confront Meiyo, but she and the other three Samauri had already gonc.

"I was a fool to think that this would work with only three blades, we needed five. Ashia died for nothing." He fell back onto the floor and cradled her dead body. His tears poured like gushing streams and he wailed pitifully, "Why? W-h-y?"

Joash sat on the other side and held onto her daughter.

As she held her limp, bloody body, she sensed something new, a deeper level of love, brought about by loss and she too wept. Her tears mingled with Jeru's tears and the blood, as the Elafrian remnant of light began to fade.

Abaddon saw the light dim and he stepped forward into a crouch position, ready to pounce. His ears tuned to the sounds that echoed inside the temple building and he heard the weeping and wailing. He sensed his victory at hand and signalled to the horde that waited in an impatient manner. At once they began to gnash their teeth.

Haru, bowed down at Ashia's feet, he could no longer conceal his sense of loss and sorrow; with his body crumpled in a heap, he added his flow of anointing tears. They cascaded down from her toes to her heel and merged with the flow of blood.

Tommy Lopez crawled through the blood like a broken man. Never before had he allowed his real emotions to show, he always bottled it all up with an image of laughter and craziness, but this was far too much for him. He arrived at her drenched torso and broke down. He cried a release, as his entire life's hurts, bitterness and frustrations spewed out all at once. He moaned and wept with deep screams of sorrow and the distraught scene became too much for the rest of the Sixers. They all huddled around their friend and leader. Not one of the 11 that remained was able to hold back the tears, as each one expressed their great love for her.

Jeru looked up at his comrades and friends, forced a smile and sniffed back the snot that had filled his nostril. They all nodded and similarly tried to smile back, so much as to say, *'we did our best, but it's over.'*

As the oil in a lamp runs out, the light fades to nothing and that is how it seemed as they dimmed into darkness. It was over and they could do no more. Abaddon knew that his time had come and he leapt forward, unfurled his wings and soared to lead the final onslaught.

The tears of many, the tears of love, had flowed. The blood of sacrifice had been released, freely given and also flowed, then mixed with those tears. As soon as Abaddon pounced, so too did the Pneuma power; it rushed into the temple like wind and as it swirled among the gathered crowd, it gathered up the blood and tears, then Jeru understood.

Abaddon gave an evil laugh as he was about to crash through the roof of the temple, but he never made it. The force of the power of blood, love and spirit exploded outwards from the temple, blew the roof off and the walls fell outward. The scene inside revealed the group of mourners within; all were still safe. The blast of the wind didn't stop and it swept across the mountainside. As the full force and power of the Pneuma, smashed into Abaddon like a tsunami, he knew that it was over.

Similar to a vacuum cleaner on reverse, the gateway began to suck and the force grew stronger. Abaddon felt his neck held in an invisible, vice-like hand. The hand taunted him, and spun him around in the wind, before being released towards the direction of the portal. The Erebusian leader let out a scream of disgust as he was thrown back into the pit that he had climbed out of and was swiftly followed by his army. In the same instant, the land and air were restored to how it was meant to be. Even the cherry blossom grew on the trees. The shockwave didn't stop, as the Pneuma shield over Japan dropped.

The northern ice mass disappeared and for the first time in decades, green shoots appeared. When the wind blew over Siberia, Akiono and his family rejoiced in the knowledge that Ashia had succeeded. Hanson took Trenchant to the surface, without breaking through the ice. At the equator, the Pneuma stopped blowing and removed the barrier to unite the whole earth, though not all were aware of the sacrifice that had made it possible.

It all happened so fast. In the second after the roof blew out, the huddled crowd squinted their gaze into the rising sun and cheered. Jeru though, struggled to find a cheer in his heart. For him, the cost of freedom was far more than he could bear, but he hoped that it wasn't the end and that one day he would meet his love again. Hope was all that he had left.

Ashia walked peacefully beside the river that she had once climbed out of. Elio held her hand like the father that she wished she had known. She felt so calm, peaceful and even familiar, so referred to him by the name, *'Father.'* They talked nonsense, simply enjoyed each other's company and had fun together. She felt happy, although missed Jeru greatly and decided to ask a more serious question.

"Father, how was it that my death, my sacrifice saved the world?"

"Ashia, my daughter, I am so sorry that you had to go through that pain and suffering. If there had been any other way, I would have spared you. Yes, your blood was spilt and the Pneuma played a part, but it was love that really made the difference. The world had been in great need of love. For far too long mankind had been unable to love; they had forgotten how. Your demonstration of love was needed as a spark to light the fire. Your love for Jeru poured out to your team and continued over the rest of humanity. Love, as you know, has to be two-way, but what you are not aware of is that all love comes through me…I am love. I love all of mankind."

"But how can you love those that do so much wrong?" She wasn't sure if her question had overstepped a boundary and apologised, "Sorry. That was wrong of me. Who am I to judge?"

"No, you are right to ask, Ashia, yet you may not understand the answer. I love them, because I love them, because I love them, because I love them. I love them unconditionally, regardless of what they do, I still love them, because I made them."

As if a switch had been thrown in her mind, she understood and held his hand tighter.

He continued, "Every person that ever lived has desires, some are good and some are bad. They also have choices to make, these too are good and bad. No matter what they choose, I will always love them, but

I also have desires. My greatest desire is to be loved by mankind. I hope that they can love me, because they love, because they love me, because they love me. However, there is much to do to bring that about." She smiled and thought to herself, *'Nothing is impossible.'*

Glossary

Not quite... More like interesting points

- Sagami Province is today known as Kanagawa Prefecture, it is in Cipangu which is known today as Japan.
- Masamune actually is the greatest Japanese sword maker in history.
- Damascus steel is real and often was plunged into the body of a muscular slave to cool during the forging process. It was believed that the strength of the slaved passed into the blade.
- Shuriken named Honour.
- Wakizashi called Sure & Steadfast.
- Katana called Truth & Justice.
- Elafria is Greek for light – where Elafrians come from *(Angels)*.
- Erebus is from Greek mythology and was the personification of deep darkness – where the Erebusians come from *(Demons)*.
- Fonias is Greek for slayer.
- Mortem is Greek for death, therefore Mortemus is the Bringer of Death.
- Skia is Greek for shadow.
- Agonia is Greek for agony.
- Penthos is Greek for grief and mourning
- Chaos is Greek meaning Chaos.

- Abaddon — Hebrew for "destruction" *(Satan)*.
- Choani is Greek for hopper.
- Ketsueki is Japanese for blood.
- Cipangu is an old name for Japan.
- Nephilim – thought to be descended from angels.
- Shison is Japanese for descendant.
- Meiyo is Japanese meaning honour.
- Mitéra is Greek meaning mother.
- Elio is a take on Eloi which is Derived from Aramaic/Syriac meaning: He Is.
- The Elafrian language used is Aramaic.
- Haru is a real Japanese name and means spring of light.
- Kurai is Japanese meaning darkness.
- Akiono Musuko is Japanese meaning son of Akio.
- Tsuma is Japanese meaning wife.
- *'Zmey Gorynych'*, meaning dragon or snake of the mountain, it is an actual mythological creature from Russian folklore.
- Mount Osore, has been called the entrance to the next life, in Japanese folklore.
- Gisei is Japanese meaning sacrifice.

**If you have enjoyed reading this book, please visit
Amazon and/or Goodreads
and leave a quick review.
Thank you.**

**Please also continue reading for the story of how
God made me an author.**

I Am An Author

The story behind the author and
how this book came into being

This book and the other books that have since followed almost didn't happen. I feel that it is important to include this story in each of my published books, which you will find listed at the back of this book.

My mum died in 2011 and while sorting through her belongings, we found the start of her life story, in her scribbly handwriting. It was only a few pages long, but it exposed her pain and struggles in life. It was inspirational and it planted a small seed in me. I had the idea of doing the same. That idea rolled around in my head for a couple of years, but I questioned it, "How would I find the time to write"? Life was already busy running a charity (see my book, 'The Golden Thread').

Then, in 2013 I shared my thought with a person that I considered to be a friend. I hoped to receive some encouragement and reassurance that I could do this, but I didn't!

This is how the conversation went:
"I'm thinking of becoming an author."
The response somewhat surprised me, "You couldn't possibly be an author."
I respected this person's opinion so I asked, "Oh, why not?"
"Because authors write 3,600 words in an hour and you could never do that."

It was said with such authority, such confidence and knowledge that I just accepted it. "Your right, I could never do that." I knew that my crippled finger would always slow me down, but I now know that no disability should EVER stop anyone from following a dream. This one throwaway comment would delay my writing like a curse. God was speaking to me, leading me, but a massive barrier had just been built and it would hold me back for years.

In 2015 I stepped down from full-time charity work and managed to free up some time. It was then that I pushed the barrier out of the way and I wrote and published my first book, my biographical story called, 'The Golden Thread'. It felt good to have a book published. I knew that my story could impact the lives of many and to share it was a way of glorifying God, but I still struggled to consider myself as an author, with my 'friend's' comment still echoing in my mind, *"You could never be an author."*

In agreement, I now found myself thinking, "Yeah, it's a one-off, a fluke, anyone can write ONE book. It doesn't make you an author."

That then was that, decision made, I'm not an author and it's time to move on. Yet, God is patient and He had other plans, but it would take another three years before I knew exactly what He would require of me.

In 2018 my kidneys had failed so badly that I had been on dialysis for two years. We went to a Christian summer camp festival, called,

"Naturally Supernatural". It was organized by Soul Survivor and this was our third year of attending. Halfway through the week, during the loud worship time, in the throng of thousands of people, I became angry with God. I sat and I cried out aloud, "O God! What am I supposed to be doing with my life? Have you given up on me? Do you no longer have any use for me? Why have you abandoned me?"

Then, amid the noise and hubbub, I heard Him. It wasn't an audible voice; it was like a brain download. Some may say that it was a thought, but it was more, it originated from a supernatural source. It was so powerful, "You still have skills and tools that I have given you! I want you to use them. I haven't finished with you yet."

I felt the warming presence of the Holy Spirit course through me and I instantly knew that God had heard my cry and He had responded, but I still didn't know what it meant. Skills and tools? Did He want me to continue in youth work? He had equipped me for that role, but now it didn't seem right.

Later that week, a woman that I had never met

before prayed for me. She told me that she feels that God hasn't finished with me yet. She had a picture of me walking and said, "I believe God wants you to walk with your Gospel shoes on and that you will be ready to speak the good news of the Gospel."

For a brief period, once again I found myself angry and confused. I tried to explain to her, "I have end-stage kidney failure and I'm waiting for a transplant! I don't think I'll be walking far too soon."

I was bang-out-of-order, yet she humbly apologised, "I'm sorry, I'm new to this and maybe I have it wrong."

We both returned to our seats, but something caused me to watch where she went. She was four rows immediately behind where I sat. Now her words echoed around my head, just like the words from five years earlier had echoed, *"You can never be an author."*

She had said, *"God hasn't finished with you yet."* God had told me the same, *"I haven't finished with you yet."* Little did I know, that this was the five-year-old curse being undone, I was being released! *"I have given you tools and skills…"*

My mind raced through my life, "What tools? What skills?" My racing mind stopped in my first year of knowing Jesus and instantly I knew what He was telling me. I ran back four rows to the woman that had prayed for me. "I'm sorry, I need to apologise. God spoke to me through you and I was too angry to hear or understand, but what you said was spot on. I now know that He wants me to write".

In that first year of knowing Jesus, He had given me the gift (tool) and the ability (skill) of rhyming words and I had used it to become a rap artist. That skill had since developed and my writing skills helped me to develop The Door Youth Project charity.

I felt the power of the Holy Spirit already form words in my head; I was so excited! When I went home from Naturally Supernatural, I had the idea to write some teen fiction. I had previously gathered a collection of teen fiction books, which I now intended to read, to gain inspiration. Now, as I pawed my way through the books, I came to an abrupt halt, as I once again heard God's voice in my heart, *"I have*

I left the books on the shelf, then doubt tried to have a final word. *"You can NEVER be an author! An author writes 3,600 words an hour!"* Was that true? I decided to Google it and discovered that most authors write 1,000 words in a day. The figure of 3,600 is how many words a copy typist can produce in an hour. I had been cursed and lied to. Now though, I knew the truth and I started to write my first novel. "Issues" was written in just over a month. Then, as soon as it was published, I felt inspired to write, "My Foundation for Life". I had used the skills and the tools but still struggled to call myself an author (the curse was strong) – *"You can never be an author!"* The fire faded in my heart and I didn't write anything for nearly two years (recovering from a kidney transplant slowed me down). Then at the end of my transplant year of 2019, it started to snow and I was once again inspired to write my first science fiction novel. When "The Invasion of the MIMICS" was eventually published, I could at last call myself an 'author'. The curse had been lifted and with it came a full-on release.

Just a month later, I published my poetry book,

"Rhyme Time." Soon afterwards, I was in a prayer meeting, when these words came into my head, "ONE GOD – Many names." I instantly had the thought that I had to produce a film (yes, I also make films) with this title. As the film was being made, I also knew that God wanted me to publish a book with the title and so in November 2020, I started to meditate on the many names and titles of God (over 900 in the book). I wrote my thoughts and life-related stories for many of the names and sensed the Holy Spirit's presence grow in me. Then, after just three months and halfway through writing the book, He gave me another 'commission'.

'Commission' is the word that I like to use and I see it as **COM**e together on **MISSION** with God. This time, the call was to use the 'base' writing skill that He had given me *(use the skills and tools)* – 'rhyme'. A friend of mine had recently rewritten Psalm 23 as a rhyming poem. I had produced a poetry book and several 'spoken word' films. Now, I felt God speak to me again, "I gave you these tools and these skills for this time. Work with me and write the 'Psalms in Rhyme.'"

I write to bless others and to give God the glory

and so I was obedient and did as He had commanded. The whole experience was an incredible journey of five months, during which I was immersed in God's presence.

The writing now flowed, like a supernatural river of words. The curse was broken, "I AM AN AUTHOR"!

Writing two books at the same time is quite incredible and only possible (for me) with God in the mix, but as if that wasn't enough, He also gave me my first illustrated children's book to produce, "The Land of Make Believe". He continued to pour other poems into my mind regularly, plus He gave me the first four chapters of the sequel to, "The Invasion of the MIMICS."

Just a few negative words telling me that *'I CAN'T'* had held me back, but I had learnt. Never let ANYONE tell you that you can't do something or be something.

**Brendan Conboy has an active speaking
MINISTRY for GOD
And is looking forward to
hearing from you**

*Contact Brendan at the following:
Email – <u>bmconboy@gmail.com</u>
Phone - +44 (0)1453 731008
Mobile – 07980 404873
www.brendanconboy.co.uk*

**The following pages contain information
about Brendan's book titles (Bibliography).**

The Golden Thread – Biography
A true story of fear, forgiveness and faith
First published – 1ˢᵗ September 2015

Brendan Conboy grew up in fear and confusion, struggling with many personal issues. These experiences formed a foundation that could have ended in disaster, but instead, became the motivator to want to make a positive difference.

Issues – Teen / YA Fiction
We all have issues… Can a bully change?
First published – 23ʳᵈ January 2019

Marcus Daniel was a caring, intelligent, larger-than-average ten-year-old. His parents changed and then so did he. Now Marcus is thirteen years old and a spiteful bully, full of anger, rage and pain. His actions have changed others. Will the fear, pain and rage win?

My Foundation for Life – Semi Biog / Scriptural Teaching
14 underpinning and impacting scriptures
First published – 19th February 2019

What is it that makes some of us more resilient than others? I am sure that psychologists will have several long-winded explanations to answer this question, but I believe that we can increase our resilience by building our lives on a foundation of truth

Rhyme Time – Poetry
Poems with a message for you to read.
Poems of truth that plant a seed.
First published – 13th November 2020

The Invasion of the MIMICS
Science Fiction / Dystopian / Fantasy
They're already here… Invading your country…
Dwelling in your home… Living in your body!
First published – 21st October 2020

Climate change had been predicted long ago, but not one person could foresee the events that had unfolded. Humanity is defeated, civilization lost, all hope has gone. Enlightenment is the new belief, but there are those who refuse to believe.

The Land of Make Believe – Children's fantasy in rhyme
Based on the story of doubting Thomas
First published – 4th March 2021

ONE GOD Many Names
First published – 14th July 2021

When we meditate on the many names of God, something powerful can happen to us. Brendan Conboy shares his thoughts and personal stories of what some of these names mean and how they had a transformational impact on his life.

The Book of PSALMS in Rhyme
First published – 24th August 2021

**POWERFUL…
POETIC…
RHYTHMIC,
RHYMING
PSALMS…**
**A fresh expression
to ignite your soul.**

Yellow Dog
Publishing

www.ingramcontent.com/pod-product-compliance
Lightning Source LLC
Chambersburg PA
CBHW051010180726
48291CB00006B/2047